Want to understand what is going on right now between China and America? A murder investigation exposes systemic deception, crime, election rigging, information dominance, mass manipulation, corruption and outright theft at the highest levels of China and the United States. This gripping, thoroughly researched novel reveals—as sometimes only fiction can—the raw, excruciating truth behind today's headlines.

More real than the news: *Slay the Dragon* is destined to awaken America from its slumber! This novel of civil unrest, murder, espionage, kidnapping, wild escape and so much more lays bare the titanic, all-too-real geo political struggle of our epoch: China vs. America!

Whitewater Press
El Sobrante, California

Slay the Dragon: An Adam Weldon Action-Adventure Mystery Suspense Thriller is available in print, ebook, and audiobook from your favorite retailer.

Published by Whitewater Press

www.WilliamMcGinnis.com

bill@whitewatervoyages.com
(510) 409-9300
5205 San Pablo Dam Road
El Sobrante, CA 94903-3309

Printed in the United States of America
First Edition: September 2021

10 9 8 7 6 5 4 3 2 1

McGinnis, William
Slay the Dragon: An Adam Weldon Action-Adventure Mystery Suspense Thriller

ISBN: 978-1-7336547-8-4

Cover design: My Awesome Book Cover Design
Book design by Andrew Benzie: www.andrewbenziebooks.com
Technical Assistance: Will Farley McGinnis
Editing & Proofreading: Toni Hall

To the United States Constitution
and
All Who Defend It

"Supreme excellence (in war) consists in
breaking the enemy's will without fighting." —Sun Tzu

"The line separating good and evil passes not through states,
nor between classes, nor between political parties either—but right
through every human heart—and through all human hearts.
This line shifts. Inside us, it oscillates with the years.
And even within hearts overwhelmed by evil, one small bridgehead
of good is retained." —Aleksandr Solzhenitsyn

"The whole problem with the world is
that fools and fanatics are always so certain of themselves,
but wiser people so full of doubts." —Bertrand Russell

Lo! The caravan of civilization has been
ambushed. Fools are everywhere in charge." —Rumi.

Foreword

Slay the Dragon is a work of fiction. The events and characters herein sprang from the author's imagination. Any similarity to actual people and events is entirely coincidental. That said, however, the elements of unrestricted warfare and the background world portrayed in this novel are based on extensive research. To learn more about subjects touched on in the story, please see the reading list at the back of this book.

CONTENTS

Character List

Listed in order of appearance

Adam Weldon—Former Navy SEAL, military police investigator, black ops commando

Aiguo—Commandant in secret branch of Chinese military

BC/Billy Calhoun Davis—Tech-savvy black Oakland cop

Bohai—Wuzhou People's Armed Police (PAP) detective

Cao—Wuzhou People's Armed Police (PAP) detective

Chung Bo—Chung Qichang's father

Chung Jia—Chung Qichang's young daughter

Chung Mei—Chung Qichang's mother

Chung Mingshu—Chung Qichang's wife

Chung Qichang—Chinese Falun Gong computer genius

Da—Wuzhou People's Armed Police (PAP) detective

Dave Dorman—Oakland police officer

Fang Fang—Longhu police chief

Gong Dongfeng—Chinese owner of a building supply company

Harry Bellacozy—Silicon Valley billionaire, owner of Prophecy, etc.

Ike/General Eisenhower—Right hand man to Harry Bellacozy and head of cyber research and security for Prophecy

Ling—Pro-democracy Chinese dissident

Peace Weldon—Adam's cantankerous ex-Zen monk uncle

Rasheed—Young, black, viral filmmaker, former child hitman, buddy to Vocab

Roe Rosen—Ex-con cop killer, founder of Freedom Highway

Su Jingfoi—Chinese-born, East Bay real estate agent

Sun Changing—Young novice monk at Mt. Longhu Monastery

Tripnee—FBI agent, drone expert, Adam's girlfriend

Vocab—Young, black, viral filmmaker, former child hitman, buddy to Rasheed

Dr. Robert Whitehead—University chemistry professor, also works at Lawrence Livermore Lab

Wong Yoo—peasant fish farmer

Wuzhou PAP detectives: Cao Ai, Long Bohai, and Du Da

Xu—China's Supreme Leader, head of Communist People's Party (CPP)

Master Zhang—Mt. Longhu Monastery Tian Shi, top Taoist priest

Zhuliang—PAP commander

List of Acronyms

ACAB—All Cops Are Bastards

CPP—Communist People's Party

CRC—Communist Republic of China

CRT—Critical Race Theory

FH—Freedom Highway

GLA—Global Liberation Army

MAP OF THE SAN FRANCISCO BAY AREA

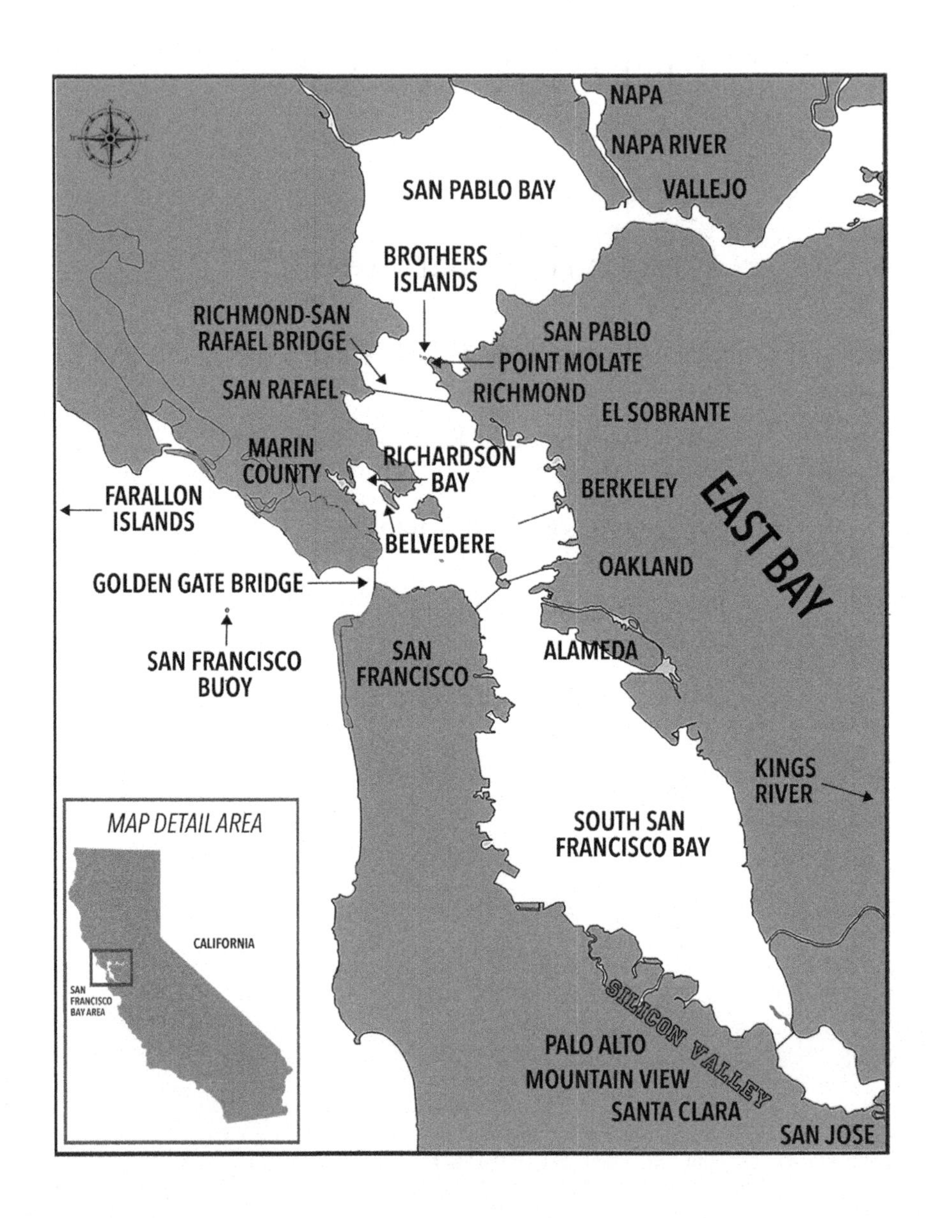

MAP OF SOUTH CENTRAL CHINA

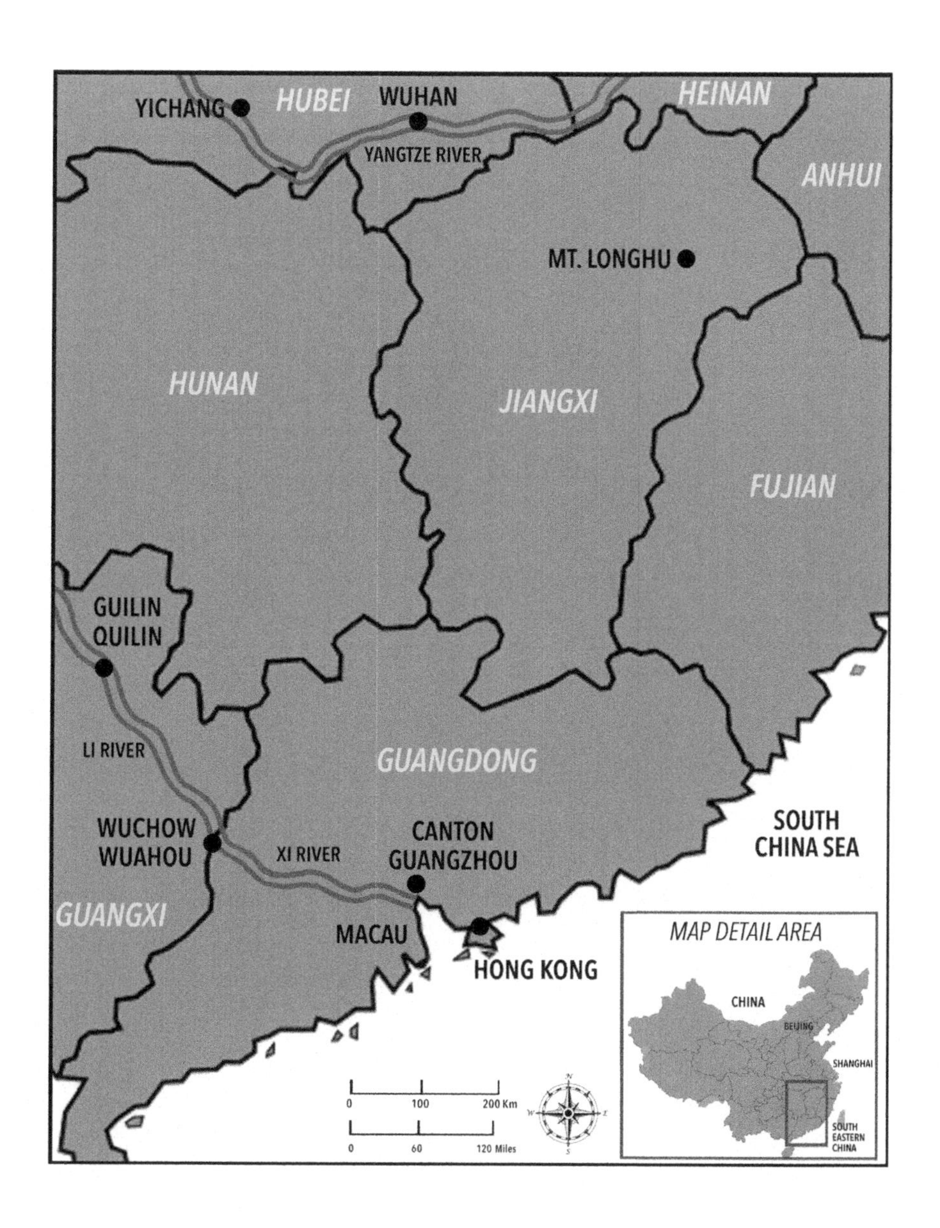

CHAPTER 1
DAVE DORMAN

Dave Dorman wasn't thinking about the throbbing pain in his legs from two gunshots received during a drug bust gone bad the year before. Nor did he dwell on the lingering soreness from multiple deep lacerations to his hands and forearms incurred six months earlier while breaking up a knife fight between two homeless men on fentanyl. Also, at least for the moment, he stopped worrying about the reprimand from his superiors admonishing him for even getting involved in that knife fight—their implicit message being: turn around, walk the other way.

Dave stood on his front porch in the East Bay hills breathing in the crisp morning air, looking out over Oakland and the shimmering waters of San Francisco Bay. He smiled and laughed, realizing for the millionth time that despite its challenges, life was good.

His two darling little girls, Debbie age three and Darla six, were getting along for a change and were looking forward to being with their grandma for the day. Due to the pandemic, schools and daycares were closed, but his mom, oddly laid off from her Kaiser nurse's job, leapt at the chance to spend time with her beloved grandchildren.

If you were going to be a single parent of two little girls, it was a blessing to have a mom like his. And if you're going to be an Oakland cop, it was good to be a big strong—even if wounded and cut up—African-American man.

As he dropped off his girls, his mom said, "You be careful Davy. You know what's been happening at these marches. They're turning violent and police are getting attacked."

"Don't worry mom. I'll be fine."

"Don't give me that 'I'll be fine' talk. You're too much of a risk taker. You gotta remember: You're everything—EVERYTHING—to your girls and me. You hear me now? You gotta be careful!"

Picking up on their grandmother's concern, his bright, cute-as-a-button girls chimed in. "Daddy, daddy, please please be careful today!"

As Dave drove into the center of the city, the homeless encampments seemed quiet and hunkered down. The few joggers and bikers around Lake Merritt seemed bent on finishing early and heading for cover. Even the vibrant multistory murals along Webster Street—which normally seemed to dance and shimmy—appeared muted, subdued. Something felt off. Was it him? Or was this the lull before the battle?

In the squad room at police headquarters, the morning briefing made no mention of protecting lives and property, but instead emphasized keeping one's head down. This had been the message for a while now. Not good.

His assignment for the day, as he knew it would be, was to cover the latest in a long string of protest marches through downtown Oakland. He and Payton, his partner for the day, drove along Broadway toward their assigned location, the federal building at Huey Newton Plaza.

Many of the storefronts lining the boulevard were shuttered in plywood, others were empty, charred, burned-out caverns—former Footlocker, Target, and Walgreens storefronts. Mute testimony that this was indeed a favorite protest route.

Dave and Payton parked their squad car, and got out to survey the intersection in front of the federal building they were to protect. Sitting on the curb thirty yards away was a three-foot-wide by three-foot-deep by three-foot-high pallet of bricks. Where did it come from? Looking around, here and there along the street, he counted not just the one—but four full pallets of bricks. Hundreds, maybe thousands of bricks. There were no construction sites in the area. Whoever put them here did so to incite violence, to turn a peaceful protest into a full on mob riot. Once windows got smashed, Dave knew, inevitably, inexorably, protestors transform into rioters hell bent on looting, burning, and fighting—especially attacking police. The bricks guaranteed trouble. But there were too many for the two of them to move or hide.

Vehicle traffic was light, and then gradually vanished altogether. Foot traffic also died out. Leaving the boarded-up, burned-out, war-zone of a downtown eerily quiet—except for a slowly increasing hubbub emanating from the distance: the sound of approaching marchers.

Then they arrived. At first it was just a few people hurrying to stay in front of the crowd, people with cameras stopping to film and then scurrying ahead again.

Then came the surprisingly scraggly main column. Except for an occasional denser mass of people here and there, the crowd was sparse and spread out. Not really that many people if you counted heads. Maybe three or four hundred.

People of all races, sizes, and shapes. Very few masks.

Many—maybe a majority—of the banners and signs proclaimed "All Cops Are Bastards" or the shorter acronym "ACAB." Some placards read "Defund the Police" and "Freedom Highway," while others touted a wide range of causes.

Some marchers seemed innocent enough. Citizens simply out to exercise their right to peacefully protest. But Dave saw that a sizable percentage were looking for trouble. These picked up bricks as they passed the pallets.

Several solid 'black blocks' of marchers—each twenty or so strong—were dressed head-to-toe in black and marched in tight formation shoulder-to-shoulder, belly-button-to-back-bone. Black helmets and extra large black face masks left only narrow slits for the eyes. These 'black blocks' endlessly chanted "All cops are bastards," and carried black shields, black batons, hammers, paint spray cans, and what Dave identified as bottles of fire accelerant.

Payton, standing beside him, yelled over the din, "Come on, Dave. It's getting dangerous out here. We better go inside."

Dave said, "What's the point of us being here if we're just going to hide?"

"I hear you. But doggone it, look at those bricks. Look at this crowd."

"Let them see the uniforms. See the blue."

"They're not paying us enough to get ourselves hurt. Besides, they specifically told us to play it safe."

"Us being here, being visible, makes a difference. Reminds them to be civilized. Reminds them of what Abe Lincoln called the better angels of their nature."

A brick sailed through the air and bounced across the sidewalk, missing them by only a few feet.

Payton said, "I'm going in," then turned, unlocked a steel service door behind them, and disappeared inside.

Dave stayed outside. But he was no fool, so he called for back up. He reported to his sergeant that bricks were flying up and down the street, the situation was about to explode, and he urgently needed back up.

"No can do," was the response. "A bunch of shop owners—

the ones whose stores are still open—have already called pleading for help. But the mayor's orders are to stay clear. It's too dangerous. Besides, going in could escalate the situation."

"You've gotta be kidding. We have to do something. We're the thin blue line. Doing nothing is exactly what will escalate the situation. We have a responsibility—"

"Nope. From the mayor on down, our orders are to de-escalate, stay away." Click.

Directly across the street, a guy moved differently, more independently, with a greater sense of purpose than those around him. Wearing a huge black face mask and all-black but tailored, well-fitting clothes, he ran up to one of the few remaining intact windows—of a small, single-proprietor clothing store. Pulling a hammer from his backpack, he smashed the glass, sending shards flying. Then the nifty dresser stepped aside to let the rabble pour into the store through the shattered window.

Dave started across the four lane toward the store, but several bricks suddenly sailed out of nowhere. Most missed, but one caught him square on the left side of his head. Thank God for his helmet, but still the heavy brick stunned him, knocking him down.

As he struggled to get up, more bricks came at him, too many to dodge. Again most missed, but one clobbered his shoulder and another knocked his left leg out from under him, toppling him again to the pavement.

The situation, predictably, continued to escalate. More and more bricks flew. More of the few remaining windows up and down the street were getting smashed.

Half a block away, the guy in the nifty, tailored, all-black outfit threw a burning Molotov cocktail into a building. Then he did the same thing twice more, to two other buildings. The guy was systematically setting fire to Oakland's entire downtown. As

Dave watched, lasers directed by malicious rioters played across his face, searching for his eyes.

Vehicle traffic was near zero. What few vehicles there were had blundered by pure accident into the melee, their oblivious drivers suddenly surrounded, mobbed, terrified. Rioters jumped up and down on their hoods, their roofs. The mob rocked the unfortunate vehicles back and forth, rolling some over. One driver got pulled out and beaten.

Dave called the station again and again to report the worsening situation, begging for back up. But each time the response was the same.

The total abdication of responsibility by the mayor and the police chief simply could not stand. After four calls to his sergeant—all with the same result—he had no choice but to call the mayor directly. After all, he knew the woman, and she knew him. One month earlier, on stage in the Prophecy Arena, in front of a crowd of thousands, she had praised him to the heavens and presented him with an award for his work with the Oakland Youth Non-Violence Program.

He was going outside the chain of command and there would be hell to pay, but he was at his wit's end. If law and order, if Oakland, if civilization was to have any chance, people with the responsibility and the power had to act, had to fight chaos. Someone around here had to act like a fucking adult.

The phone rang and rang, finally, someone said, "Yeah?"

"!t's an emergency! I have to talk with the mayor!"

"Not possible, the mayor's busy. This is Conrad, her assistant. Who's this?"

"I'm officer Dave Dorman, Oakland Police. The Mayor knows me. I absolutely have to talk with her. It's an emergency. I've got fires and a full-on riot here on Broadway. It's out of control. I need back up—"

"That won't be possible. You need to stand down. Get out of there."

"We can't stand down. Oakland is burning—"

"Officer, you've got a lot of nerve calling this number. We can't risk escalating the situation. Get out of there. Don't call this number again." Click.

The steel service door of the federal building opened and Payton's blond head popped out. His eyes went wide as he took in the pandemonium up and down the street. He yelled, "Dave, get in here!" Then he pulled his head back in, slamming the door.

The guy had a point. It was time to go in, to live to fight the tide another day.

Dave, limping, backed away from the street, moving toward the steel door.

A white van approached. Unlike other vehicles, which instantly got stopped, surrounded and mobbed, this one rolled easily through the crowd, which parted like the Red Sea. It was as though the vehicle was known and had some special permission.

The van pulled up to the curb thirty feet from Dave, who had now backed up to the steel door, his hand reaching behind him for the doorknob. The van's sliding side door opened a crack. A gun barrel appeared. Shots rang out. Dave's body armor stopped the first seven bullets, but the eighth tore away half his throat, and the ninth caught him in the forehead right between the eyes.

As the shooting stopped and the van moved away, there was stunned silence. Then a woman with a bullhorn whooped, "A cop is down! Hurray!" At first only a small coterie cheered. Then more joined in, and soon the crowd took up the chant, "A cop is down! Hurray! A cop is down! Hurray!"

CHAPTER 2
JACK LONDON SQUARE MARINA

"It's bad?" asked Adam Weldon.

"Real bad," said BC Davis.

"An Oakland cop, a black cop, shot down in broad daylight. You'd think the department would be all over it."

"Damn straight," said BC, his big black hands clenched into fists. "We're on it, but we're getting blocked, shut down."

"You've gotta be kidding."

"Nope. We're being defunded, decimated. We're getting zero support from the mayor and city council. We're getting crucified in the media. Even the FBI, at least the local office, is against us."

Adam shook his head. "I just don't get it."

"While you've been out sailing the world, things here, frankly, have gone insane."

"Yeah?"

"Just one example," said BC. "I myself was suspended for stopping a mob from tearing down a statue of Jack London just a hundred yards from here."

Sitting on the high quarter deck of BC's Chinese junk Big Zen, the two men turned to look at London's still-standing statue in the middle of Oakland's Jack London Square.

"Didn't you and Dave Dorman go through the academy together?"

"Sixteen years ago. Me and Dave. We were rookies together, and later, partners for ten years," said BC, his eyes wet. "I can't believe he's gone."

To give his old friend a private moment, Adam, forehead furrowed and jaw clenched, watched a weathered sloop motor upwind against the tide along the Oakland estuary, creeping toward open water on San Francisco Bay—and maybe far beyond.

"It's fucked up crazy town," resumed BC. "But I owe it to Dave and to whatever vestige remains of law and order, to bring his killers to justice. And I need your help."

"You got it," said Adam. "How did Dave die?"

BC, his face a portrait of agony, summarized what he knew of Dave Dorman's death. "Dave was guarding the federal building—a mile from here—standing out front. About 400 people were moving along the street. Started out peaceful. But people started throwing bricks, smashing windows, looting, lighting fires.

"Dave's phone shows four calls to his sergeant and one to the mayor's office requesting urgent back up. But none came. Then a van pulled up. Automatic fire from inside the van tore into Dave. His body armor stopped most of the bullets, but one tore open his throat and one hit him between the eyes."

Both men hung their heads, eyes welling, fists clenched.

"Five calls for back up?"

"All refused by order of the mayor." Eyes now shut, nostrils flared, BC's whole body shook. "She didn't want to fucking escalate the situation."

They went below into the belly of Big Zen to BC's electronics/video/drone lab to study Dave's body camera and nearby surveillance camera footage. In one video, a white, new-looking Ford van pulled up in front of the federal building. The van's side door opened for a moment, then the vehicle raced away. No license plates. And a balaclava covered the driver's face, leaving only a narrow opening for the eyes.

BC ground his teeth. "Not very useful. Can't see the shooter at all. No way to ID the driver or the van."

"You've exhausted every avenue to track down the van?"

"Yeah," said BC. "There're tens of thousands of vans like it in Northern California. It'd be easier to find a needle in a haystack."

They looked for news articles, social media commentary and YouTube footage covering events surrounding the murder.

"Amazing. So little coverage," said Adam.

"Not so amazing. A cop's death doesn't fit the narrative," observed BC. "Don't you know cops are bad?"

One of the few newspapers to report the murder was a San Francisco publication nicknamed the 'Comical.' A stripped-down parody of its former, historic self, the 'Comical,' it seemed, no longer had the staff nor the inclination to even attempt objective reporting.

Going through a stack of newsprint copies—and also checking online—Adam found that Dave's death garnered only a single brief mention: a two-paragraph article buried deep on an interior page of the print edition and virtually hidden on its website.

However, because the 'Comical' allowed readers to post comments online, Adam found it valuable reading. The commenters spanned the full political and sanity spectrums, but a salient few provided telling perspective and details. Several described how pallets of bricks had been pre-positioned beforehand along the demonstration route—in places with no construction sites nearby.

When the demonstrators came upon the stacks of bricks, first one person, then a few more hurled them through windows, threw them at cars and at anything that would break.

Soon, a herd mentality took over, the allure of brick throwing became irresistible, others joined in, order disappeared, and chaos and looting erupted. Before long, Molotov cocktails flew right and left, igniting stores, cars, anything that would burn.

Other posters described how they'd been swept into vehicle caravans that descended on suburban downtowns such as that of Walnut Creek, sixteen miles inland from Oakland. There also, pallets of bricks had been pre-positioned. Egged on by the actions of a few, soon there too all hell broke loose.

"Coordination behind the scenes," said Adam. "Somebody's deliberately creating chaos."

"I see what you mean. Those bricks put right where they'd create mayhem," said BC.

CHAPTER 3
BRICKS

"Dave's murder and those bricks," said Adam. "Gotta be connected."

Adam surveyed BC's thirty-by-fifteen-foot tech lab. The low-ceilinged space down in the belly of Big Zen was crammed with computers, flat screens, drone paraphernalia and piles of electronic gear. "You still a state-of-the-art white-hat hacker?"

BC grinned.

"Can you tap into video cameras in the riot areas? Maybe we can get images of whoever dropped off those bricks?"

"Gotta crack some passwords." BC winked. "Just so happens, I've got something perfect for the job. NSA stuff released by Ed Snowden. Also, I'll use AI recognition software to scan the videos for pallets of bricks."

"Sounds good. In fact, amazing."

"Oh yeah, AI's advancing by leaps and bounds."

BC set to work. Soon video of downtown Oakland and Walnut Creek moved across a half dozen flatscreens. Most of it flashed by, but every now and then a screen would pause to zero in on an object.

"When the AI finds bricks—or what it thinks might be bricks—it shows us the image. If it's what we're looking for, we'll save and study it. If not, we click continue. Very rapidly, it'll get better and better at identifying pallets of bricks."

The two men settled in, scanning images of bricks and brick-like objects. Sure enough, the AI learned fast, and soon found images of bricks—mostly of people carrying and throwing them. But it found no brick stacks, on or off pallets.

"Well, the bricks were there alright," said BC. "But whoever supplied them somehow avoided the cameras. Careful, clever devils."

Scratching his head, Adam asked, "Let's go at it from the other direction. Can you tap into the records of building supply and truck and forklift rental companies?"

Soon, computer and video surveillance data from building materials suppliers and truck and forklift rental companies scrolled across the screens.

"Look for anyone who bought multiple pallets of bricks and rented brick-hauling equipment in the days and weeks before the riots," said Adam. "Ignore contractors and people who pulled building permits."

"Also," said BC, "When people use cash, I'll run the store video footage through facial recognition software to see if anyone went around making multiple purchases."

The computers churned data and the screens scrolled. Time dragged. The low-ceilinged space below the water line felt stuffy, oppressive and reeked with the pungent odor of sea water. Again the search came up empty.

"Okay, okay." Adam let out a long sigh. "Let's cast a wider net. Instead of just six Bay Area counties, let's search all of Northern and Central California."

Two hours later, still nothing. As the wakes of passing ships occasionally rocked Big Zen, the air closed in, offering no oxygen. The two big men slumped, immobile.

Adam looked up and pumped a fist in the air. "I've got an idea. What if these guys have deep pockets?"

"So?" asked BC.

"Maybe they'd buy an entire company. Let's search for building supply companies that changed hands since the rioting began."

"Makes sense," said BC. "With a single purchase they'd get bricks, trucks and forklifts. Everything they'd need to drop off pallets of bricks."

"All without having to rent anything or go around making a bunch of separate brick purchases."

BC returned to his computers, and after a while said, "Interesting, I found six such outfits."

"Which ones carried a big inventory of bricks?"

After consulting his computers for several minutes, BC said, "All six. That's doable. But it'd be nice to narrow it down."

Adam sat, staring into space, rubbing his chin. "Let's take another look at the killer's van."

"Sure," said BC. "But I've gone over it a hundred times. There's not a distinguishing mark on it."

The familiar, horror-filled footage, shot by multiple cameras, appeared on BC's big screen. There was the white van, the side door opening and closing, the balaclava covering the driver's face, leaving only a narrow opening for the eyes.

"Can you magnify and enhance the driver's eyes?" Adam asked.

A few moments later, filling the high-definition screen, loomed a pair of distinctly Asian eyes.

BC's jawed dropped. "Son of a gun."

"Interesting. Not what you'd expect," said Adam.

"Our stats show there aren't many Asian rioters," said BC. "And darned few Asian members of ACAB."

The black Oakland cop consulted his computer for a few minutes, then turned again to Adam. "One of the six companies was purchased by someone with an Asian-sounding name.

Diablo Building Supply in Concord. The buyer was Gong Dongfeng."

"Of course," reflected Adam, "it might be just a coincidence—"

"But something tells me otherwise," said BC.

CHAPTER 4
AIGUO'S REPORT TO GRANDFATHER

All goes well, sir. Just as you so wisely foretold, the gweilo barbarians are gullible, have few scruples and are easy to bribe. Thanks to your leadership, we are sowing division, hatred and chaos. It's beautiful.

Drug addiction, technology transfer and the disappearance of their middle class are going as planned. Recently, our valiant agents—with the assistance of bought politicians and unpaid useful idiots—have been transforming peaceful protests into full on riots rampant with looting, fire, mayhem and, when we can manage it, murder.

The gweilo penchant for costly, counterproductive foreign wars is a sweet bonus speeding their decline. Another bonus is the widespread disrespect for authority and the breakdown of the family. I am frankly amazed by how little regard sons and daughters show their parents and grandparents. Such disintegration of natural kinship, I would not wish on anyone—except gweilo ghost devil Westerners.

The American left, along with most of Hollywood, academia, pro sports, the media and the tech sector, are proving to be our best allies. Wonderful for us, crazy for them. They're defunding police, eliminating bail, opening borders, emptying prisons, and even claiming that robbery is not violence.

Police officers can be 100% right but still be found guilty and sent to prison just for doing their jobs. The predictable result,

Americans call it the Ferguson effect, is police won't go into high crime areas. It's wonderful. What better way to undermine law and order, create anarchy, and destroy a country.

Anyone who disagrees with the orthodoxy of the left is canceled, punished, ostracized. No one has the stones to disagree.

Tech companies shadow ban and de-boost contrary, conservative ideas. Google employees voted not to cooperate with their own Pentagon. Independent thinkers self censor. Groupthink and enforced political correctness rule. It's wonderful.

The Green New Deal agenda is brilliant. It's guaranteed to collapse their economy and undermine free enterprise and the Western world. What better way to hamstring America. Hats off to you, grandfather, for your role in that.

Here's the best part. Your idea to foment racial hatred and stereotypes was pure genius. Gweilo culture, with our help, is approaching civil war. Racial issues are tearing the place apart. The left is screaming that capitalism itself is racist and oppressive. A popular song goes, "We cutting the throat of the old system" and you "better run" if you aren't with them. More and more voices are demanding reparations for slavery, and even claiming the white race is genetically inferior. Thanks to our efforts, people arguing against these policies are being drowned out, lost in a wild chaos of mistrust, judgment and hatred.

Our historic campaign is something to be deeply proud of, grandfather. China's power and influence are growing, and America, despite all its energy, ingenuity and resources, is in decline. And best of all, our campaign has remained completely below the radar. American politicians are saying that even talking about China is a diversion.

Your devoted grandson, Aiguo

CHAPTER 5
FOOTHILLS OF MT. DIABLO

Adam, wearing jeans and t-shirt, and BC, in dark slacks and sport coat, walked from the marina to the garage under Jack London Square where they unplugged and climbed into BC's dark blue Tesla Model 3. Following Hwy 24 through the Caldecott Tunnel and then Hwy 680 north, they drove 22 miles inland. Under the shadow of the eponymous Mt. Diablo, on the outskirts of Concord, which itself was on the outskirts of the Bay Area, they found Diablo Building Supply's metal building and yard.

Filling the building and yard were pallet upon pallet, row upon row of flagstone, pavers, concrete building blocks, and a seemingly infinite variety of other building materials. But, after walking through the entire layout, they found only a single pallet of bricks.

Looking around to make sure they were alone, BC said, "The inventory shows forty pallets of bricks. Now where do you suppose all those bricks went?"

Adam grinned, but with narrowed eyes. "You're a smart guy. Don't you know bricks are hard to keep track of?"

Interestingly, both the staff and the clientele seemed to be mostly Asian. Although Adam had learned Chinese in the military language school at Monterey, he thought it best to keep this to himself. Two Asian men manned the counter, one tall, skinny and smiling, the other short, muscular and serious.

Adam walked up to the counter and said in English, "I need ten pallets of brick."

The tall, thin clerk said, "No problem," and turned toward the cash register to ring up the sale.

Overhearing this, the other clerk, the guy who looked like a body builder, said in Chinese, "I'll deal with this gweilo." And then in English he said, "I'm sorry sir, we only have one pallet of brick in stock."

"When will you get more?"

"Two weeks."

"Oh, okay. Thanks." Adam moved away a short distance and pretended to study a display of brick-laying tools.

The skinny kid said quietly in Chinese, "Our brick inventory is wrong—"

"Shut up," hushed the muscle-bound guy also in Chinese. "I told you, let me handle all brick orders."

Turning a shiny brick-laying trowel in his hands, Adam thought he saw muscle-guy's reflection looking his way suspiciously.

Bingo. They'd struck pay dirt. But better not alert these guys they've been found out by asking more questions.

Come to think of it, maybe it wasn't such a good idea for the two of them to show up together. There was no getting around it. To an experienced eye, BC, plain and simple, had the bearing and look of a cop—and, under his sailor's tan and casualness, Adam's alertness and physicality betrayed his Navy SEAL past.

Walking back to the Tesla, they both had to smile. This was the place. But, how to learn more about its owner Gong Dongfeng?

CHAPTER 6
RICHMOND'S MARINA BAY

Gong Dongfeng's address on the real estate purchase documents was a P.O. Box in Hong Kong. A dead end.

But Adam had an idea.

By the time Adam and BC returned to Jack London Square, northbound traffic on Highway 80 from Oakland to Richmond was in full late afternoon gridlock. No problem. He had a better way to go: his seventy-foot sailboat Dream Voyager. And the tide was right.

Adam fired up the Yanmar engine, cast off mooring lines, and motored West straight upwind along the Oakland Estuary toward central San Francisco Bay. Out on open water, still headed into the wind, he stepped on a deck button to send the mainsail racing up the hundred foot mast. Next, he unfurled the genoa.

Then he turned to starboard, shut off the motor, and trimmed both sails for a broad reach due north. Dream Voyager glided under the tiara of the eastern span of the Bay Bridge and carved a path parallel to the East Bay shoreline. Adam savored the full gorgeous curves of sails, the gentle listing of the deck, the quiet murmur of the water sliding under the hull. As the sun descended in the west, headed for the horizon directly beneath the Golden Gate Bridge, a twelve-knot evening breeze propelled him past gridlocked traffic over on the East Bay freeway. Death, mayhem, riot. The troubles of the world were real, but no more real than this beautiful moment.

Rounding the Richmond breakwater, he turned to starboard.

Keeping the red channel markers on his right, he ran east along Potrero reach toward Richmond's upscale Marina Bay, a half-mile-square small-boat harbor surrounded by shoreline trails, parks, restaurants, and gated condos and townhouses. In the marina's northeast corner, Adam tied Dream Voyager to the T-end of a guest dock, locked all hatches, activated the security alarms and walked along floating piers to the ramp to shore. A series of manicured pathways led him to a certain three-story townhouse. After ringing the door bell, he admired the home's small well-tended garden, then turned around to take in a sweeping view of the marina and the Bay beyond.

An Asian woman opened the door a crack, looked him up and down, then stuck her head out and looked all around.

When setting up this meeting earlier on the phone, Adam had said only that he was investigating the murder of an Oakland policeman. The woman had seemed unusually apprehensive. Now, seeing her in person, he saw she was borderline terrified. It was going to take some kind of miracle to get her to open up and talk freely.

"Su Jingfoi?" Adam asked. "I'm Adam Weldon."

It was amazing. The woman suddenly smiled broadly, opened the door wide, and ushered him in.

Adam found himself lounging on a luxurious high-backed sofa, drinking tea, munching Chinese cookies and appreciating the friendly vibe of this elegant woman sitting opposite him on a similar posh couch. Su Jingfoi's warm smile grew even broader, if that was possible, and she asked, "You're Adam, Peace's nephew?"

Adam's jaw dropped. What were the odds!? Then he too cracked a big smile. This woman was friends with Adam's goofy, ex-Zen monk, school librarian uncle! It turned out that Jingfoi had helped Peace finance and run a community urban farm on empty land next door to one of her apartment complexes. Well, considering Peace's countless Bay Area endeavors—ranging from the philanthropic to the quixotic to the downright insane—maybe it wasn't such a miracle. After catching her up about his uncle, Adam got to the point of his visit and described the murder.

"That's terrible!" Jingfoi exclaimed. Then, calmly but with force, she said, "The looting, rioting, destruction and killing are just terrible. I'm so against it."

"I need to talk with Gong Dongfeng. You brokered a real estate deal for him not too long ago."

"Not just one deal. Many."

"Yeah?"

"Like many of my clients, Dongfeng is buying up real estate in the Bay Area. Lots of it," Jingfoi said. "Paid cash for two apartment complexes, a shopping center, and ten houses. Nice properties."

"Cash?"

"Lots of money coming out of China. Rich Chinese want to get their wealth beyond the reach of the Chinese Communist Party by investing overseas, especially in United States real estate."

"It sounds like you're well connected with Chinese elites."

"Not really," Jingfoi said. "I was born in China and my father was an official in the Party, the Communist Party. To show loyalty, he sent his daughter—me—to a farm for three years during the Cultural Revolution. I was the sacrificial daughter. Funny thing was, I actually liked working on the farm, growing things. Later though, I got fed up with the lack of freedom and at age 24 I was granted permission by the US government to immigrate."

"Fascinating," said Adam. "Seems like you've done very well for yourself."

"It's been a wild ride. I made and lost one fortune. Went bankrupt in a bad divorce. But since then, I've been in real estate and now I own four apartment complexes, some condos and this townhouse, mainly so I can take take care of my daughter."

"Good for you. I'm curious, why did you leave China? Will you ever move back?"

"There is no freedom in China. Also terrible pollution and the entire food supply is unhealthy. I go to visit family. But I never move back."

"Where can I find Gong Dongfeng?"

Jingfoi said, "Dongfeng is a shadowy guy. All I have is his cell number."

"No address?"

"Just a P.O. box in Hong Kong," Jingfoi replied. "Have you heard of Guanxi?"

"You scratch my back," Adam said. "I scratch yours."

"That's it. In China, no transaction is simple or straightforward. Every time someone does something for someone else, obligations are incurred, favors are expected."

"So, because Dongfeng buys real estate through you, he expects things in return. What things?"

"Airport pickups. 24/7 chauffeur. Party, dinner invitations. Introductions to my girlfriends."

"And you do all that?"

"I used to. Chinese expect it. It's part of the deal."

"Used to?"

"Recently I've tapered off. I guess I'm becoming American. I like things simpler, more straight forward. I'm tired of all the endless obligations. Also, I've made plenty of money and I'm trying to retire."

"When you pick this guy up at the airport, where is he generally flying in from? Hong Kong?"

"Almost always from mainland China."

Adam looked out Su's huge picture window at the Bay shimmering in a golden sunset. This was going better than he could have hoped. Emboldened—and struck by a thought, he asked, "Does guanxi include keeping the guy's secrets?"

"Definitely."

"You're talking with me why?"

"Because of Peace, really," Su said. "I love the rascal, and you're his family. I know from all he's said about you that I can trust you."

Adam nodded, patted his chest over his heart and took a deep breath. Jingfoi did likewise.

"Just talking with you," Jingfoi said, "crosses the red line."

"The red line?"

"There's no clear line, but in Communist China everyone self censors. Limits what they do and say, because you never quite know where the line is. And if you do go too far, the penalty can be sudden, drastic, terrible."

"Are you in danger?"

"Dongfeng has never threatened me. But there's something about him. He's got connections. You would never want to be on his bad side."

"He trusts you?"

"Not exactly. Not enough to tell me his real address. I think he works with me because I practice good guanxi—at least until recently. Also, of course, he knows my father was a lifelong party member, and I'm known as the good daughter. But, like I say, there's something about the guy. If he ever felt crossed, I'd be in trouble. Serious trouble."

"So Dongfeng is connected to the CPP, but he's still moving his money to the United States?"

"No matter how well-connected a person is in China, no one feels secure," Song said. "Even Dongfeng. All wealthy Chinese hedge their bets by investing at least a portion of their wealth overseas."

"What's he do? His profession?"

"Journalist."

"You buy that?"

"Not really."

"And you have no idea when he might show up?"

"None."

Su Jingfoi then picked up a pad and pen from a side table, wrote a note, and handed it to Adam: "The CPP surveils not only its own citizens but also many people outside China—probably including me. I sweep my house for bugs, but I think I have already said too much out loud. I will try to learn more about Dongfeng and let you know."

Adam wrote a reply and handed the tablet back. "Thank you. You're wonderful. Be very careful."

Walking back to his boat, Adam couldn't help but grin. That went better than he could've hoped. He'd just learned a lot. Clearly, though, he'd just begun to scratch the surface investigating Gong Dongfeng.

Pulling out his cell phone, Adam called BC.

BC said, "Can't talk. You remember where we hid out from Reamer Rook. I'll meet you there."

Oh oh. It would take something big to spook BC. With time of the essence, Adam hailed an Uber.

CHAPTER 7
NAPA RIVER

Adam remembered the place well. A remote, gunk-hole marina far up the Napa River in the middle of wine country. The last-place anyone would ever think to find a 65-foot Chinese junk, let alone an entire marina.

"It's the damnedest thing," BC said. "Out of the blue, I got a call from a guy—sounded Asian—said my boat was rigged to explode. Guy wouldn't say who he was or how he knew. Just told me a bomb on a timer was attached to my boat. Yeah, and he said I should disappear for a while."

Under a bright full moon, BC and Adam sat on Big Zen's elevated quarter deck, their eyes roving from the sweet lines of the Chinese junk to the familiar derelict marina to vineyards stretching into the distance and then back again to BC's beloved home on the water, all visible in the ethereal lunar light.

BC continued, "Sure enough, right where he said—amidship just below the water line—where I could reach it from my dinghy—there it was: an IED big enough to sink my boat in a heartbeat."

"Damn."

BC chuckled. "I pried it off and deactivated the sucker."

"And I thought you were asleep the whole time you were in the bomb squad."

"I told you a thousand times I was awake for part of it."

They both smiled.

"I'm guessing," Adam said "they traced your license plate from our Concord visit."

"Must have somebody inside the police or DMV?"

"Or some hot shot hackers."

"They sure picked up on us fast. They're fast—clever—and deadly."

"True," Adam agreed. "But that tip-off call tells us a lot: Someone or some group has infiltrated them."

"Undermining their efforts."

"Thank God for that phone call."

BC said, "I did a DMV search—back dated this time—and guess what? A month ago Diablo Building Supply reported that it scrapped a late model, white Ford van."

"Nothing suspicious about scrapping a new van."

"Course not," BC said. "Oh yeah, also, the IED is military grade Chinese hardware."

CHAPTER 8
ADMIRAL TY JEPPESEN

"This is big," Adam said. "Almost certainly international. Very likely the People's Communist Party."

"Bigger than you and me for sure," BC said.

"Time to call in the professionals, the specialists, the experts in dealing with this stuff."

Adam knew just the person: Admiral Ty Jeppesen. As young Navy SEAL officers of similar rank, Adam and Ty had shared many a black ops mission and remained lifelong foxhole buddies. Ambitious, smart, dedicated and by the book—although a little softhearted and whimsical at times—Jeppesen had risen steadily to become not only an admiral but also a key player in United States national security and a trusted advisor to the president.

BC, who was also friends with Jeppesen, said, "Good idea. He's a good man."

Calling on Jeppesen's private line, Adam learned that, by a stroke of incredible luck, his old Navy SEAL buddy was right then enroute to the west coast. Not wanting to say more on an unsecure line, Adam simply said he was onto something urgent and big. His old fox-hole buddy took the hint and offered to have his agency jet land at the Napa Airport. Adam suggested the three of them meet the next morning aboard Big Zen for breakfast.

Adam did the cooking river-guide style, down and dirty. In under thirty minutes, on the massive table of Big Zen's main salon, he served up fried eggs, thick sliced uncured bacon, sweet potato, fresh hot toast, vegetable smoothies and thermoses of hot tea and café au lait.

While they ate, Adam and BC filled in Jeppesen on what they'd learned about Dave Dorman's murder—and on events since. Adam concluded, "Everything points to the CPP. This is big. Too big for me and BC. We need to hand this off to you and the feds."

"Hold on." Jeppesen, with palms down, gestured 'slow down.' "First, congratulations and hats off to you both. You've done a top notch job. Brilliant, in fact."

Such praise should have felt good, but something told Adam something less than ideal was coming next.

"Second, I'm going to level with you. All is not good. At the very highest levels, we've got problems."

"Meaning?"

"Bottom line: I need the two of you to continue this investigation."

"But this is exactly the sort of thing that your agency is for," BC said.

"My agency—and Washington DC as a whole—is hamstrung by bought politicians. To go straight to the naked, horrible truth:

The Communist People's Party has corrupted the US government and literally owns who knows how many key people."

BC was incredulous. "You got to be joking."

"Believe me, I wish I was," Jeppesen said.

"No!" BC yelled, his big hands pounding the table. "No way man. That's crazy. I hear shit like that in Oakland all the time. Every perp and criminal and nut case spouts cockamamy conspiracy theories just like that. Identical."

"You're correct. It's unbelievable," Jeppesen said quietly, "But it's true. Horribly true."

Meanwhile, Adam put a hand on his friend's shoulder. After a while BC grew less agitated, took some deep breaths, and seemed calmer.

"Let me give you a little example," Jeppesen said. "A little glimpse into the corruption. What I call 'the horror.'

Let's say you're leading a delegation to hammer out a trade deal with China. Maybe fifty billion, maybe a hundred billion, maybe two hundred billion dollars are at stake. The CPP are old hands at under the table bribery. They offer to put a hundred million dollars in a secret Swiss or Hong Kong bank account in exchange for just a few little changes here and there in the treaty. Changes that don't seem like much, but that open loopholes worth multiple billions to the Chinese."

"I can see," Adam said, "how that would be difficult to impossible to even detect—let alone prove."

Calmer now, but looking depressed, BC reflected, "That kind of money can literally change the course of a presidential election or of any number of Senate and Congressional races. Even for someone who started with good intentions, the temptation could be irresistible."

Jeppesen continued, "Combine this with black ops guanxi."

"Black ops guanxi? What's that?" BC asked.

"That's using the vast powers of a sovereign government—especially a one-party, totalitarian, gangster-run country like China—to provide special services."

"Special services?"

"Taking care of any and all problems including assassinations on request. Do you think that all the suspicious deaths among people on the fringes of power are suicides?"

"That's so fucking messed up," BC moaned. "I was afraid of something like this."

"Black ops guanxi special services can include, let's say, the satisfaction of any sexual appetite you could name," Jeppesen said. "And, of course, once you get in bed with all this, there's no getting out. The CPP own you from then on. They're very good at recording every, shall we say, indiscretion."

"To blackmail the shitheads forever." BC hung his head, his hands still balled into fists.

"An open, rather naive society like ours," Adam observed, "is so vulnerable to a gangster outfit like the CPP."

Jeppesen asked, "Ever wonder how former secretaries of state, vice presidents and presidents wind up worth hundreds of millions? And why their enemies often encounter mysterious deaths?"

Jeppesen continued, "The fact is DC is a mess. Our intelligence agencies are hamstrung. Outright spies, leakers, bought politicians—and a few well-intentioned but wrong-headed useful idiots—thwart us in every way they can. Constantly breathing down our necks, they hold hearings, block our investigations, expose our operations."

The three men sat in silence. Did Jeppesen seem older, diminished, shrunken?

"That's why I need the two of you to stay on this. BC, you've got the tech and computer skills, and, Adam, you've had more success dealing with exactly this sort of thing than any of my regular agents."

"This is a battle that has to be fought," BC said, "but you're asking me and Adam to tackle this alone?"

"You won't be alone," Jeppesen said. "I have people who will help."

BC asked, "Can we access your top secret databases?"

"That would alert the corrupt double agents, the swamp,"

Jeppesen replied. "We'll have a much better chance of success if you stay under the radar, stay off the agency computer networks."

BC shook his head. "That sucks."

Jeppesen leaned forward, tense, his voice exploding with force. "Believe me, the two of you are our best shot. You're perfect. You're smart, tenacious. Your skills are top-notch. I couldn't ask for anyone better."

"This could lead to Hong Kong, mainland China," Adam said. "To the elites of the Communist People's Party."

"So be it," Jeppesen said. "I need you to do whatever it takes. Follow this investigation wherever it leads,"

"You mean that?" BC asked. "Shit gonna hit the international fan."

Jeppesen replied, "This could be our golden opportunity, the opening I've been hoping for!"

Adam took a deep breath. "It's gonna be huge."

"This is our chance," Jeppesen said, "not only to expose the whole corrupt system, but also—hold onto your seat—to spark major reform both here and in China."

BC's cell phone rang. He picked up, talked some, but mostly listened. Putting his phone away, he said. "That was my marina neighbor Bruno. A little while ago somebody opened the door of my Tesla. Musta tried to steal it. Both the thief and the car got blown to smithereens."

CHAPTER 9
BIG ZEN

Kablaaam! Kablaaam! Kablaaam! Kablaaam!

In the middle of the night, jolted awake, Adam leapt from his bunk in BC's guest cabin. Big Zen was going down. The explosions must have ripped holes in the hull below the waterline. Fortunately, they'd also activated the ship's emergency interior lights. Sloshing through already knee-deep water toward BC's cabin, Adam yelled, "BC. BC. Are you okay?"

Adam's big friend heaved open his cabin door. "Yeah. I'm fine. But my boat sure as hell ain't."

Adam, wearing only shorts and t-shirt, and BC, in purple pajamas, pushed through already waist deep water toward the ladder to the main deck.

When they reached the ladder, something made Adam pause and yell to his friend, "Hold on. Let me check something."

As desperate as the situation was, they were both still unhurt, and Adam wanted to keep it that way. A 6-foot-long cushion from a salon bench floated nearby. Grabbing it, Adam climbed halfway up the ladder and thrust one end of the cushion up into the night air.

Pssst. Pssst. Pssst. Silenced automatic fire ripped into the cushion. Whoever set off those bombs was waiting, no doubt with a night-vision scope, to cut them down the second they appeared on deck.

Adam asked, "I don't suppose you have scuba gear?"

"No man. You know me. I don't swim." Already stressed, BC looked even more shaken at the mention of swimming.

"What about a hose?"

"Damn. Left that back on my dock."

"No problem. We'll use tubing." Adam pointed at the inside ladder to Big Zen's elevated stern cabin, which would be last to flood. "For now, go up to the stern cabin. I'll join you soon."

With the water chest-deep and rising, Adam pushed his way to the galley, felt around for a knife, grabbed it, sucked in a big breath and dove down. He opened the cabinet under the galley sink and groped around for plastic tubing. None. It was all metal pipe.

He swam up, desperate for air, but water filled the cabin clear to the ceiling. With lungs screaming, he remembered. Swimming under water, he kicked, stroked, and pushed his way along the passageway. The head was this way? Where? He should have reached it by now. Gotta keep going. No. Gotta go back, get air. No. Gotta keep on. Gotta get tubing. Gotta. Gotta. Finally, the head. He swam to the shower and reached in. His hand closed on plastic tubing. Thank God. The hand-held shower hose. He cut it free. His oxygen-starved brain shutting down, blacking out, he kicked, pulled, stroked and clawed. Where was that interior ladder? Where? Where? Blackness.

Strong hands gripped Adam's arms. BC propelled his friend's limp form toward and then up and up the ladder. When Adam's unconscious head finally broke the surface near the ceiling of the high stern cabin, some animal instinct took over, some primordial will to live arched Adam's back, expanded his chest and opened his windpipe in a violent gasp, an enormous sucking in of sweet, sweet air.

But there was no time. The air space between water and ceiling was less than six inches and diminishing fast. Adam sucked in one last breath as it disappeared entirely. Amazingly, the tubing was still in his hand. He swam toward the cabin's door to the main deck. Now completely underwater—equalizing the water pressure on both sides—it opened easily. Careful not to let his head break the surface, he extended the shower tube upward until the end poked into the night air. Using all the air he had, he blew the water up out of the tube, clearing it. Then, carefully testing it, he sucked. Aaahhh. Sweet air! Cupping his palm over its end to keep it clear of water, he passed the tube to BC, who drew in a huge lungful. BC too must've been moments from passing out.

Adam expected it to happen a little later. But suddenly, when the cabin roof was only two feet below the surface, Big Zen hit bottom and settled onto the mud.

No doubt it would take a while for the bomb-wielding shooter or shooters to satisfy themselves that everyone aboard Big Zen was dead. Determined to out wait the assassins, Adam and BC passed the tube back and forth, grateful just to be breathing.

The Napa River was much warmer than the Bay, but still they steadily lost body heat. Before he got too numb to function, Adam swam down to retrieve stuff: weapons, wallets, shoes, clothes, iPhones. Everything was completely soaked. Amazingly, the phones—little infinity machines—seemed just fine.

After a half hour, before they slipped into hypothermia, they had to move. Instead of surfacing over the boat, they came up under a nearby floating dock. Ahhhh, at last, air. Free, abundant air straight into mouth and nose. Not through a tube. Time to slip away silently and fast. To play it safe, the two sopping wet men stayed off roads as much as possible, and instead walked through the middle of vineyard after vineyard.

In the early morning light, Adam asked, "How does it feel to be perfect, smart and tenacious?"

BC grinned. "And to have top-notch skills."

"Better than any regular agent." Adam rolled his eyes.

After a while, Adam said, "By the way, I know what you did. I was a goner. And you figured out how to swim all in an instant. Facing lifelong fear takes guts, real guts. Totally saved me."

"And I know what you did," BC replied. "That thing with the cushion—and the tubing. Totally saved me."

CHAPTER 10
FIVE-FOOT-TALL VINEYARDS

As they walked, BC called a detective buddy with the Oakland police. After asking a few questions but mostly listening, he put away his phone and said, "They're drawing a blank on the car bomb. Before the Tesla exploded, someone shot and blinded the garage security cameras with a paintball gun. The explosive was military grade C-4. Impossible to trace exactly, but probably of foreign manufacture."

The light of dawn was breaking, and the two tall men would soon be clearly visible as they walked among the rows of grape trellises. Come to think of it, they could already be seen by anyone using night vision goggles.

In the distance they saw a roadside cafe, already with a row of cars parked out front. Probably vineyard workers grabbing breakfast before another day tending the vines and figuring out how to make the world's best wine even better. Taking refuge inside, they ordered breakfast and basked in the warmth of the place, hoping their clothes would dry out already.

As they waited for their food, BC said, "The world and Oakland being what they are, I activated sentry mode in my Tesla."

"What's that?"

"It means fourteen motion activated cameras record anything and everything that happens in and around the car. It's still cutting edge enough that most car thieves—and car bombers—don't know about it."

"Could a savvy bad guy break in and erase or steal the video?"

"Nope. I set it to instantly upload to the cloud."

"You can access the footage on your cell phone?"

"Yeah, and I can feed it to your phone as well."

BC got busy tapping his phone, and soon they both watched video of a robust-looking Asian guy drop down next to BC's Tesla, reach under and attach what had to be a bomb. Later, a hapless car thief—guy with the look of a meth or fentanyl junkie—smashed a side window. And that was all she wrote.

The bomber struck Adam as fit, savvy and relaxed.

Exuded strength and confidence. Well dressed but not flashy. The guy was a pro.

Adam said, "We could show this to Su Jingfoi and see if it's Gong Dongfeng."

"That's worth a try," BC said. "But it's probably just some low-level operative."

Adam selected a good frame showing the guy's face clearly, and texted it to Jingfoi.

BC ran the photo through Oakland Police and national law-enforcement databases. All came up dry.

"It really sucks," BC said, "that we can't use the agency database. Seems like they'd have cameras on the Chinese embassies or something. Maybe this guy's a known spy."

"Sometimes, when you're forced to be resourceful, you come up with something even better," Adam said. "I think I know something even better, way better."

At that moment an inner alarm sounded in Adam's brain. A nondescript light colored sedan had just pulled up in front of the cafe and six very alert-looking Asian men were getting out and looking around. One was the bomber!

Adam immediately spun on the booth bench seat to face away from the window. Signaling BC to do likewise, he said, "Speak of the devil, the bomber and five of his friends just pulled up out front. They're coming in. Follow me."

Adam slid out of the booth, and, stepping around a server, speed walked straight into the kitchen. Seeing the back exit, he broke into a run with BC hot on his heels. They raced through the door and BC slammed it shut. Hunching down to stay below the level of the five-foot-tall grape trellises, they ran into the vineyard.

Deep among the grapes, Adam said, "Those men looked way too alert for us to take them by surprise."

"And that was no place for a fire fight."

"Besides, they damn near took us by surprise."

"Them finding my boat way up here, and now finding us like this, they've gotta be tracking us somehow."

"It's gotta be our cell phones," Adam said. "Follow me again."

Still hunched over, they raced through the vines toward a gas station in the near distance. A pickup and a van towing a ski boat were parked at the pumps, while, apparently, the owners used the restrooms, paid for gas, or maybe got coffee. After glancing around and seeing the coast was clear, Adam slipped his phone under the cover of the ski boat while BC hid his under a pile of trash in the back of the pick up truck. Just in time. The owners soon climbed into their vehicles and drove away. In opposite directions. Beautiful.

Seeing a phone booth on the far side of the gas station, Adam said to BC, "I'll join you shortly out in the middle of yonder vineyard."

Before discarding his phone, Adam had pulled up and memorized a number which he dialed.

"Yellow,"

"Harry, you rascal. It's happening again. Me and BC are up to our necks—actually way over our heads—in a quest to save the world. Literally. And we need your help."

True to his blessed, eccentric, fearless nature, Adam's, Peace's and BC's old friend, tech billionaire Harry Bellacozy, quickly grasped the situation. Minutes after their brief chat, Harry's personal Sikorski helicopter was in the air on its way to pick up the two large damp men.

CHAPTER 11
SILICON VALLEY

The nearly silent Sikorsky flew the full length of the blue, shimmering Bay, from the vineyards of Napa in the north to the heart of Silicon Valley in the south. Instead of going to Bellacozy's mansion in Woodside, the helicopter delivered them to the sprawling Menlo Park campus of Prophecy.

Harry Bellacozy's empire included his private Hawaiian Island, the Golden Gate Yacht Club, an electric car company, an international energy extraction outfit, and more than a dozen major tech firms, foremost among which was the tech giant Prophecy. Under Harry's leadership, Prophecy, his flagship enterprise, had built and continued to maintain much of the world's internet infrastructure.

The Prophecy campus was vast, beautifully manicured, and exuded wealth. The roofs of the buildings and the surrounding grounds were an exquisitely landscaped oasis of trees, exotic plants, pathways, and inviting conversation nooks and gathering places. Pump-driven waterfalls and streams, created, frankly, an ambiance of paradise.

Indoors, luxurious cafeterias overflowed with the trendiest in chef-made California cuisine—all free to employees. A spacious beautifully equipped gym, zany game rooms, private soundproof sleeping/meditation pods, and on-site child and pet day care centers both nurtured and, let's face it, addicted the Prophecy team.

Harry Bellacozy was a casually dressed, six-foot, trim, somewhat weather beaten guy in his sixties, who looked and moved like a much younger man. General Eisenhower—General was his name not his rank—was a small, round man with busy hands and a military bearing—though he'd never served a day in the military. It was obvious the two had a special bond, not just because Ike brought an insane level of talent to his role as Prophecy's head of cyber research and cybersecurity, but also because he was totally honest and loyal.

Adam and BC, who knew Harry and Ike from past escapades, briefed the two men on the investigation and recent events. They concluded by sharing a Tesla photo of the bomber Gong Dongfeng.

Harry Bellacozy asked, "How'd these guys zero in on you so fast?"

"Beats me," BC said. "All we did was walk through the Diablo yard and ask about bricks."

"It's actually not surprising," Ike said. "That walk through and single question were enough for them to run a check on both of you."

"Here," Adam asked, "in America?"

"These guys are Chi Coms," Ike said. "The Chinese Communists maintain an ever-growing database on people inside and outside China. Their AI facial recognition cameras and BeiDou satellite system work hand in hand. They must've identified you and linked you to your cell phones. From then on you were surveilled and tracked 24/7."

"Everywhere?"

"Yep. Up until you ditched your cell phones."

Adam shook his head. "Orwellian."

Ike agreed, "A surveillance state with worldwide reach."

Harry moaned, "And they couldn't have built it without us, without the big US tech firms."

BC asked, "Why for God's sake did you do that?"

"I wish to hell we hadn't," Harry said, his brows bunched. "We thought if we worked with 'em, the Chi Coms would mellow and become more democratic. But they've only grown more totalitarian and aggressive."

BC said, "That's for sure. They're destroying democracy in Hong Kong. Demolishing the indigenous culture of Tibet. Obliterating Uighur culture and putting millions of people in reeducation camps. They're forcing organ harvesting on Falun Gong prisoners. And they let loose the Covid 19 pandemic."

"Not to mention," added Ike, "intellectual property theft, forced technology transfer, ongoing cyberwarfare and a whole lot more evil shit."

"All true," Adam said. "So where do we go from here?"

"Fortunately," Bellacozy said, "we left a back door."

Ike added, "After all, we're not fools."

BC said, "Thank God!"

"Yeah, tell me about it," Harry said.

The four men left the billionaire's posh office, passed through an internal heightened security check point, and entered his huge, private, inner-sanctum computer suite. "Their firewall, facial-recognition, surveillance, social-credit, censorship system is interwoven with artificial intelligence, AI. The whole thing continuously improves, refines and protects itself. If we didn't have a secret back door mostly hidden from the AI, we'd be shit out of luck."

"So we can use their own system against them?" Adam asked.

"Exactly," Harry said. "Pretty much."

"What do you mean by 'mostly hidden'?" Adam asked.

Ike jumped in. "Means we have to be very, very careful to blend in, to not call attention to ourselves, to leave no trace."

"It's a tightrope, a delicate balance," Harry said. "Gathering data while hiding in plain sight."

Ike sat down in front of an especially complex keyboard. As his hands moved in a blur over the keys, he said, "I'm searching, very carefully, all Chinese systems for information on the bomber."

The others looked on in hushed anticipation. Amazing. What a world. With a few key strokes they'd soon have the full scoop on Gong Dongfeng. Adam took a moment to survey the room, appreciating the rosewood panelling, the forest of big screen computers filling the space, the soft natural light filtering in through floor-to-ceiling windows, the exquisite redwood grove rustling in a light breeze just beyond thick, no-doubt bulletproof glass. The minutes ticked on, but nothing happened.

"Odd," Ike said. "There's no sign of this guy on any of their databases."

"Just a hunch," Harry said. "Remember the massively encrypted database for the secret police division of the Chinese Ministry of Public Safety? Try that."

Harry paused, then put his hands together as though praying to the gods of cyber, "But whatever you do, don't alert the AI."

"That won't be easy," Ike said as his fingers danced over the keyboard. "I'll have to use quantum computing."

BC whistled as he looked over Ike's shoulder. "Multiple ever-changing kaleidoscopic passwords. This isn't just secret-police-level encryption. This is top secret CIA-level stuff. Is this guy a regular Chinese James Bond?"

Then, after several minutes, images of Gong Dongfeng appeared on the giant flat screen. A dozen or so images and a chunk of data.

"Son of a gun," BC said, "That's him alright. Ministry of

Public Safety my ass. This guy's one bad dude."

The data, though limited, allowed a profile to take shape. Gong Dongfeng, it seemed, posed as a journalist while in fact he was a major in the Global Liberation Army and an impressively versatile black ops agent and hit man.

As part of the CPP's 'Fox Hunt: Tigers and Flies' and 'Thousand Talents' programs, Dongfeng brought Chinese researchers and academics working in the United States back to China as a way of stealing US technology. Often these Chinese living aboard complied willingly—but when they resisted, Dongfeng forced compliance by threatening and sometimes actually imprisoning family members still in China. Often, he tapped the more willing of these people to help with other operations, all with the goal of undermining and dominating the United States.

As a sort of propaganda puppet master, he fed carefully crafted articles and "background information" laden with CPP propaganda and disinformation to mainstream western news outlets, which printed it without question or criticism. This propaganda, more often than not, was accompanied by jaw-dropping bribes and other incentives directed to key editors, publishers and influencers.

One thread that particularly caught Adam's eye involved Dongfeng's close relationship with a woman named Roe Rosen.

As a member of a Marxist revolutionary group, Rosen had received a near life sentence for her role in pulling off a series of robberies, bombings and cop killings. Amazingly, she had been granted a presidential pardon a dozen or so years earlier. Currently, as a founding board member and vice president of a nonprofit called 'Thousand Rivers,' Rosen oversaw the flow of millions upon millions of dollars—much of it provided by Gong Dongfeng—to ACAB and Freedom Highway.

Dongfeng and Rosen were working hand in hand to turn

protests violent by sending in paid agents provocateur, scouts, communication teams, pallets of bricks, vans filled with rocks and fire accelerants, and armed shooters. Through the manipulation of social media, the mainstream media, and a horde of witting and unwitting accomplices, they fanned the flames of political and racial division, mayhem and hate. Clearly, Dongfeng and Rosen did not seek reform or improvement, instead they were doing everything they could—often with devastating effectiveness—to destabilize the United States and aid China in its pursuit of world dominance.

CHAPTER 12
THE BATTLE ROYAL

Adam turned to Harry, who was just finishing a phone call. "So we can use the CPP BeiDou system to track Dongfeng?"

Harry replied, "Yep, provided we have his cell phone number."

Ike added, "Also, if you can pinpoint where he is in real-time, the system can lock onto his phone and track him from there."

BC said, "Trouble is, I'm not seeing the guy's cell number anywhere. This is a lot of information, but no cell phone."

"That in itself is significant," Ike said. "It could indicate Dongfeng's independent, a bit of a rogue. If true, that's amazing. In the CPP, to keep your cell phone secret from the system is no small thing. Basically everyone is supposed to be tracked and surveilled by the system. Only the people at the very top are above this. Certainly freedom from surveillance wouldn't normally apply to an army major, no matter how much he might be like James Bond."

Adam said, "There's no address for Dongfeng, but there is one for Roe Rosen."

"I see it in your eyes," BC said. "An idea."

Adam opened his mouth to speak, but paused when he noticed Harry Bellacozy tightening his jaw, balling hands into fists, and smoldering with unconcealed anger. Adam said, "Harry, I don't think I've ever seen you so pissed off."

"The gall," Harry spoke through clenched teeth. "The sheer audacity. The evil. I knew the CPP was bad. That they're essentially a bunch of gangsters who dump the spoils of a state run fascist economy into their own dictatorship. But I had no idea they were moving so fast to bring us down, to destroy us."

Harry faced Adam and BC. "You came to the right place! This is a battle that absolutely has to be fought, and the sooner the better."

"That sounds so good."

"Thanks, man."

"This calls," continued Harry, "for an all-out response. I'll be damned if we'll let our brand of wild, goofy, chaotic freedom go down without a fight."

"It's fight or be swallowed," Ike said.

"Amen to that," BC said.

Harry smiled at BC. "You're a true tech wizard BC. I'd like you to team up with Ike here and some other American tech warriors, a group I call my cyber ninjas."

Ike added, "Also, we're sending a crew to float and tow Big Zen to a boatyard in Richmond where it will be fully restored."

BC broke into a huge smile. "That all sounds fantastic. You guys are the best."

At that moment, in walked two dozen or so diverse young techies—including, holy mackerel, Vocab and Rasheed, both grinning broadly. Adam and BC hugged and chatted up the two young black men, who, they learned, were full time staffers for Prophecy—making viral videos right and left for the tech giant.

Harry welcomed everyone, introduced each person by name, and then outlined the situation. With arms spread wide, he concluded by saying, "You, in this room, are literally the top tech geniuses on this planet. It's time to right a terrible wrong. It's time to tear down the CPP Great Wall. We helped create a monster, and it's high time we civilize it, teach it some manners.

I'm talking, of course, about the Communist People's Party, the CPP, not the Chinese people."

No one batted an eye. This larger-than-life, sometimes grandiose billionaire had more than once transformed much of the modern world, and was capable of anything. The task, everyone knew, was damned near impossible. But if Harry Bellacozy said do it, they were going to pour themselves into the effort with total dedication, with every ounce of sinew, heart, soul and brain power they possessed.

For these young people, of course, paychecks were important.

But even more important were the challenge, the camaraderie, and, for many, the chance to join with this charismatic billionaire in the defense of freedom. Also, it didn't hurt that chef-prepared California cuisine—and unlimited pizzas—were in the offing.

Harry turned to Adam, grinning. "In this room, we'll fight the cyber war."

Adam grinned back. "Meanwhile, I'll be out there, in the physical world—"

"—doing what you do so well," Harry said.

"Well," Adam said, "doing my best."

"Cyber only goes so far." Harry continued. "Sometimes there's no substitute for actually going into the dragon's lair, being there, seeing, piecing things together, doing what has to be done, and, of course, along the way, out smarting the booby-traps and assassins."

"The fight's on," BC beamed, "the battle royal."

CHAPTER 13
BELVEDERE

The whisper-quiet Sikorski flew Adam north. Far below, bridges spanning the Bay sparkled like bejeweled bracelets in the twilight.

He was going to miss having BC at his side. But Harry had a point: BC would be more valuable as a cyber warrior than as an undercover sleuth, where his identity as a cop was difficult to hide. Fortunately, BC's role as liaison between the cyber war room and Adam would keep them in frequent touch.

In the copter's luxurious, captain-of-the-universe main cabin, Adam familiarized himself with a duffle bag of high tech gear provided by Ike: untraceable ear-piece, throat-mic comm gear; cell phones; jammers; a drone shield; high-resolution night-vision scopes; tiny cameras; a long-range parabolic listening device; and other spy wizardry.

Testing out one of the phones, he punched in the number for Tripnee, his undercover-FBI-agent, world-class-sniper girlfriend. One of the smartest people he'd ever met, she was impetuous, a force-of-nature, and often a major pain in the ass. But she made his heart pound like no one else. Damn, no answer.

The chopper dropped Adam off in a tree-studded, grassy park on the north side of Marina Bay. As a warm Santa Ana wind swept west, off the land and out across the Bay, he walked along the shoreline trail in the fading twilight toward Dream

Voyager's mooring. Right there, adjacent to the trail, was Su Jingfoi's townhouse. A lot had happened in the two days since they'd talked. Was she OK?

When Adam knocked on Jingfoi's door, she opened it only a crack. With quivering lips and eyes big and scared, she scribbled a quick note, and handed it to him. Then she whispered, "Go away," and shut the door. Oh oh. Something had terrified this strong, elegant woman.

The note read, "The photo you sent is Donfeng. We're all in danger. Be careful."

Troubled, Adam continued to his boat. Interestingly, the closer he got to Dream Voyager, the less heavy and more energized he felt. The challenges of the world were still there with a vengeance. But as he climbed aboard his floating home, his sanctuary in a wild universe, it was as though he stepped out from under the problems and bubbled up to see them from above, from a sort of meta perspective.

Wait! The boat was dark, but the alarms had been deactivated and the companionway hatch stood open. Had CPP agents tracked down his boat, disabled his security system, and forced their way in? Were they lying in wait with guns drawn? He didn't think so. "Tripnee, is that you?"

"Adam, is that you?" Came a playful, melodious, familiar voice.

They came together at the top of the companionway. After hugs and kisses, Adam filled her in on recent events. When he told her his plan, naturally, she wanted to go with him.

"I dunno. These guys are bad, really bad," he said. "They're lethal and evil. They use the latest technology to track and surveil. They're doing everything they can to kill me and BC. I don't feel good about exposing you to that. It's just too dangerous."

"To hell with that." Tripnee said. "I'm coming. You're going to need me."

The woman had a point, and Adam knew what to do. Starting from the beginning, he began filling her in on all that had happened. Also, at the same time, they fired up hot drink in the galley, slipped their moorings and got underway. For the moment, it was a beautiful night. The extraordinary, warm Santa Ana wind flowed out of the east, headed across the Bay and out to sea. For the sheer sensual pleasure of it, even as they talked, they hoisted the main and unfurled the genoa, putting one to starboard and the other to port. Gliding downwind wing on wing, they knifed along Potrero Reach, across the open Bay, and up the center of Raccoon Strait, the narrows between Angel Island and Tiburon. After passing the southern tip of Belvedere, they jibed the main to turn north—to starboard—up into Richardson Bay.

An inlet off San Francisco Bay, Richardson Bay was roughly one mile wide by three miles long. The lights of ritzy Sausalito sparkled on its west side while the designer lamps of far more ritzy Belvedere glowed on its eastern shore. In between, covering much of the bay's ever-sloshing surface, floated a vast armada of boat dwellings known as anchor outs.

Adam was still bringing Tripnee up to speed as they lowered the main, furled the genoa, and started the motor. Moving slowly, steering carefully, Adam threaded his way into the motley flotilla of anchor outs. In the moonlight, they slid by all manner of craft, from handsome, well-kept power and sail boats to beat-up, barely floating derelicts. All swung at anchor, living rent free, basking in the view shed of multi-multi-million-dollar homes.

The nice thing, from Adam's perspective, was that this worked both ways. The anchor outs were in full view of this

Valhalla of the super rich, but at the same time, these opulent homes were in full view of the anchor outs.

It took a while, but eventually they found a spot large enough for seventy-foot Dream Voyager to drop and swing at anchor. Perfect. They were lost in the middle of this menagerie. Still, to further ensure they would be the observers and not the observed, they draped netting around the bimini awning, encircling the cockpit.

Digging into the bag of spy gear provided by Ike, Adam brought out a powerful night scope and a high-tech parabolic microphone system that could listen in on conversations up to a mile away.

Tripnee brought out six drones the size of bumble bees and put on special augmented reality AR glasses and a wrist device that looked like a big watch. Moving her hands through the air as though operating an invisible control board, she sent the tiny, powerful quadracopters out into the night.

Their focus, the reason for this stake out, was Roe Rosen, the ex-con, Thousand Rivers board member linked to Gong Dongfeng.

Tripnee looked toward Rosen's estate on the northern end of the Belvedere shoreline a quarter mile away. "Can you believe it? How does someone running a non-profit, a convicted cop killer, after being sprung from prison, own such a big chunk of the most expensive real estate in the world?"

"Hard work?" offered Adam, rolling his eyes. "Whole-heartedly embracing the American dream?"

Tripnee grimaced, "More like totally selling out and destroying that dream."

Adam peered through his powerful scope, which poked out through a crack in the netting. Like many Belvedere homes, Rosen's opulent mansion featured floor-to-ceiling glass windows facing the water. Perfect. Made Dream Voyager's location an ideal vantage point.

Interesting. An Asian man and a blonde Caucasian woman were having a wild time in bed. Adjusting his scope, he zeroed in on the woman. The similarity to the photos he'd seen earlier was unmistakable. It was Roe Rosen. Maybe she wasn't the most beautiful woman Adam had seen, especially considering present company, but Rosen was good looking alright—and clearly had an animal magnetism. The man was beside himself, delirious with crazy joy. The woman obviously had gifts.

One of Tripnee's drones attached itself to a high corner of one of Rosen's bedroom windows. A miniaturization miracle, the device allowed her to monitor voice and electronic communications, and—via her AR eyeglasses—allowed her to see as though looking through the camera-eyes of the drone.

"Why would anyone," she wondered, "do this in plain view of the world with the lights on?"

"From those houses," Adam said, "the anchor outs and the world look far way. There's an illusion of privacy."

"That's an illusion alright." Tripnee handed Adam a pair of AR glasses. "With these we'll hear and see through the drones' mics and cameras."

The man in the lit up bedroom a half mile away pleaded, "Say it! Say it!"

"Hegemon."

"More. Louder."

The woman yelled, "Hegemon! Hegemon!"

"Aaaaah, yes! Yes! Yes!"

"HEGEMON! HEGEMON! HEGEMON!"

"YES! YES! YES! Aaaiiieeeee!!"

After the man crescendoed in a paroxysm of screaming and writhing, the pair grew still.

Rosen asked, "What's it mean: Hegemon?"

"Is very special word," said the man, who was slight of build with a baby face and looked to be in his twenties. "It means supreme ruler, owner of everything."

"Everything?"

"For six thousand years the emperors of China ruled and owned everything under heaven. With one ruler, everyone knew their place. It's the only way to create peace and harmony."

The man leapt up and began pulling on clothes. The woman also rose, but instead of dressing, arched her back and paraded nude back and forth across the large bedroom, seeming to relish how the man's gaze followed her every move. She said, "I like it. But what about recently, the last two hundred years?"

"Unspeakable humiliation," the man said, sounding wounded, casting his eyes down. "But temporary. Soon China will again take its place as the most powerful nation in the world, as the hegemon."

The man left the room. Within moments a chauffeur-driven limousine emerged from behind the house and drove away, followed by a second long black car carrying four men. Probably some kind of security detail.

Adam relayed photos of the couple plus their exact GPS location to BC at Prophecy headquarters. Soon, BC called and Adam put him on speaker phone. "That's Roe Rosen alright. But the guy isn't showing up at all in the facial recognition system. Or, to be more precise, the system automatically blurs him out. Could be a glitch, but I don't think so. I think this guy is some kind of super Chinese elite. So high-level the system won't track him."

"For a big shot," Tripnee said, "he's damed young—and green."

"Too young to have made his own mark," Adam said, "Probably riding on somebody's else's coat tails."

"Maybe the relative of some super big shot," Tripnee said.

"High up enough to think he has a chance to become the hegemon."

BC said, "This BeiDou system is impressive. Just knowing his exact co-ordinates a few minutes ago—even without knowing his name—we identified his phone. Now we're tracking him."

"That's excellent—and, of course, terrible," Adam said. "Give us hourly updates on where he goes. For now, we'll stay on Rosen."

It was past midnight. Adam had been going nonstop for two days, so Tripnee kept watch while he slept. Later, they switched and Tripnee went below while Adam kept an eye on Rosen.

At first light, a black Porsche pulled onto a flat parking area just south of the house. Out got—whoa!—Gong Dongfeng.

The guy must've had his own key, because he let himself in through a side door near Rosen's bedroom. He slipped in, took off his clothes, and jumped into bed like it was his house.

Dongfeng seemed to be at least as excited and infatuated as the previous visitor. The woman, compared to her romp the night before, seemed more eager, more into it. This guy, it could be seen, had the muscular, filled-out body of a more mature man in his prime. His passion was intense but more measured and longer lasting.

The tiny surveillance drones stuck to the bedroom window did their job perfectly. Adam, soon joined by Tripnee, watched and listened as though they were in the room, and recorded it all.

After their romp, Dongfeng and Rosen jumped out of bed. They dressed, grinning and laughing, all the while casting appreciative glances at each other—and touching and kissing each other.

Suddenly, Dongfeng, as though remembering something unpleasant, frowned and seemed to lose his swagger.

"Oh yea, I should let you know, a couple of gweilos are investigating our Oakland protest, and they're getting a little close."

"Who are they?"

"One's an Oakland cop. Not sure about the other one."

"Goddammit!" Rosen yelled. "You said Oakland would only pretend to investigate. You said you had that taken care of."

"This cop's a renegade, doing it on his own," Dongfeng said. "We think he was a friend of Dorman's."

"Goddammit to hell!"

"Don't worry," Dongfeng said soothingly. "I tell you only because—"

"I made you promise to keep me informed."

"Exactly. So, most assuredly, for harmony, put it out of your mind. Meditate. Stay calm. I'll handle it. There's no way they can trace anything back to us. Everything's fine."

"Shit, shit, shit, shit." Rosen hunched over, her hands pulling her long blonde hair. "We did what we had to do. Thing is, there's no way to create mayhem without spilling a little blood."

"Like Americans say," Dongfeng said, "you can't make omelet without breaking egg."

Rosen seemed to perk up. "That's right. And things are looking up. We're winning. The revolution is rocking and rolling!"

Rosen moved close to Dongfeng, her tits almost touching his face. "I just can't go back to prison. You've got to do whatever it takes to kill these investigators. Remember ACAB: All Cops Are Bastards!"

Dongfeng said, 'Don't worry. I'll take care of it."

Rosen stood back, fists on hips, and snarled, "Don't fuck it up!"

Dongfeng, his expression unreadable, left the bedroom, let himself out the side entrance, and roared away in his Porsche.

This time BC was able to confirm this man was in the BeiDou system. He was indeed Gong Dongfeng. And now that they had him linked to a cell phone, they could use the worldwide Chinese system to keep tabs on the guy. So far so good.

Tripnee asked, "You think the two guys know about each other?"

Adam mused, "Maybe they have an understanding? One gets evenings and the other gets mornings?"

"Something tells me they know each other," Tripnee said, "but somebody doesn't know the whole picture."

"What do you say," Adam said, "we learn more about these two rich Asian men."

"One a lot richer than the other."

"You got that right."

CHAPTER 14
DONGFENG'S DAY

Tripnee brought in most of her drones, leaving just two wedged in high corners of Rosen's bedroom windows. Keeping more in place could be too risky if Rosen did security sweeps for bugs.

Adam and Tripnee locked all hatches, set the alarms, packed some select equipment into two backpacks, and rode the skiff across glassy water to the dinghy dock at Schoonmaker Point in Sausalito.

You can't save the free world running on empty. So they ordered breakfast at a nearby dockside restaurant overlooking the bay. As they dug into eggs, bacon, sausage, fried tomatoes, pancakes, fresh squeezed juice, and coffee, they turned on their earpiece coms and checked in with BC, who was tracking Dongfeng.

"Dongfeng's already made two stops," BC said.

Tripnee said, "Busy guy."

"On his first stop," BC said, "he parked in the Point Richmond driveway of Chen Lao. Google and Chinese system searches show Chen is president of a pro-democracy Hong Kong student group at the University of California Berkeley. Dongfeng stayed there only fifteen minutes."

Adam said, "Something tells me Chen didn't enjoy those minutes."

"On his second stop," BC continued, "Dongfeng went to the East Bay hills home of Ma Lanying. Ma was born in China, immigrated to the US in her twenties, and is now a doctor with a successful medical practice and chairman of an East Bay Republican group. Also, she's a big donor to the Independent Institute, a conservative think tank. Dongfeng was there for about half an hour. Right now, he's on the Bay Bridge heading into San Francisco."

"This BeiDou tracking system's excellent," Tripnee said, "and terrifying."

"Yeah," BC said, "No kidding! BeiDou not only tracks, it also monitors phone calls and even off-line conversations. Our cyber team just hacked the system so we can turn on the microphone on Dongfeng's cell phone."

Adam asked, "So we can listen to his conversations wherever he goes?"

"Yea, pretty much," BC said, "as long as he has his cell phone with him."

"This is a total game changer," Tripnee said. "But you didn't eavesdrop on his last two stops?"

"No. We didn't get any audio on those," BC said. "His cell phone might've been in his briefcase or maybe there're things about the system we're still figuring out."

"So where is Dongfeng now?" asked Adam.

"My screen shows him heading toward the Sunset district, on the west side of the City."

"We'll rent a car," Adam said, "and pick up his trail there."

Adam and Tripnee walked a few blocks to a car rental agency, where they selected a Ford Taurus with a sunroof.

Tripnee said, "The ultimate incognito vehicle. You know how to treat a girl right."

Adam grinned. "Only the best."

Later, as the Taurus crossed the Golden Gate Bridge, BC

checked in. "Dongfeng's meeting with someone out near Ocean Beach. I'll patch the audio through to you."

Dongfeng's voice came through loud and clear. "How's it going with Whitehead?"

A woman's voice replied, "Very good, sir."

Dongfeng said, "And?"

"He already loves me and wants to get married."

"And?"

""He's on Tier One. He feels positive about China. And he's ready for Tier Two."

Dongfeng said, "For Tier Two, we need copies of his latest secret research."

"Yes, sir."

"Very good," Dongfeng said, "this will show in my report on your work. Keep doing your job, and your family will be very happy. They will get to stay in their very nice apartment."

The conversation ended, and Dongfeng departed.

BC patched the BeiDou data stream through to Tripnee's iPad. A moving dot on a Google-like map showed Dongfeng driving, and then stopping at an address in the upscale San Francisco neighborhood of St. Francis Woods.

"This system blows me away," BC said. "It's already telling me Dongfeng's walking up to the home of a Dr. Robert Whitehead. Whitehead's a chemistry professor at California State University in San Francisco, and also works at Lawrence Livermore lab."

"The lab's a national defense contractor," Tripnee said.

BC again patched through the audio from Dongfeng's phone. They heard the sound of Gong Dongfeng ringing the doorbell. When the door opened, he introduced himself and was ushered in.

"As I said on the phone," Dongfeng said, "I'm writing an article about you and your impressive achievements."

"Who did you say you write for?"

"My articles appear in China Daily, China's largest newspaper, and also in the London Times, the New York Herald, and newspapers worldwide."

"Main stream. I like it." Whitehead said.

"How was your recent trip to China?" Dongfeng asked. "I understand your talk went extremely well."

"They said that?"

"Yes. Everyone I've talked with was deeply impressed with both your presentation and with you as a very perceptive, brilliant man."

"Really? They sure rolled out the red carpet."

"For you, of course."

Whitehead said, "The students were so engaged and asked excellent, in-depth questions. It really was great. I felt like a celebrity."

"Sir, if I may say so, you deserve the attention. You've written over fifty cutting edge papers."

"I'm afraid that doesn't get you much recognition here in the US."

"That makes no sense."

Tripnee looked skeptical. "Gag me. Dongfeng's laying it on thick."

"Yep," Adam said, "Praise and flattery. Spy recruitment 101."

Dongfeng continued, "My article and, I hope, future articles will lead to you receiving the recognition you deserve."

Whitehead said, "You're too kind."

"Sir, you're a great scientist. I know what I'm talking about."

"Well, I did love my trip. I learned a lot about China, and I can tell you, I'm all for you guys."

"Coming from you, that means a lot."

"Why is it that US academics criticize China?" Whitehead

wondered. "Seems so unfair."

Dongfeng said, "We'd love to continue following your brilliant work. Would you do us the honor of coming to China to make another presentation? All expenses paid of course."

"I'd love to," Whitehead said. "Would it be okay if I bring my new girlfriend? You wouldn't believe it. Since returning from my trip, I've met a very special woman. She's absolutely amazing. It just so happens she's Chinese."

"Of course. That would be wonderful," Dongfeng said. "I have to hand it to you, sir. It is well known that Chinese women are the best. They're loyal, know their place, and they will take care of you in every way."

The encounter went on in this vein for awhile, then Dongfeng excused himself and drove away.

Tripnee said, "That's how they do it. Getting the guy to see China and the CPP system in a positive light is the first step, the so-called First Tier. Just achieving that is considered a win."

"And Tier Two," Adam said, "is getting them to reveal classified material. What's Tier Three?"

"That's when they help recruit other spies."

Tripnee's iPad, thanks to BC hooking it into the BeiDou system, showed the Chinese agent driving north across the Golden Gate Bridge and then taking Highway 1 toward Stinson Beach. Adam and Tripnee kept pace a few miles back. Despite all that was going on in the world, as they drove they couldn't help but marvel at the pristine beauty of Mt. Tamalpais, the towering redwoods, and the wide Pacific stretching to the far horizon.

Dongfeng continued on through the quaint town of Stinson Beach, and turned in to a large estate near the quirky town of Bolinas, which was famous for the frequent disappearance of any and all directional signs pointing to its location.

Adam tucked the Taurus into a redwood grove two hundred

yards away. Tripnee opened the sunroof and, with her wrist controller and AR glasses, deployed a swarm of drones. Flying single file, the tiny but powerful quadracopters raced to the Bolinas estate, where they fanned out around the lavish home. The camera eyes of one, peering through a window, located Dongfeng talking with a woman in a blue pants suit. The drone attached itself to an upper corner of the window to peer in and listen.

In the meantime, BC had begun feeding the audio from Dongfeng's cell phone to their earpiece coms.

Adam, who also wore AR glasses, said, "Something tells me this is gonna be good."

The woman in the pants suit, who had her back to the window, was saying, "—too sensitive to include in any message. Some things can only be communicated in person."

"Of course," Dongfeng said. "Your precautions are very wise."

"We've got a problem. A very high profile guy in a New York City prison who knows too much. You've got to act fast. But you can't leave any sign of foul play." The woman handed a thumb drive to Dongfeng. "This contains all the information you need."

"I understand, no problem. We will handle it as we have for you so many times before."

"I sure as hell hope so," the woman said. "But this time I don't want there to be any fuck-ups, you understand? There'll be guards, security cameras and the coroner's report you've got take care of. It's got to look like suicide."

"Of course. It will not be a problem."

The woman's voice rose, gaining force, "I don't want there to be any rumors floating around the web. It's absolutely got to be seen as suicide."

"I understand."

"This is of paramount importance. We both know what this means for the next election."

Dongfeng bowed. "I understand. Consider it done. We have the best network, as you know. Our teams will totally handle the event. Make it look like suicide and leave absolutely no clues indicating otherwise. There will be absolutely no clues leading back to you or us."

"We're fucking counting on it. Don't fuck it up."

The woman turned—holy mackerel—no facial recognition software was needed. It was a face known throughout the world. Adam and Tripnee sat stunned. It was the wife of a former United States president, who herself had held major positions in the U.S. government.

Adam said, "Talk about big-time black ops guanxi."

Tripnee held her face in her hands. "This confirms my worst fears. I feel sick."

"Makes too of us."

"So the rumors are true. She and her husband—they're totally corrupt and in bed with the CPP!"

Adam said, "BC, have you been monitoring this? Let's send a super secure copy of this to Jeppesen."

"Good idea," BC said. "Wow! But I'm not surprised."

"Another thing," Adam said, "let's use BeiDou to track and tap that woman's phone."

"Consider it done," BC said. "Also, got some updates for you on the people Dongfeng visited earlier. The Cal Berkeley student Chen Lao resigned from his pro-democracy Hong Kong group. And Dr. Ma Lanying resigned from the East Bay Republican group and cut all ties with the conservative think tank."

"So fast. He must've scared the shit out of 'em." Tripnee's gaze turned hard. "This guy is definitely one evil asshole."

"Must've done something like that to Su Jingfoi. She was scared out of her wits too," Adam said.

"Sounds like their Thousand Talents program," Tripnee said.

"Or the Fox Hunt: Tigers and Flies Program."

Dongfeng had silently handed a briefcase to the woman and left the room. Soon, Adam and Tripnee heard his Porsche roar past the redwood grove where they were tucked out of sight. The iPad showed him driving at breakneck speed heading 'over the hill' back into the main Bay Area.

Back in the elegant home, the woman, now alone, opened the briefcase. As luck would have it, the drone's camera angle showed her smiling down upon row upon row, stack upon stack of hundred dollar bills.

Tripnee retrieved most of her drones, leaving just two to monitor the place. Then she and Adam followed Dongfeng. As they drove, BC reported, "Dongfeng's just asked his assistant to book a charter jet to take him to New York."

CHAPTER 15
NEW YORK CITY

BC's voice crackled over Adam and Tripnee's earpieces. "Dongfeng sent a super encrypted message. Took us a while, but we've hacked it. Here's the translation:

"Dragon Team: Top Top Priority: Immediate Action Required: Research, plan and begin no-trace hit on high-value inmate X in the Metropolitan Corrections Center in lower Manhattan. We need full details on:

—Warden, shift commanders, guards, kitchen staff, janitors, and medical examiners including names, work assignments, backgrounds, extended family and vulnerabilities"

Tripnee swore, "These guys are pros."

Adam added, "Yeah, they are. Sounds like for them this is routine."

The message continued:

"—Construction plans for entire prison complex including nearby federal courts, NYC police headquarters and nearby sewer and tunnel systems

—Prison rules and routine, timing of rounds, meal and exercise routines, etc.

—Alarm and lock systems, keys & codes for entire complex

—Location of prisoner—floor, section, cell number

—Cell mate info (move cell mate)

—CCTV

—Dragon Team entry/exit

Note to Tao: Make Harmony offer to frontline guards and medical examiner. I want everything to be in place ASAP to do the deed."

Adam and Tripnee caught the next commercial flight to New York.

As they settled into their seats, Tripnee frowned. "The Harmony offer?"

"Sounds like the sort of offer you can't refuse," Adam said. "Let's see: If you choose harmony, you do everything we say, keep mum about it, and maybe even get well paid. Otherwise, you and everyone you care about dies a horrible death."

They both fell silent. Later, Adam said, "The Metropolitan Correction Center. Isn't that where they kept Bernie Madoff and "El Chapo" Guzman?"

"That's the place. The MCC," Tripnee said. "Twelve stories high. Built for 350 inmates, but usually stuffed with over 700. Infamous for violence, bad sanitation, crowding, noise, rats, short staff and suicides. It's so bad, prisoners transferred from Rikers Island—itself an infamous hell hole—ask to go back to Rikers."

When the pair landed, BC called. "I'm patching you into a secure conference call with Ty Jeppesen, Harry Bellacozy and Ike."

After quick initial greetings, Jeppesen said, "We just intercepted a communication to Dongfeng from his Dragon team. The message said they've already made five so-called Harmony offers. The first two, a shift commander and a guard, refused and are dead. Two other guards and a medical examiner agreed to cooperate, and each has been promised a million bucks."

Tripnee blurted out, "How in hell are they moving so fast?"

"Several years ago," Jeppesen said, "the CPP hacked and downloaded the entire US federal employee database—

including all federal prison staff info."

"Through Tik Tok and other apps," Ike said, "The Chi Coms collect massive data worldwide—especially in the US."

"In other words," Jeppesen said, "Most of the information they need is already in their system, available at the touch of a button."

"Makes sense," Harry said, "when your goal is world domination."

"What about the inmate? Adam asked. "Did they kill him already?"

"Not yet," said BC.

Tripnee said, "I say we arrest—or better yet kill—Dongfeng and his Dragon team before they kill anyone else."

"Although tempting—" Jeppesen said.

Ike said, "But we can't intervene without revealing our back door."

"Agreed," Jeppesen said. "We've got to play a long game. After all, we want to win the war, not just this skirmish. The back door is our ace in the hole. I'm not sure how yet, but somehow we've got to use it to stop not only the CPP but also the rot, the corruption in the US."

"Besides," Harry said, "who cares about that piece of shit pedophile."

"What we do need," Ty said, "is video of the CPP committing the murder."

Harry Bellacozy added, "But we've got to do it on the down low, so we don't tip 'em off that we're watching."

"Eventually, when the time is right, some how, some way," Ty said, "All of these people will be held accountable. The truth has got to come out."

CHAPTER 16
CELL 1204

Adam and Tripnee sat at a table in a Manhattan office tower adjacent to the Metropolitan Correction Center. Arranged by Jeppesen, the corner suite featured a long balcony overlooking the roof of the notorious MCC—a roof entirely covered in exercise cages of heavy mesh.

Using the CPP's astonishingly comprehensive database, Adam and Tripnee studied all of the same information as the Dragon team, including building plans, location of the cell, guard routines, etc.

Tripnee leaned back, rubbing her eyes. "The prison operating plan calls for the guards to check the cell every thirty minutes and shows multiple cameras continuously monitoring both the approach hallway and the cell itself."

"With the guards all harmonious and all," Adam said, "none of that is likely to happen."

"The way in for the drones," Tripnee said, "is through the ventilation system."

"Sounds good."

"But there's a problem. The rooftop filtration system will block 'em."

"I guess that's where I come in," Adam said.

They had anticipated this. At first, he'd considered getting onto the MCC roof by sliding down a rope from a silent helicopter. Then a simpler solution occurred to them: a zip line.

Usually, the simpler the plan, the less that can go wrong. Usually.

Jepson had come through with the equipment they'd requested. The key item was a pneumatic line thrower. Powered by compressed air, it had to be way quieter than the old rocket-driven models. Or so he hoped.

The question was: Would the 330-foot spool of 7 mm climbing line be long enough? And would the grappling hook find purchase? Or would it slide off, swing back and crash through some window far below?

Adam and Tripnee both wore full tactical gear, including black-ops clothing head-to-toe, body armor, and silenced Glock pistols in shoulder holsters. They studied the scene through night vision goggles. Since nightfall many hours earlier, the prison's rooftop exercise cages had been empty. No sign of activity. Mentally crossing his fingers, standing on the corner balcony several floors above the top of the MCC, Adam aimed the line thrower and pulled the trigger. Whooosh. Good. Not too loud.

The hook arced through the night. The line spooled out. All looked good. But suddenly the grapnel jerked to a stop in midair, then fell—and fell—until it swung to and fro through the city darkness like a big pendulum.

Son of a gun. Some kind of utility cable was in the way, invisible even to their night vision glasses. Hmmm. Even though they couldn't see it, maybe they could pull it out of the way. Reeling in the 7 mm line, Adam brought the hook up until it latched onto the wire. Then, going to the far end of the terrace, he kept pulling until whatever it was that was out there was pulled to one side.

Fortunately, they had an extra line and hook. Again, Adam aimed—this time with a flatter trajectory to miss the errant cable—and fired. Whoosh. The hook flew straight—and looked good—at first. But as the line spooled out, the arc curved downward—ever more downward. Until it clearly was just plain too low. Then, amazingly, instead of banging off the side of the prison, the grappling hook caught a lucky rebound on a protruding ledge. Seeming to defy gravity, it bounced up over the roof edge and snagged the corner of an exercise cage.

Whoa! That was cutting it close. Not only was the bounce a pure miracle, but also a mere twenty feet of line remained on the spool.

Adam tightened the 310-foot line with a z-rig, buckled on his tool-kit fanny pack, and hooked his climbing harness onto the line with a carabiner and pulley. Then he zipped through the darkness, wind whipping through his hair, over to the MCC roof edge.

Pulling himself up onto the cages, he walked across the heavy mesh. Finding the ventilation tower between two cages, he dropped down to examine the unit. Hmmm. The filtration system filled the bulk of the tower, but the bottom ten inches seemed to be straight ventilation shaft formed of one thickness of sheet metal.

He set to work. With a portable drill he made a tight row of small holes so close together they touched, forming a slot. Driving the lower jaw of a pair of metal snips into this slot, he cut a u-shape and pushed open the flap, creating a hole roughly six inches in diameter.

Opening a small case, he carefully lifted out and activated the latest in drone tech, a hybrid bumble bee/cockroach device able to both fly and crawl. It could pretty much fly anywhere. But where flight was impossible, it could crawl under doors, up walls, across ceilings, and, of course, throughout air ducts.

Adam had just packed his tools and was about to move, when Tripnee whispered into his earpiece com, "We've got company. A stealth helicopter directly above you. I count six guys sliding down black ropes onto your position."

Adam drew his Glock and slid low on the backside of the ventilator tower. Sensing the Dragon team dropping down and moving across the cages, he tensed, his Navy SEAL instincts kicking in. He was sorely tempted to take down the bunch of them then and there. After all, he'd often faced worse odds and had each time managed to come out alive—somewhat more so than his adversaries.

But the moment passed. The Dragon team climbed down through a mesh hatch, and then filed through a door into the building—both no doubt left unlocked by harmonious guards.

Alone on the roof, Adam made his way back to the grappling hook. He rigged a remote-controlled quick-release system on the hook, pulled on combat gloves, swung down onto the line, and briskly hand over handed his way 310 long feet back up to Tripnee on the balcony. Once there, he touched the remote control, releasing the grappling hook, and rapidly reeled in the 7 mm line.

Putting on drone AR glasses, Adam was in time to see, through the drone's camera eyes, the Dragon team strangle the infamous pedophile in cell 1204.

CHAPTER 17
AIGUO'S REPORT TO GRANDFATHER

Dearest Grandfather,

Exceptionally excellent news report! Grandfather, your brilliant long-term multifaceted strategy is unfolding just as you foretold.

Per your directions, we are providing our American barbarian associates with both great wealth and solutions to every problem, and, sure enough, for them this is not only irresistible—it is addictive! We have them hooked!

I have eliminated, with the assistance of my subordinate Gong Dongfeng and his Dragon team, the high-profile pedophile. It's fantastic. This simple guanxi step has enhanced and solidified our relationship with that whole group. Also, as always, we have recorded video that will allow us to control them like never before.

I am happy to report that, due to your brilliant leadership, the American barbarians are more bound to us and more dependent upon us than ever! As they say in English, we have the whole bunch wrapped around our little finger.

Dearest Grandfather, there is something I need to explain so you understand my motives—I do everything for you and our Party! It is, of course, very wise of you to personally review surveillance reports on all of your key people—with me, I like to think, being foremost among them. The thing is, I fear reports about me may be wrong or incomplete, so here is the true, complete picture:

In order to better carry out your inspired strategy, I am keeping close tabs on the gweilo woman Roe Rosen. As you no doubt already know, she is an influential baizuo, a rising star, a powerful dynamic player on the American left. Like most white lefties, she thinks she's saving the world, whereas in reality she's naive, ignorant, and arrogant. Also, in her case, she's a raging fanatic—and has killed five US police. These traits, of course—as you have taught me so well—make her all the more useful to us. So useful, that I am watching her closely myself.

To be frank, Roe Rosen is a full-on shengmubiao bitch goddess. In the name of selfless empathy, she advocates politically correct causes such as affirmative action which claim to help minorities but in reality discriminate against Asians. The real effect of her zealous work is to sow racial tension, division, and hatred—which is just what we want!

As well suited as she is to our purposes, this woman has rogue maverick tendencies and is in some ways too talented. For one thing, she is one hell of a fundraiser. In addition to the millions of US dollars we give her, she brings in millions upon millions more in voluntary donations from virtue signaling American celebrities, athletes and corporations. While this is in some ways good (and unbelievable!), it also could spell trouble. Her having independent funding might lessen our hold on—and control of—her. Hence the need for me to keep a close watch.

Just between you and me Grandfather, I am amazed at the hate this woman and all her donors and followers have for their own country—a country that, despite all its problems, has given them so much. Of course, their hypocrisy and intellectual shallowness are exactly what make them such useful idiots.

We will, as you have wisely mapped out, continue to express

support for our American co-conspirators. But as you have also made clear, this entire alliance is temporary and simply one of convenience for the CPP. These barbarians, so easily manipulated, so full of hate for their own homeland, are not people to be trusted. They are tiresome, and it will be a relief, as soon as we no longer need them, to cast them off—as they say in English—to throw them under the bus!

Please forgive me Grandfather if this letter is impertinent. You already know all of this, of course, as you must in your position. If I have overstepped, please attribute it to my infinite love for you and everything EVERYTHING you do. I want there to be no secrets between us. I am honored beyond measure that you are my Grandfather! Everything I do is for you and our Communist People's Party!

One additional note: My team and I are in the process, if I do say so myself, of pulling off a great miracle. The information we will gain is likely to be the key to finally and forever subduing subversive American barbarian resistance to our goals. This project promises to be so important, so game changing, that I myself will step in and take charge to guarantee the right outcome. I am going to make you very proud.

Your devoted grandson, Aiguo

As Sun Tsu and you yourself so wisely say, "The best victory is won through intelligence, without fighting."

CHAPTER 18
ROSS

"Adam, you're not going to like this," BC said over their secure phone connection. "Dongfeng—the guy moves fast—grabbed Su Jingfoi and is right now taking her to Marin."

After a day catching up on sleep and taking in a Broadway play, Adam and Tripnee were just then descending into the San Francisco Bay Area, this time aboard a posh agency Lear jet.

"I'll keep you updated on where he takes her," BC said. "Ty says do what you gotta do, but whatever you do, don't tip them off to our backdoor."

Adam and Tripnee had their pilots land at San Rafael Airport, a small private airstrip in the heart of Marin County. Picking up a rental car, they plugged BC's BeiDou tracking data into a laptop and picked up Dongfeng's trail.

As they followed, the screen showed the Chinese agent head into the leafy upscale enclave of Ross, and stop at an estate on the northern slope of Mt. Tamalpias. They drove slowly by. The place was a large, impressive estate surrounded by thick, towering hedges. Adam parked a quarter mile away in a trailhead parking lot, where paths led up to reservoirs and redwood groves on the slopes of Mount Tamalpais.

They put on AR glasses and sent out drones. The sensation, for Adam, always felt amazing. When he turned his head, the drone did likewise giving him the sense of actually being the drone and looking out through its camera eyes.

BC spoke into their earpiece comms. "County records show the place Dongfeng parked is owned by an international holding corporation, which in turn is owned by another shadowy corporation. Very likely it's some kind of secret CPP safe house. It's probably well guarded with a state of the art security system."

It was late in the day when Adam and Tripnee flew their drones over the high perimeter hedge. Wow. A full-on Wuthering Heights haunted mansion with three floors topped by multiple turrets and gables.

So where in this vast place had Dongfeng taken Su Jingfoi? Figuring the ground floor was the least likely, Tripnee took the second floor and Adam the third. Flying around the building, peering into window after window, they spied plenty of armed guards, but no sign of Adam's friend.

Then, on the far, back side of the structure, Adam's robot bee peered into a third-floor window. Bingo. There, tied to a plain, heavy, upright, wooden chair with a bag over her head, was a woman. Had to be Su Jingfoi.

Adam and Tripnee's timing was good. They had no sooner located Jingfoi when an inner door opened. In walked Dongfeng and right behind him Roe Rosen! Gong pulled off Jingfoi's hood, leaving her squinting into the bright room. Then he and Rosen sat in comfortable-looking recliners facing their prisoner.

"I apologize for bringing you here like this," Dongfeng said, "but it's a matter of utmost importance, great national importance to China."

As her eyes adjusted, Jingfoi studied her surroundings and her captors. Instead of cowering in fear, the refined woman seethed with anger. "Are you kidding me?" she yelled, her voice strong. "You're kidnapping me. Where am I? This is no way to treat a friend."

"Again, I apologize," Dongfeng said. "Yes, we are friends—and I appeal to you. I need your help. China needs your help."

"What? What are you talking about?"

"I would prefer to gain your willing help," Dongfeng said. "So please bear with me and allow me to give you some context, to help you understand. For thousands of years China was the most advanced civilization under heaven."

Jingfoi replied, "Every Chinese person knows this. So what?"

"As you also know," Donfeng continued calmly, "for the last hundred or so years, China has suffered unspeakable humiliation. But now this degradation is coming to an end. China is rising, fulfilling its destiny. Given who we are, our talent, our work ethic, our chi, our numbers and so much more—which transcend all other nations—it is only right and fair and harmonious that we reclaim our rightful place.That we return to the top. Unstoppable, ascendant, dominant. The truth is our ancient civilization will bring new order and harmony to the world."

Jingfoi replied, "You sound like the old Chinese emperors. Their talk of order and harmony was simply a soft disguise to hide harsh tyranny. Same with the CPP, which only cares about power and money."

"We really do embrace harmony," Dongfeng said. "Unlike the chaos and cacophony of the West, China has the world's most sophisticated Internet and AI system to encourage harmony and good behavior."

Jingfoi turned to Roe Rosen, "Will you help me with this man? Please let me go."

"Believe me," Rosen said, "I'm here to help you. And to appeal for your help."

"You'll free me?"

"Of course," Rosen said. "Provided you help us."

Jingfoi's eyes narrowed. "Help you how?"

"Dongfeng and I," Rosen said, "are leading the charge toward imperative change."

"What change?"

"We're on a huge campaign. A campaign to liberate people from circumstances that enslave them. You should join us."

Jingfoi asked, "What're your goals?"

"Cultural revolution."

"So, you're out there promoting riots? ACAB?"

Rosen sighed heavily and now her eyes narrowed. "We support progressive ideals: Defund police. Abolish bail and prisons. Liberation for all marginalized people."

Jingfoi asked, "What's your role?"

"Special Projects Director for the National Workers Alliance."

Jingfoi shook her head. "You sound like a communist."

Rosen's back straightened and her nose tilted up several degrees. "I am a communist. I've always been a communist."

Jingfoi gave the statuesque woman a silent look. "I suppose you like ACAB?"

Rosen's nose rose higher. "Of course."

Jingfoi's nostrils flared. "You support rioting, cancel culture and critical race theory?"

Rosen, her eyes gleaming, said, "All three dispense justice—and they're exciting. There's a reason they're sweeping the nation. They're our cultural revolution."

"You actually think all this has a future?"

"We've worked long and hard. We've got academia, Hollywood, and the media. Absolutely." Rosen paused, tilted her head sideways, and asked, "As a Chinese woman, you must see that the accusations against the Communist People's Party are xenophobic and racist.'

Jingfoi took a deep breath, and seemed to change tack. "Look. I'm uncomfortable. If you want my help, untie me."

Rosen smirked. "Hey, revolution is uncomfortable."

Jingfoi said, "You need my help. I'll tell you my decision. But first you have to hear me out. After all, this is still America."

Dongfeng rolled his eyes, then nodded.

"You're doing exactly what the Chinese Communists did," Jingfoi said. "You indoctrinate, control, censor, silence, intimidate and threaten violence. You're destroying what's most precious about America: free speech and the rule of law—the essential foundation of a thriving and healthy society. These are the very things the Chinese people crave—but don't have."

Both Dongfeng and Rosen reddened with suppressed anger and looked like they wanted to scream, 'Shut up.' But somehow they managed to swallow their words and remain silent, listening.

Jingfoi continued, "Growing up in China, I learned about America. I can't believe I'm seeing, right here in America, such horrible behavior by the left. I can't believe the American left is just like the evil Chinese Communist Party: controlling thought, speech, choice, life, even driving people out of their jobs for having different views. I can't believe democracy in America means left win, left rule, and left speech."

Jingfoi pulled against her bindings. "This is what the Communist People's Party does. But even they admitted the Cultural Revolution was a mistake. I pray Americans will not go down this same disastrous path. It wouldn't happen in one night, but it really could happen."

Jingfoi paused, seemed to appraise her captors, then continued, defiant yet trembling. "If people like the two of you gain power, America could gradually become like China. The future of this great nation is in terrible peril!"

Dongfeng stood quiet, smoldering.

In the rental car, Tripnee said to Adam, "Way to go Su Jingfoi! Tell it like it is!"

Jingfoi concluded, "Thank you for letting me speak. I could tell that wasn't easy or natural for you."

Earlier, during Jingfoi's talk, Adam had slipped his tiny drone in through an open window. Taking advantage of the way Jingfoi frequently turned her head to her right, away from her captors, Adam was able to fly his micro device right into her right ear while staying out of their line of sight. In a super low volume only Jingfoi could hear, he whispered, "It's me Adam. Don't let on you can hear me. We're outside. I'm speaking to you through a tiny drone. We'll do our level best to rescue you, but in the meantime, don't play the hero or get yourself tortured. Go ahead and cooperate so they don't hurt you."

Jingfoi concluded, "The fact you kidnapped me and now you won't untie me, tells me everything. My answer is: Hell no I won't help you."

Both Dongfeng and Adam said, "Don't—"

But Jingfoi blurted out, "This is still America. You can't kidnap people here. You can't intimidate and coerce people. You won't get away with it. Dongfeng, it's you and your friend who are in big trouble."

Dongfeng stuck a hypodermic needle in Jingfoi's arm and pushed in the plunger. She was unconscious before the plunger touched bottom.

"Transparent, xenophobic, racist slander," Rosen said, her nose rising. "This silly woman has been brainwashed."

"Misguided child. Needs re-education," Dongfeng said. "Now for Operation Black Bag."

CHAPTER 19
OPERATION BLACK BAG

Adam said, "I'm going in."

Ty Jeppesen, who had been monitoring their drone audio and video feeds, spoke into their earpieces, "Don't. It's too heavily guarded. Too many unknowns."

"Thing is," Adam said, "I'm responsible. If it weren't for me, she wouldn't be in this mess."

"I'm telling you, don't. If they grab you, they have ways of extracting everything you know—which is way too much. Besides, I've got a bad feeling."

"Yeah, I know what you mean. Me too," Adam admitted. "Still, it's gotta be done."

Tripnee insisted on going in too. But he convinced her that she'd be far more help flying drone surveillance.

It was night and the trailhead parking area was deserted except for them. With the Ford backed in among redwoods, Adam stood at the open trunk and unzipped the bags from NYC. After pulling on dark clothing, body armor, and night vision, he strapped on a hip holster with his suppressed Glock and extra clips, a combat knife, and a fanny pack of goodies.

What the heck was Operation Black Bag?

As Adam moved through the night toward the house, Tripnee flew a quiet, invisible drone swarm around him. Two out front, one off to each side, two bringing up the rear. Six in all for 360 awareness.

Tripnee said softly in his earpiece, "Got a sentry in the back yard."

Adam snuck up, squeezed the guy's carotid, and put him out cold.

Tripnee whispered, "Su's still in the same third-floor room. Stretched out on a narrow bed, handcuffed to the bed frame."

Adam climbed a drain pipe, thankful that it was solid and well attached. Once on the roof, being somewhat old school, he turned off his earpiece so he could concentrate on his immediate surroundings. Careful not to slide off the steep roof, he crept to the edge directly above Su's window. Pulling a rope from his fanny pack, he looped one end around a vent pipe. Running the line through two carabiners on his belt, he stood up, leaned back out away from the building, and belayed down over the roof edge, until he hung, feet against the clapboard siding, next to Su's window. The window was ajar and opened easily.

The room appeared unusually dark, and apparently was without even the faint trace of ambient light needed to make his night vision work. Something felt completely wrong, but he'd come this far and Su had to be rescued. So he swung in and dropped soundlessly onto the floor, landing in a crouch ready for action.

In a flash, the room filled with bright light, blinding him. Ripping off his night vision goggles, Adam struggled to regain his vision. Before he could, many pairs of strong hands seized his arms and wrenched them around behind his back.

"Welcome," Dongfeng said. "We've been expecting you."

Adam's vision returned just in time to see a black bag drop over his head. Next, he felt a hypodermic needle plunge deep into his upper right arm.

CHAPTER 20
GUILIN, CHINA

Adam's eyes opened. His arms, legs and torso were strapped into a heavy metal chair. Facing him across a bare table was Gong Dongfeng. The room was small and without windows. Adam sensed they were underground, probably many levels down in the basement of some large building or military installation. Something—the humidity? the smells? the air?— told him he was no longer in the San Francisco Bay Area but in a far land, probably China.

Adam's limbs were sore and his gut seethed with nausea. His whole body felt like it had been driven over by a truck. Probably the after effects of the knock out and wake-up drugs.

Dongfeng finished putting a hypodermic needle into a small case, snapping it closed, and sliding it into his pocket. "Hello, Adam. I apologize for abducting you. But you and what you know are of vital interest to my country."

The guy spoke quietly, in a polished, utterly cold manner that sent tremors through Adam's tortured body.

"You will tell us everything you know. The only question is: will you share willingly with minimum harm to yourself. Or will you force us to inject you with more damaging drugs and subject you to pain—excruciating pain—leaving you, well, not so good. I assure you, we are skilled in such things."

A tall, powerfully-built uniformed soldier entered the room

and whispered into Dongfeng's ear. Frowning, Dongfeng got up to leave, saying, "I'll be back and you will begin talking."

Left alone in the room, lashed to the chair—which Adam saw was bolted to the floor—the direness of his situation sank in.

Dongfeng had been many steps ahead and had just plain outsmarted him. He saw no way to play this man. The guy had lured him into a trap, thwarted his night vision, and bagged him like a sitting duck. A willful, blind, foolish sitting duck. Now he was the prisoner of a no-nonsense, serious, professional badass. A Communist People's Party black-ops assassin badass.

Even if he managed to escape—and that was an absolute urgent top priority—yeah right! Even if he pulled off the impossible and got out of this interrogation cell and the surrounding building, he guessed he was lost somewhere in the middle of the most locked-down, controlled, high-tech surveillance state in the world. An entire vast country with facial recognition cameras literally every few feet. And him locked in a steel chair with nothing but a badly fitting yellow jumpsuit, bare feet, and a body wracked with pain. He was, to put it mildly, in deep shit.

He inwardly grabbed himself by the scruff of the neck and somehow came into the moment. This was real. Face it. Shaking himself, he took stock. He was alive and breathing. His body was intact and would heal. He had his wits. And he knew some stuff. Taking deep breaths, he resolved to take things step by step, play for time, and somehow figure out a way to survive.

The solid steel door opened and in walked Roe Rosen's twenty-something, baby-faced princeling lover, who said, "Do you have any idea who I am?"

Now here was someone he could work with—or rather, play. Slowly, subtly hunching over in a submissive, defeated posture, Adam said, "It's obvious by your very bearing that you are a person of great importance."

Hearing this, the young man's chest ever so slightly puffed out and he stood a little straighter. "You have information. Are you ready to talk?"

Adam said, "Absolutely. First, there is something you personally need to hear. But you're not going to like it."

Babyface's eyes narrowed with suspicion. "Tell me. Out with it."

"Okay, if you say so. Your subordinate Gong Dongfeng is playing you for a fool."

"No way! How dare you," Babyface said. Then, cocking his head, he asked, "How so?"

"He's sleeping with Roe Rosen."

"You lie. I trust Dongfeng."

"I'm afraid it's true."

"You lie! He wouldn't dare! And she wouldn't dare!"

Adam said, "I have video."

"Where is this video?"

"A few minutes online and I'll show you proof. But you're not going to like what you see. I would not blame you if you refused to look at it. It's bad. Most men would not have the strength to see it, to face the truth."

Gnashing his teeth, nostrils flaring, Babyface jumped up, leaned forward, and jabbed a finger in Adam's face. "I have to see it! But I warn you, if this is some kind of trick, you will die the most excruciating death imaginable!"

This was going far better than he could have hoped. Of course, it was all too human—and just like a princeling hegemon—to descend into a fit of jealousy over one's lover. But this young man wasn't likely to stay sidetracked for long.

Babyface said, "There is only one computer in this complex that can access the world Internet: mine."

Babyface left the room and soon returned with six very fit,

very big soldiers—all bigger than Adam. Each had a pistol on his hip, an earpiece radio with throat mic, and what Adam recognized as a Chinese military bullpup 5.8 mm QCW-05 submachine gun in his hands. All pointed their weapons at Adam. He'd read about China conducting tests to create biologically enhanced super soldiers. Was this the result?

After unstrapping him from the chair, they marched him out of the interrogation room, along several corridors, and into an elevator. All the while the six kept the muzzles of their submachine guns aimed point blank at him, with, it looked like, all safeties off. Adam moved slowly, as though weak and defeated, signaling, he hoped, that he was no threat and they could relax. Four of the six seemed to be buying this act and appeared relaxed. But the two biggest men, who were each more than a head taller than Adam, weren't. Their eyes remained alert, on edge, constantly moving, and their gun barrels poked him, urging him along.

In the elevator, one of the soldiers punched the button for floor 35, the top floor. On their way up from the subbasement, the elevator stopped and the doors opened on the ground floor, giving Adam a glimpse of a barricaded and heavily guarded main entrance. The area looked impregnable. No way to escape through there.

As the doors closed, the two wide-awake giants smiled. They'd seen him surreptitiously view the place—and enjoyed his deflation at the sight.

On the top floor, wide, thickly carpeted corridors led to an especially large door of handsome hardwood. A bold plaque in Chinese characters translated to: Commandant Xu Aiguo. This explained a lot. Babyface, who walked apart from his elite squad of bodyguards, was not just a member of China's wealthy oligarchy, he was a scion of its ruling family.

Not letting on that he understood Chinese, Adam shuffled

along meekly, head bowed, eyes downcast, looking forlorn and hopeless. All the while, though, through half closed eyes he took in every detail, including Babyface's—Aiguo's—door keypad code.

Aiguo's office suite was a palatial expanse of elegantly furnished rooms. Floor-to-ceiling windows looked out on an other-worldly landscape of tall, sheer-sided hills jutting skyward like giant thumbs: it looked like the famous karst limestone hills of Guilin China. At least now he had a clue as to where he was.

Going behind a massive desk, his back to the view, Babyface fired up his computer.

Still hunched and downcast, Adam was almost—but not quite—able to glimpse the reflection of the screen in the window behind the desk. If he could move just a few feet to his right, there was a chance he could catch the login username and password. Damn! The two wary guards noticed the same thing and spun him around, spoiling his chance.

Once he'd logged into the computer, Aiguo stood back and motioned for Adam to come around the desk. Adam gestured with a tilt of his head toward his hands, which were still cuffed at his back. While the other five kept their weapons trained on him, one guard unlocked the cuffs, then relocked them with Adam's hands to the front.

BC had taught Adam a thing or two about computers. But how do you send an SOS while retrieving video with seven people watching every keystroke?

Instead of attempting the impossible, and probably getting shot for the attempt, he pulled off something even more immediately useful and important. He palmed a paper clip. It's a little-known fact that most handcuffs—although built to restrain people of all sizes including giants—can be defeated by a simple short bit of stiff wire.

Once Adam had downloaded the video of Dongfeng and

Rosen from the cloud and queued it up, Aiguo ordered him and the guard squad to the far back of the room. Turning the screen so only he could see it, Aiguo, pale, sweating, and lips trembling, hit play.

The video began. Aiguo's skin flushed, spittle formed at the corners of his small mouth, and his hands clenched as though strangling a small animal. As the wild sex scene unfolded, he foamed at the mouth, threw things, and kicked a chair across the room. Towards the end, he was stabbing the air with his pistol, screaming, "I'll kill the son of a bitch," and, "I'll kill his whole family." When the clip finished, in between guttural howls, he dispatched three of his giant, bio-enhanced guards to fetch Dongfeng and sent the other three off with Adam with orders to lock him in a basement cell.

During the video, the guards—including the wide-awake pair—couldn't take their eyes off their stressed out commander. Adam took advantage of the opportunity to unobtrusively work on the handcuffs with the paper clip, loosening them just enough to free his hands. When the moment was right he'd throw them off, but for the time being he kept them on his wrists, looking as tight as ever.

Adam was immediately marched out of the commandant's office by his three assigned guards. Unfortunately, the trio included one of the keen-eyed individuals—a sharp, alert guy who wasn't falling for Adam's listless, docile act. Adam kept up the performance for the sake of the other two, but Keen Eye was going to be a problem. While the others carried their weapons pointed down at the floor, this man kept his muzzle aimed straight at Adam's torso.

In the elevator, Adam saw his chance. After the doors closed, the two relaxed, sleepy soldiers inadvertently blocked Keen Eye's view. Seizing the moment, in a blur of speed, Adam pulled free from the handcuffs. With his left hand, he reached around Sleepy to push down Keen Eye's gun barrel. Simultaneously, with his other hand he grabbed the pistol from Sleepy's hip holster. Keen Eye reacted badly, shooting Sleepy in the foot. In that same moment, a split-second before Keen Eye forced up his weapon, Adam shot him dead, sending a bullet through the heart. Sleepy went down writhing in pain, clutching his foot. Sleepy guy #2 was just bringing up his machine gun when Adam leveled the pistol at him yelling, "Drop it," in Chinese. Slowly, the soldier lowered his weapon to the floor and raised his arms over his head. The whole thing was over in under ten seconds. Fortunately, it unfolded without any of these physical giants—all broader and taller than Adam—getting their hands on him. Whew!

Adam hit the emergency button, stopping the elevator between floors, and rounded up all the weapons and radios. At gun point, Sleepy #2 accepted the baggy yellow jumpsuit in exchange for his slightly loose but usable boots, socks, and army uniform. Adam handcuffed the soldiers tightly together—including the dead guy—with all three back-to-back. The corpse and the wounded guy, he hoped, would weigh Sleepy #2 down enough to prevent him from doing much. Adam cut up Shot-in-the-Foot's shirt to bandage his wound and gag both him and Sleepy #2. He gathered their earpiece comms, cell phones, IDs, money, ammo, keys, and—from the dead guy—a combat knife.

Adam took the elevator down to floor 22 and as he did so pulled on one of the earpiece comms. Had the gun shots raised an alarm? Holding down the button to keep the door closed, he listened—both to the earpiece and to the direct sounds of the building. Hearing nothing, he tucked into a corner and pressed the open button. Oh oh. Trouble. Voices and footsteps! He instantly hit the close button, but the doors kept opening. Not far down the corridor, four soldiers were talking—and walking.

Peeking out, Adam saw they were, thank the universe, going

the other way. Employing an old elevator hack, he waved his hand in the doorway, breaking the sensor beam. This made the elevator think someone had left, and sped up the closing of the doors.

On the 18th floor, and then on the 15th, he repeated the procedure only to encounter more close calls—each more hair raising than the last. On every floor the building swarmed with soldiers. If he got recaptured, Aiguo's people wouldn't make the same mistake twice. There would be no second chances. He absolutely had to make this first escape succeed.

Remembering how the doors seemed to open automatically on the ground floor, he ruled out trying to make it to the basement. Instead, better to go up, way up.

On floor 34, finally, some luck: the doors opened on an empty, quiet corridor. Then he got lucky again: next to the elevator he found an empty unlocked utility closet. Still at gun point, Sleepy #2 and Shot-in-the-Foot dragged themselves and the corpse of their companion into the windowless space, and Adam locked them all to an exposed pipe at the far end from the door.

Very soon these guys would be missed, an alarm would be sounded, and a building-wide search would begin, giving him just minutes to disappear. Trying to walk out of the building right when an alarm sounded seemed like a bad idea—especially considering the fortified ground floor. Better to use the little time he had to hide. But where?

To throw off his pursuers, he sent the empty elevator to the subbasement. Back in the utility closet, brandishing a pistol, he persuaded Shot-in-the-Foot and Sleepy #2 to share their phone passwords. But sending an SOS proved impossible. The phones could not call outside China, not even Hong Kong.

Because the phones and radios probably had location tracking, he removed the batteries from them all. Then, with the three machine guns on his back and the three pistols and other stuff in his pockets, he climbed to floor 35. He peeked along a section of the luxurious top-floor corridor. Empty.

Feeling exposed, he made his way to Aiguo's huge ornate door. Inhaling deeply, he thought, 'What the hell. Gotta commit.' He took a submachine gun in one hand, and with the other punched in the key code. Swiftly, silently, he opened the door, stepped in, and closed it behind him.

Aiguo's raging voice reverberated from the office at the end of the short hallway, but no one was visible. Choosing a door at random, Adam slipped into a side room, which turned out to be a bedroom. A moment later, he heard what sounded like several soldiers leave Aiguo's office in a hurry and race out the big door.

Someone could enter this bedroom at any moment. Gotta get out of sight. Fast. But how? He ruled out going under the bed or into a closet. His eyes went up to a large ceiling vent. Was it big enough? The ceiling was low enough for him to reach up and pry open the vent with the combat knife. Holy moly. The ventilation system, at least the one on this floor, appeared to be super-deluxe, military grade, and massive. Probably designed to keep the 35th floor elites alive and comfortable in any and all conditions, including heat waves, bio-weapon attacks, anything. Still, considering his size, it looked like it was going to be tight, maybe too tight, but at that moment he was out of options.

He pulled himself up and in, machine guns and all. The air duct was a little snug, but even bigger than he'd expected. He slid over to a much larger main shaft, where he was able to turn around. Then he slid back to close the vent cover.

Crawling deeper, he found himself directly over Aiguo's office looking through a vent down on the man's desk. Aiguo, who was alone, paced back and forth, swearing and muttering.

Without knowing exactly why, Adam sensed a golden opportunity. He inserted a battery into one of the cell phones and began recording a video. The thing had telephoto zoom. Terrific. A few minutes later, Aiguo's computer blared a unique ringtone. The sound shrieked: Urgent! Imperative! Aiguo frantically typed in his username and password, and a world-famous face appeared on the screen.

"Grandfather, what a surprise—and honor," Aiguo said. "Unfortunately, this is not a good time."

"Quiet, Chickpea. Immediately cancel your order to kill Gong Dongfeng!"

"But why?" Aiguo replied. "Why are you concerned with something so minor? I have my reasons."

"Chickpea, shut up and listen. Dongfeng reports to me. He is my eyes and ears in your organization. Also, he's a very useful and skilled black ops agent. Right now, we need him to find, interrogate, and then kill the American gweilo. Dongfeng is very good at all three."

Aiguo's body slumped and trembled. "Dongfeng has been stabbing me in the back, over and over, sleeping with my woman. And I can't believe she'd betray me. I bought her that house and I pour money into her ACAB organization."

"My little Chickpea, don't worry. The money is all part of the plan. The woman and ACAB foment rioting, looting, racial tension, division. The money is well spent. But you, Chickpea, are fucking up. You're letting your naïve personal emotions cloud your judgement."

"No way."

"I said shut up and listen. Sex with a gweilo is fine. I do it myself. But you are being weak. You let yourself become infatuated. You let your little head scramble your big head. You disgrace not only yourself. You disgrace our family."

Aiguo began to sob, tears streaming down his cheeks.

"I see what you did. You tried to mislead me. You tried to make me think that you were spending time with the Rosen woman for strategic reasons. While, in fact, you did it out of puppy love obsession. If you were not my grandson, I would have you shot."

Wide-eyed with shock, baby-faced Aiguo opened his mouth to speak, but no words came out, just an anguished guttural sputter.

"Okay, my little Chickpea, I see I've gotten your attention. You will not kill Gong Dongfeng—at least not yet. Yes, he overstepped and does not know his place. He should not have trespassed on your plaything. But right now we need Dongfeng. We need him to deal with the American, find out what the Americans are doing, and stop them. Afterwards, when this is over, then you can kill Gong Dongfeng."

Chapter 21
Chung Qichang

Adam figured the longer he stayed hidden in the air duct the better. But how long could his already sore and depleted body go without food and water?

By a small miracle, one of the pockets of his recently acquired military cargo pants held two Chinese candy bars. These he cut into pieces—twelve bite-size bits in all—which he made last three days. Four meals per day. Who could ask for more?

In truth, though, the hunger proved unbearable. A monster gnawed on his hollow interior, driving him into delirium and hallucinations. But somehow, clinging at the very edge, he kept on holding on.

For the first couple of days the office suite below him ebbed and flowed with a constant tide of soldiers coming and going, all in a hubbub, all searching for him. At first the focus was inside the building, and then in the vicinity, and then far and wide. As time passed, however, signs of an active search gradually diminished.

Late on day three, after he'd eaten the last candy bar tidbit, Adam experienced two lucky breaks. By then he was so delirious from excruciating thirst, hunger, and an ever increasing claustrophobia that he couldn't determine which of the two was more wonderful.

The first goodie from the universe was a trio of big rats.

Waking from a fevered sleep as they crawled over his face, he killed them with his bare hands and ate them raw, savoring every juicy, chewy bite.

The second gift came soon thereafter. Adam overheard Aiguo say he was going away. The little commandant did not mention how long he'd be gone. But finally, at last, Adam could leave his crawl space at least long enough to get a drink of water!

After the hustle and bustle of Aiguo's departure, the rooms were quiet. Adam waited a couple of hours, then crawled to the bedroom vent and dropped out of the ceiling.

Being careful to leave no fingerprints, he checked the rooms for surveillance devices, but found none. He quickly used the toilet and shower. Sitting down in at Aiguo's desk, he typed in the user name and password recorded on the phone video, and voilá Aiguo's computer sprang to life.

Wow, full secure access worldwide! Adam made a Skype call to BC. The moment his friend's face filled the screen, he asked, "Are Tripnee and Su Jingfoi OK?"

"They're fine, but worried sick about you. Are you OK? Where are you?"

Adam summarized the situation, concluding with, "Someone could walk in here any minute. So let's install a root kit on this computer ASAP."

Fabulous! The root kit would allow BC to download Aiguo's compete files, examine his full history, and monitor everything the young commandant did in the future—including all communications between grandfather and grandson. Best of all, this state-of-the-art spyware was designed to fool intrusion detection systems by hiding in plain sight while mimicking other routine programs—software that runs in the background of every computer.

Adam was about to shut off the machine when a message

labeled "Top Secret" arrived in Aiguo's inbox. He had already pushed his luck past the breaking point. It was way past time to get out of there. But instead, he stayed, riveted by what he read:

"From: Ministry of State Security

"Top Secret: Commandant Xu's eyes only

"Subject: Chung Qichang—Immediate Elimination

"A member of your cyber warfare staff, Chung Qichang, must immediately be sent under close guard to the Xiangchiang Organ Transplant Hospital. Chung, although he is a member of the banned Falun Gong, has himself not done anything wrong. In fact, he's one of our best programmers. He's performed valuable work for China, including writing software for Domain Voting Systems to rig US elections. Chung created the key chip that allows elections to come out "right."

"The problem is Chung knows too much. If what he knows were to get out, it would set us back decades and make China an international pariah. Who knows what the Americans would do to retaliate! Our entire American network of old friends and useful idiots would go to jail. And that would just be the beginning. So you must eliminate this risk immediately.

"Total secrecy is essential. Many people, including members of your own staff, would not understand the need to eliminate someone so talented, who consistently does outstanding work. We have determined, in fact, that there is a high potential for dissension and mutiny by friends of Chung Qichang. So, for morale's sake and for the greater good, handle this sensitive matter of national importance swiftly and with utmost secrecy.

"Due to the ultra-secret, super-sensitive nature of this matter, we are sending this order directly to you and only to you, and not through regular command channels."

Adam photographed the order, then erased all trace of it. He found a staff directory showing Chung Qichang's photo and his office location on the 17th floor.

After shutting down Aiguo's computer, Adam took care to leave no trace of his visit. Then he slipped out of the suite, taking with him the weapons and other stuff he'd entered with.

Oops. Outside Aiguo's office, voices came toward him from around a corner in the hallway. Gotta vanish. But nowhere to go. Except back. Moving fast, he tapped in the code, stepped in, and got the door closed. But was it too late? Had he been seen? Two pairs of footsteps approached the door. With no time to hide, he grabbed and aimed a machine gun, expecting the door to open. But the footsteps passed with a quiet slow swishing, the soft sound slowly diminishing into the distance.

On the next attempt, he made it to the stairs, which he took silently, two and three at a time, down to floor 17. When he found Chung Qichang's office door, he couldn't very well stand there in the corridor, so he whipped it open, jumped in, and snapped it closed behind him.

"You must be the American everyone's looking for," said a pleasant male voice.

As Adam's eyes adjusted to the dim light in the small, cell-like room, he saw Chung Qichang sitting at a computer, smiling. Instantly sensing he was going to like this guy, Adam smiled back and said, "That's me."

Not knowing how much time they might have before someone walked in on them, Adam briefed Chung Qichang on his perilous situation, then showed him the cell phone photo of the order itself. When he finished reading, Chung Qichang looked up.

Adam said, "We've got to get you out of here."

The fit-looking young man sighed and said, "I'm not going anywhere."

What? Was the guy nuts?

"They have my wife, my little boy, my parents. If I bolt, the communists will harvest their organs without anesthesia."

Chung Qichang looked miserable. His smile gone, he chewed his lower lip, making it bleed. "It's what they do to Falun Gong families."

"We'll just have to stop that from happening." Adam said. "Can you hack the CPP firewall? I need to talk with my team back in the United States."

"No problem. But you'll need to keep it short to minimize the chance of the call tripping an alarm."

The guy really was a computer genius. Moments later, Adam was talking with Admiral Ty Jeppesen.

Adam summarized the situation, concluding with, "This is a golden opportunity for us. A total game changer. But, understandably, he won't leave without his family."

Ty said, "It's you I'm worried about. It's a miracle that you're okay and that we're talking. It'll take an even bigger miracle for you—just you—to get out of there alive." Adam's old friend paused, swallowed and seemed to almost choke up. "I'm really sorry, but getting this man's family out of China is impossible. We don't have enough people in place to pull it off. Besides, the priority is you. Not only for your sake, but if they find out what you know, it'd blow up everything we're doing."

Chung Qichang, seeing Adam's expression as the call ended, said, "I thought so. It's impossible."

CHAPTER 22
LI RIVER

"It can't be impossible," Adam said. "There has to be a way, and we'll going to find it."

"You 're serious!"

Adam cracked a resolute smile. "The journey of 1000 miles begins with small steps. One at a time."

Chung Qichang 's eyes narrowed as he appraised this American. For some mysterious reason, due perhaps to something that passed between the two of them, he came to an inner decision. Then he nodded, chortled, and made a thumbs up gesture.

Turning to the subject of how to get out of the building, Adam asked, "What about surveillance cameras?"

"Hidden cameras are everywhere. But Aiguo had me turn most of them off. His priority isn't really surveillance, it's keeping his activities hidden."

"Top secret state espionage?"

"That's part of it," Chung said. "But his main obsession is keeping his real business as secret and out of the public eye as possible."

"His real business?" Adam cocked his head, eager to hear what was coming.

"This kid is the biggest fentanyl dealer in China—which makes him the biggest in the world."

Adam rocked back. "That stuff's a hundred times more deadly and addictive than heroine."

"And he ships it out by the container full. Also, he sells the ingredients in bulk to cartels. In fact, one of his biggest distribution hubs is a little way south of here."

"You know this how?"

"For years I've quietly kept an eye on the guy."

"Wishing you could do something?"

"Wishing someone would do something."

Adam said, "So you turned off some cameras, but not all? Which ones still operate?"

"Mainly just the ones surveilling people considered suspect."

"And those people would be?"

"The forced labor work areas. The slave labor cubicles. People like me."

Adam looked around the windowless room. "Why do I get the feeling the cameras in this room are not working?"

Chung Qichang gave a short laugh, "I turned them off so I could do my Falun Gong exercises in peace."

"So, bottom line, are cameras going to be a problem?"

"Most are turned off. But instead of shutting them down outright—which would get noticed pretty fast—I set them to play repeating loops from a year ago. So far no one has noticed."

"Lucky for me," Adam said. "That explains a lot. So there's a way out of here—a way that avoids active cameras?"

"Getting out of this building is not the problem. Most GLA—Global Liberation Army—buildings have multiple secret exits."

"Interesting."

"Yeah. Probably springs from paranoia—the paranoia that goes with being a tyrannical kleptocracy."

"I see you're objective and without bias," Adam said with a wink.

"Absolutely."

"Let's blow this popsicle stand." Adam said. "That's river guide slang for: Let's get out of here. Now!"

"Sounds good. But first there're a few things we need to do." Chung Qichang's fingers began moving in a blur over his keyboard. "You can help by ripping open the false back on that closet in the corner."

At first glance the closet appeared normal. But some thumps on the back wall produced a hollow sound suggesting a secret compartment. Then he found it. A small slot where he could grip the plywood back. He pulled the panel out to reveal a fully loaded backpack.

"It's what American preppers call a bug out bag," Chung Qichang said over his shoulder. "I just sent a message telling my family to cook Peking duck."

"What?"

The techie savant chuckled. "It's our private code. It means sneak out of Yichang and go into hiding at a friend's duck farm."

His fingers continued to fly over the keys. "Now, I'm hacking into the regional surveillance system to block facial recognition for you and me and my family."

Impressed, Adam nodded approval. There was a lot to this guy.

"This FR—facial recognition—block won't last all that long. But it'll look like it was authorized by top brass above Aiguo's level. If we're lucky, that'll cause some infighting and mistrust. Anything to slow them down."

Chung zipped opened a pouch on the backpack and pulled out a small device. Adam beamed. It was a pocket-size video endoscope. Chung stretched out the four-foot tube and put a right angle at the tip. Then he slid the tube under his office door and out into the corridor. By rotating the gadget, he first looked left and then right.

"All clear," he said. Then, with trembling hands gripping his pack's shoulder straps, he turned to Adam. "Please. You lead. Go right to the far end of the corridor, then go left."

Instead of heading for the main stairway and elevator area, Chung's directions took them in the opposite direction. After a couple of turns, at the end of a remote back corridor, they came to a dead end.

Reaching into another pouch on his backpack, Chung Qichang produced a key and opened a thick metal door. Wow, a stairway!

"This is part of a secret emergency evacuation route available only to the big brass."

They descended down and down, not just to the ground floor, but to the lowest basement level—subbasement #6. Chung Qichang used the same key to unlock another door which opened onto a small low room with what looked like a deep alcove at its rear.

He threw a switch and the alcove lit up—it was no alcove. It was a tunnel entrance. The passage was just tall enough and wide enough for Chung Qichang to walk comfortably. Adam had to hunch down to keep from banging his head. The tunnel lights extended into the distance as far as he could see. Had to be a mile—maybe a lot more.

As they walked, Adam said, "You've given this a lot of thought. You've done your research. You've got one hell of a bug out bag and a family escape plan. You could have escaped any time. Why didn't you escape earlier?"

Chung said, "The question was always: Where could we go? And how? How would we pay for travel? How do we get visas? Where could we escape the long reach of the CPP?"

"Even with your super-human computer skills?"

"Believe me, it was tempting. But the levels of surveillance are suffocating. Not to mention the CPP's network of spies embedded in embassies and government agencies world-wide. If any of us applied for tickets or a visa, the overlords would know. A single misstep and my entire family would go under the knife."

Chung shuddered, his eyes looked haunted. "For a fun read," he choked out, "sometime do an internet search for 'involuntary organ harvesting in China.'"

"So a lot of the CPP's espionage is to prevent Chinese citizens from escaping their grasp!"

They both fell silent for a while, contemplating the horror of it.

"Also," Chung said, "in case you haven't noticed, I'm not exactly the tough, can-do, secret-agent type."

Adam replied, "You could've fooled me. All these preparations. You know the way out of here and even have the key. You're one cool escape artist."

"You kidding?" Chung Qichang said, his voice jittery, "I'm a bundle of quivering nerves, every single one of which is scared as hell right now. How do you stay so calm?"

"Believe me," Adam said, "I've got the same quivering nerves. But I don't let 'em make my decisions or take over."

"How do you do that?"

"Well, I do my best to breathe, notice, and sort of say hello to the nerves and anything else that's in me, I kinda just accept them and let 'em be."

"How's that help?"

"Often, when I accept them, pretty soon the quivering nerves change, evolve. I find myself seeing them not from the inside, but in a more encompassing way, kind of from above, from a meta level. Instead of being under or gripped or crushed by the quivering nerves, I kind of bubble up a little ways above them. It's like I have them, instead of them having me."

"Reminds me of Qigong."

Adam replied, "It's what my girlfriend calls, 'Making Friends with Pandemonium.'"

"You've got some kinda great girlfriend."

"Amen to that."

The tunnel ended in another small room with another heavy metal door. The door opened on a hot, pollution-hazed afternoon. Before them, a broad, smooth, meandering river glided through an uncanny landscape of tall, steep-sided hills. The thumb-shaped hills seemed almost supernatural, but they were real alright.

"Li Jiang, the Li River."

As they walked along the bank headed downstream, Adam noticed a sprinkling of long, narrow bamboo rafts here and there dotting the river's surface. After a short distance, Chung stopped and pushed a few feet into the riparian bushes. Then he pulled aside a pile of leaves to reveal a bamboo raft about 4 feet wide by 18 feet long.

The two of them squatted in the foliage next to the raft. Chung Qichang lifted a bundle of clothes from his backpack. Pulling off his army uniform, he replaced it with Chinese peasant garb, rough, durable, loose-fitting pants and shirt.

He said, "Out on the water we'll have to keep you out of sight."

Getting out a second bundle, he handed it to Adam. A nylon tarp.

They dragged their humble craft into the water and stepped aboard. Chung used a long pole to propel them out into the downstream current. Meanwhile, Adam stretched out leaning back on the slightly upturned bow with the bull-pup machine guns laying beside him. Shaking out the ground cloth, he covered himself and the weapons, leaving just a slit for his eyes.

As Adam looked out across the magnificent river, he noticed that many of the other bamboo rafts carried not just a boatman, but also, sitting on chest high wooden perches, a cormorant or two.

Following his gaze, Chung Qichang said, "Fishing cormorants. No creature on earth is more skilled at catching fish than the cormorant."

"Why don't they just fly away?"

"A small cord loop around the base of the bird's long neck prevents it from swallowing larger fish. The bird returns to the boat, spits up the fish, and is rewarded with a few cut up fish bits small enough to pass down its constricted throat."

"Sounds like slavery to me."

"Yep, probably gave the CPP its core business model."

As they glided down river, the sun slowly sank in the west.

Adam said, "The river is taking us south. Isn't Yichang, where your family is, to the north?"

"Yeah, but it can't be helped. Gliding off down the river is the best way to get away from headquarters. No police patrols. No trace of our passage."

Adam thought for a while. "It's a stroke of genius. Since the coast is south and west, if they somehow trace us to the river, it'll make them think we're heading south."

Chung Qichang had mentioned earlier that their next destination was a village where a secret Falun Gong practitioner had a motorcycle shop.

The inkling of an idea occurred to Adam. "You say Aiguo's fentanyl warehouse is around here somewhere?"

"Yeah, about 10 miles south of where we'll get the motorcycles."

CHAPTER 23
AIGUO'S WAREHOUSE

Adam and Chung Qichang brought their motorcycles to a stop near the crest of a hill.

Chung said, "Aiguo's warehouse and distribution hub should be right on the other side of this hill."

They hid their CFMoto 650 TK bikes in a bamboo thicket and hiked up to the crest, crouching low as they reached the top. Spread out below them was an industrial building about a hundred feet wide and several hundred feet long. On the far side of the building was a parking and staging area with rows of trucks and shipping containers. A 12-foot high corrugated steel fence topped with barbed wire surrounded the complex. Powerful lights lit the place up bright as day.

Several big tanks occupied a far corner of the compound. Adam pointed at them. Are those tanks what I think they are?"

"They hold what you call in English, propane."

"I like it. Could be the key to creating a nice surprise for Aiguo."

Adam dug into a pocket, got out two of the tactical wireless earbuds with throat mics, and gave one to Chung. They scanned the channels listening for a minute or two on each until they found it: the channel being used by Aiguo's warehouse staff. Over the next half hour they heard and figured out the location of eight voices: four playing mahjong inside the building and four, divided into two groups of two, patrolling the perimeter fence.

"This is doable," Adam said.

"Are you nuts? There are eight of them!"

"It's okay. You just stay here out of sight. I'll take care of it."

Visibly sweating and shaking, Chung Qichang exclaimed, "And this is a good idea why?"

Adam gently put a calming hand on his companion's shoulder. "First of all, there's the satisfaction of messing with the world's biggest fentanyl supplier. Second, it's likely to distract Aiguo. He won't necessarily know it's us, but he'll know his precious fentanyl operation is threatened. He'll pull people off the search for us to have them protect his other facilities and investigate this attack. I suspect this is his golden goose, his cash cow, his baby, the special brain child of his child brain."

Chung nodded, starting to see the logic.

"And if he does figure out it's us," Adam continued, "he'll think we're going south. Which would be perfect."

Chung, his shoulders still trembling, seemed only slightly mollified. Apparently, those quivering nerve endings were alive and well.

Chung shook his head. "If something happens to you, my family will get sliced up."

"Actually you might be better off not having to travel with a giant gweilo." Adam wrote a name and number on a scrap of paper and handed it over. "If anything happens to me, get your family to Hong Kong or to any US embassy, and call this man. That's his direct private line. He'll get you and your family into the United States and take good care of you."

Adam looked down at Aiguo's warehouse. "Just stay here. Stay hidden. I'll take care of everything. This'll be worth it."

Chung Qichang swallowed and, still quivering, said, "It doesn't feel right to let you do it all. How can I help?"

"You sure?"

Adam set up the three bull pup machine guns side by side, each with its red dot laser scope carefully aimed at a different truck fuel tank on the far side of Aiguo's storehouse. He set the weapons on automatic and tightly wedged each in place with earth and heavy rocks. All Chung would have to do is touch the triggers. After discussing his plan with Chung Qichang, Adam returned to the bamboo thicket where they had concealed the motorcycles.

He pulled some cord and two blankets from Chung's bug-out pack. With the combat knife's saw edge, he cut down a dozen thirty-foot-tall bamboo plants. Next, using the cord, he lashed the bamboo stalks together into a rough ladder. Then, carrying the blankets in one hand and dragging the bamboo ladder with the other, he headed back toward Chung on the hilltop.

Meanwhile, back on the hill's summit, Chung listened in to the radio chatter of the warehouse guards, keeping track of their locations. When both outside guard teams were moving away toward the other side of the complex, Adam, taking up the bamboo and blankets, moved down the hill.

His dark green, inside-out GLA uniform blended with the night. One pistol was holstered on his hip, another rode at the small of his back, and a third occupied a cargo pants pocket. When he got within a hundred feet of the fence, he signaled Chung Qichang to open fire.

Chung was beautiful. Sticking to the plan, he kept the barage under 30 seconds. On the other side of the warehouse, three explosions ripped the air in rapid succession, and these were soon followed by more. Just as Adam had predicted, the exploding trucks drew everyone's attention, no one returned fire, and it seemed no one figured out where the shooting had come from.

Adam rushed the fence, tilted up his odd-ball, 30-foot-long, bamboo ladder and scrambled to the top. He flattened the fence-top barbed wire with the blankets. Then, while sitting on the blankets, he slid the bamboo up and over until it sloped down into the compound, giving him an easy entry and an escape route.

He raced to a rear door. Locked. Up close he saw the place was built like a fortress. Thick steel walls, solid steel doors, no windows. Maybe his plan wasn't so clever after all. How the hell was he supposed to get in?

A drain pipe! He ran to it. It was solid, but so tight against the wall he could barely get his fingertips wedged in behind it. The climb was doable, but brutal. By the time he reached the top, his fingers oozed blood and had chunks missing.

Pulling himself onto the roof, he rushed to the far side. The three targeted trucks were already charred wrecks. Below him, he counted eight guards advancing toward the remaining vehicles—many of which were burning—with fire extinguishers. He had to hand it to them. They bravely attacked the flames and would very likely soon limit their spread, protecting Aiguo's fleet.

Gotta move fast. Skylights dotted the roof. Running to one, he looked down to see stacks upon stacks of drums, boxes, and huge bags. He smashed the glass panel with the butt of a pistol, then eased himself down onto the top of a stack of boxes a few feet below the skylight. Descending to the warehouse floor, he looked around. Judging from the labels and the rows upon rows of ceiling-high stacks, the place contained enough fentanyl and precursor chemicals to kill the entire human race many times over.

So, where were the propane pipes? Ah ha, big space heaters and a staff kitchen with stove and water heater. He darted around putting out pilot lights and opening valves. As was his nature, he did an extra thorough job—maybe too thorough. The smell of gas filled the place. The slightest spark would blow the building and everything in it to smithereens. It was past time to get out of there.

He raced to a rear door. Nuts! Locked on the inside. What to do? He could shoot the lock off—and get incinerated as the entire place exploded in a fireball. He could go out front and fight eight men—and maybe also still get blown up. Or he could leave the same way he'd come.

He climbed up to the skylight and clambered onto the roof. Suddenly, out of nowhere, an armed guard stepped from behind a ventilation chimney, his handgun pointed straight at Adam. A ninth man!

The guy was savvy. He stood well out of reach, but close enough that his gun's muzzle loomed like a portal to oblivion. If Adam made a single wrong move, not only would he instantly take a bullet in the chest, the pistol blast would ignite the gas swirling out of the skylight and blow them both to kingdom come. Having no other option, he reached for the sky, signaling total submission.

"Drop your gun."

Adam did as commanded, very slowly, making sure his weapon made no spark as it touched the roof.

Damn! A ninth man. Years ago he'd known that eventually he would make a mistake—a mistake that would get him killed. And he was right. And this was it.

Then, without warning, the guy crumpled to the roof and in the same split second the sound of a single shot tolled from the nearby hilltop.

Adam grabbed up his gun, then flew down the drainpipe, over the fence, and up the hill.

"Chung Qichang, you're the most beautiful human being to walk the earth. You're a gift from heaven!"

Chung beamed, standing speechless with the automatic rifle.

"Congratulations and a million thanks. You definitely calmed those nerves enough to make friends with pandemonium."

Chung beamed even more broadly.

"Keeping it to just one shot was a nice touch. Any stray bullets probably would've ignited the whole place, cooking me to a crisp. You went deep, my friend. Tapped into your inner power."

Chung Qichang said, "Feels more like I tapped into the mystery, the power of the universe."

"Beautifully said. That too. Those're probably two ways of saying the same thing."

WHOOOOOOOOOOSSH! KAABLAAAAAAAAAM!

The entire complex erupted in one enormous fireball. After being singed and knocked down, Adam and Chung got to their feet, gathered the automatic rifles, and ran for the motorcycles.

CHAPTER 24
HUNAN

Chung Qichang's family was in hiding near Yichang on the Yangtze River roughly 400 miles to the north. To get there, Adam and Chung would have to sneak out of Guangxi province, cross the entire province of Hunan, and slink into Hubei province, all while remaining invisible. And they would have to be quick about it. They had to get there before Chung Qichang was missed in Guilin, before his bosses initiated a massive search for his wife, his little girl, and his mom and dad.

What had Adam been thinking? He was in the world's most technologically-advanced totalitarian state. Cameras surveilled every aspect of life. A vast network—numbering in the millions—of human watchers kept tabs on every human soul. These overseers used artificial intelligence and big data to enforce a social credit system which monitored everything everyone said and did, and quickly punished anyone who stepped out of line. Jeppesen was probably right. The odds against them were astronomical.

Adam shook himself. Hey, at his side he had Chung Qichang, a true computer genius. The guy had actually erased them from the regional facial recognition system. Yeah, but how long would that ploy last? Would the next camera they stumbled upon bring all hell down on them? How long before they were tracked down and their organs harvested? Legions upon legions of GLA soldiers, Ministry of Public Security patrolmen, and Ministry of State Security secret police would be searching for them, inexorably closing in. It was just a matter of time.

Too late for such thoughts. The fact was, they'd chosen the only way forward—not just for the two of them—but also for the world. Looking over at Chung Qichang as they started their motorcycles, Adam yelled, "Hey, we're not dead yet!"

With engines revving, they pulled on helmets whose visors completely hid their faces, and roared off into the night.

China, Adam learned, was a land of countless rivers, mountains, and near magical variety—including vast landscapes of terraced farms, shimmering lakes, and lots more otherworldly limestone towers like those of Guilin.

Avoiding cities and large towns, they kept to back roads. Cunning soul that he was, Chung had a gadget that monitored radio frequencies used by the security forces. Time and again this device indicated police were up ahead, warning the pair to turn around and take an alternate route.

They drove all night, stopping only three times to siphon gas and pee. The first light of dawn lit the world around them in the far north of Hunan. They'd had phenomenal luck, and they were starving. Was it safe to stop? Was the facial recognition block still working?

They came to a sizable village with a number of cafes just opening for the day. Choosing one on the far side, the north side, of town, they parked their bikes a ways away, and approached on foot. Perfect, it was empty except for a woman, who was probably one of the proprietors. The place was about the size of an American single car garage, and, like a garage, had a wide rollup door. Ten tables—all empty—filled the space. On either side of the entrance, cages held noisy ducks and chickens, and big shallow bowls held various species of lively eel and fish.

They sat at a table in the far rear. The more they stayed out of sight and the less attention they attracted, the better.

Giving Adam an odd wink, Chung Qichang caught the proprietor's eye and asked to speak with the chef. A skinny little guy—the woman's husband perhaps—emerged from a door in the back. A long, loud, animated, racing conversation ensued. The avalanche of words flowed too fast for Adam to follow, but as it progressed a clucking chicken and various frisky fish were presented for approval, and then whisked off toward the kitchen to be incorporated into their meal. Not exactly sticking with the low-profile plan, but no harm, no foul, right?

Sitting there with just the two of them, a question occurred to Adam. "So you really wrote the Domain Voting System software? The software that flipped the whole US election?"

"Yeah, no big deal. Wrote it originally for Hugo Chavez, then fine-tuned it for use in America. The funny thing is, that's the least of my accomplishments."

"Yeah?"

"You should see my cyber warfare stuff. Malware that blinds and disables planes, warships, and even satellites."

"Yikes, God help us," Adam blurted. "Why'd you do all that— such excellent work—for the CPP?"

"Had to. To keep my family alive." Chung Qichang paused, looked around, and added, "But there's more to the story."

After awhile a succession of plates—seven in all—flowed from the kitchen to their table. Plates piled high with the most delicious Chinese food Adam had ever tasted.

It was at about this time that two thirty-something Americans, one short and plump, the other tall and skinny, pulled up out front on a pair of Chang Jiang 650 motorcycles. The two sauntered in and took a table within earshot nearby. Not long thereafter, several more groups, roughly half locals, half Europeans, came in. Within twenty minutes the place had gone from empty to packed and hopping. This set off an alarm in the back of Adam's mind, but the food was so good and his hunger so keen, he ignored his concerns and went on glorying in every mouthful.

Then, perhaps drawn by the presence of so many foreigners, three tall armed village patrolmen in the dark olive green uniforms of the PAP—the People's Armed Police—walked in and began what appeared to be a random sweep—checking the IDs of everyone in the restaurant.

Oh oh. Adam and Chung couldn't move without drawing attention to themselves. They were trapped. Adam considered the handgun at his back, another in his cargo pocket, and the knife in his boot. As the cops got closer and closer, time slowed. A part of Adam's mind tracked the exact position of each of the three officers. His muscles subtly prepared for action.

Then the cops came to the table of the two motorcyclists. The taller, lead cop politely said, "Just a routine ID check. Your ID please."

"Officer, my ID is on my motorcycle right outside," the short, plump American said, starting to get up.

The cop said, "No problem. No need to get up. We don't need it."

Bringing out his phone, the policeman snapped photos of the two Americans. Adam, from where he sat, saw the cop's phone screen instantly fill with detailed information about the young Americans.

Adam pulled out one of his phones, inserted a battery, and began tapping away. A few minutes later, the patrolmen finished with the two Americans, and turned toward Adam and Chung. The lead cop's phone rang. He put it to his ear, and moments later yelled some sort of code to his companions. All three turned and rushed out of the restaurant, jumped into their

Volkswagen patrol car, and accelerated back toward the other side of town.

As soon as the cops were out of sight, Adam and Chung paid their bill and hurried back to their bikes.

Chung Qichang's eyes were big with admiration. "What happened back there?"

Adam said, "I reported a robbery in progress in a cafe on the south side of the village."

"Quick—and gutsy."

Adam offered an 'aw shucks' grin. "Couldn't think of anything else to do, and had to do something."

"I'm with the right escape artist."

"Me too."

Then they raced away to the north like wild banshees.

CHAPTER 25

GONG DONGFENG'S CONFIDENTIAL REPORT TO SUPREME LEADER

It is my eternal honor to serve you. Per your wise orders, I would like to present to your excellency this latest surveillance report on your grandson Xu Aiguo and his secret ministry.

I hope it is not impertinent for me to begin by thanking you for so quickly interceding on my behalf with your grandson. Fortunately, Aiguo and I have resolved our misunderstanding, and I am now marshaling far-flung resources to apprehend the American Adam Weldon and our renegade Falun Gong dissident programmer Chung Qichang.

First, the bad news. I know you value the unvarnished truth, so here it is: Adam Weldon and Chung Qichang blew up Aiguo's largest warehouse last night—the one just south of Guilin. The attack destroyed hundreds of trillions of yuan worth of product. Enough product to devastate the West for a decade.

Now for the good news: On Aiguo's orders, we are closing in on the fugitives. Weldon and Chung are mice in our maze, with no chance of escape. They gave away their location when they turned on their stolen radios during the warehouse attack, possibly because they could not have pulled off the assault without doing so. Unfortunately, they turned off the radios and disappeared before we could get there to grab them.

There are other big developments. Last night Chung Qichang's wife, child, and mother and father snuck away from their assigned apartment in Yichang. Also, early this morning Weldon and Chung briefly powered up one of their stolen phones in northern Hunan, not far from Yichang. Clearly, ungrateful wretches that they are, the pack of them have formed a plot to sneak out of China—probably while attempting various acts of sabotage.

Please rest assured that we will find these miscreants soon. We are bringing to bear the full resources of our security forces and AI facial-recognition tracking system. Even now we are tracing, detaining and questioning all of their friends, acquaintances, and contacts. Every member of their network, every sympathizer, every fellow traveler, every aider and abetter and—just to make sure the message is received loud and clear—all of their family members, will be brought to justice.

A few may qualify for re-education through work, the rest, as you yourself have taught us, will 'volunteer' to become organ donors. Doing this will not only be a pleasure in and of itself, it will make China safer for the Communist People's Party—and it will generate a wonderful stream of organ donations and corresponding profits.

The good thing is these events have brought to light this festering infestation of Falun Gong, pro-democracy, counter revolutionary co-conspirators. A network far more extensive than we realized.

In seizing this wonderful opportunity to stop them in their tracks and neutralize them, we will restore harmony and move China another step away from civil war. As you yourself have emphasized, civil war between the 1.4 billion Chinese people would surely constitute the greatest calamity in human history.

Would you pardon me if I offer an observation? It's kind of funny that your grandson Aiguo still thinks you don't know about his worldwide fentanyl business. As you know, I have made sure that he shares with you 70% of all profits—and of course he is aware of these payments. But somehow he still thinks that you believe this income is generated entirely by cyber crime, patent and trademark infringement, counterfeiting, extortion, and IT theft. Of course, those sources generate tens of billions every year. But without meth and especially fentanyl, the payments to your secret accounts would be cut by half, perhaps more.

It is very clever on your part, sir, I must say, that you not only have the deniability needed in your position. Your main guy up to his neck in the operation thinks you are entirely innocent of any complicity. Very very clever, sir!

Thanks to your strategic planning and unrelenting efforts, the level of resistance among American elites has never been weaker or more pathetic. What little remains of their will to resist is fading fast. Due to you, great sir, the American experiment is in its death throes.

However, there remain a small number of troublesome Western elites and odd ball deplorables who still oppose us. These people are preparing one last desperate attempt to block us. And this wily character Adam Weldon is one of them. He knows what they are up to. Apprehending him is the key to collapsing their annoying, quixotic bid to save their outmoded, chaotic democracy.

We are closing in. Our network is all encompassing. We will not fail. Our triumph is close at hand—and inevitable.

Congratulations, great, great sir! Due entirely to your leadership, vision, and brilliance, China is on the verge of world domination and the greatest victory in all history.

Your true and loyal servant, Gong Dongfeng

CHAPTER 26
THE DUCK FARM

Adam and Chung Qichang crested a mountain ridge and brought their motorcycles to an easy stop on a wide spot in the road. Spread out below them was a spectacular sight. Barely visible through the smog-filled air, a wide and mighty river moved ponderously eastward, from left to right, through a broad gentle curve.

"The Yangtze River," Chung Qichang said. "Downstream around the bend is Yichang, where my family lives, or I should say lived. Upstream out of sight around that bend is Three Gorges Dam, the biggest in the world."

"The one that's been in the news?" Adam asked. "The one releasing water like crazy, that's on the verge of collapsing?"

"That's the one."

Pointing to a valley far below, Chung Qichang said, "The duck farm's down there."

The farm turned out to be a beaten down section of stagnant creek about two hundred feet long surrounded by a rickety fence.

Dozens of ducks moved about, gliding on the water, diving for morsels, and trampling the mud banks. No one seemed to be around, and the lone structure, a humble shack, was empty.

Adam asked, "Where could they be?"

Looking worried, Chung Qichang said, "The neighbor upstream might know something. Just to prepare you, the guy—his name is Wong Yoo—is a fish farmer and he does not like our friends the duck farmers."

"Why's that?"

"He claims the ducks eat his fish. Which they probably do."

They walked toward the neighbor's fish farm. Adam speculated, "Maybe the problem could be resolved with a good mesh fence?"

Wong Yoo's hut looked exactly like the duck farm shack. As they approached, a bony, bald-headed, elderly man emerged from the ramshackle structure.

Chung said, "Hello Mr. Wong, do you know what happened to your neighbors?"

The man gave a dismissive wave of his hand and turned away.

"Please, it's important. I need to know where they are."

As the guy ducked into his hovel, he muttered over his shoulder, "Ask the police."

As Adam and Chung retreated back to the duck farm, Adam said, "That was gruff. What's wrong with Wong?"

"According to our friends the duck farmers, the real problem is fish poop increases algae and depletes the oxygen, and kills both his fish and creates disease for the ducks," Chung said. "The problem has been going on for generations, for as long as anyone can remember. So the animosity and bad blood has been building for a long time."

"Do you think Wong Yoo tipped off the police?

"I never thought it could come to this, but I'm sure of it." Chung Qichang, now sweating and wringing his hands, continued, "I knew I never should have tried this. The CPP has too many informers, too many spies. You can't beat 'em. They're just too determined, too clever."

"Hold on, hold on," Adam said. "Your family is probably in the local village jail. We can get them out."

"Yeah?"

"No big deal," Adam said, doing his best to reassure his new friend, and hoping it was true.

"Well, come to think of it, Wong doesn't know anything really damaging," Chung said, somewhat heartened. "Very likely, at this point, the police know very little."

"That's gotta be right," Adam said. "They probably took them in for questioning simply because they don't show up in the facial recognition system."

Cheering up slightly, Chung chortled, "They've probably never encountered such a thing. For someone to not show up in the security system database is unheard of. Unbelievable."

Adam and Chung Qichang rode into the village and parked the bikes. They walked to the police station, each carrying a submachine gun covered by a blanket.

Peering in through the front window, Adam said, "I count three cops."

Sweating profusely, Chung asked, "What can we possibly do?"

Adam said, "Follow me." Whipping the blanket off his weapon, he brought it up and pushed his way straight in through the front door. Shaking, but not knowing what else to do, Chung Qichang followed suit.

They pointed their machine guns at the three armed cops. Adam yelled, "Hands up. Do not move and you will be fine. We do not want to hurt you."

One of the cops lowered a hand as though going for his pistol.

Adam aimed his machine gun at the center of the guy's chest, saying, "Move another inch and you're dead. Cooperate and you'll be fine."

Using the cops' own handcuffs, Adam secured their hands behind their backs. From a row of cells in the back of the building, Chung released a dozen prisoners—including his wife, daughter, mother and father.

Twelve-year-old Jia ran to her father and threw her arms around him, her little shoulders vibrating. The whole family, their faces streaked with tears, hugged Qichang and one another, and couldn't stop touching him, rubbing his back, massaging his shoulders.

Adam locked the three officers in the cells, and, catching Chung Qichang's eye, said, "We gotta go."

The six of them ran out the back and jumped into a police paddy wagon-type vehicle. Adam was ready to hot wire the thing, but lo and behold the keys were in the ignition. Adam took the wheel and Chung Qichang the shotgun seat.

CHAPTER 27
YICHANG

"The obvious thing to do would be to head for the mountains to get away from the whole surveillance network," Adam said. "So I say we go in the opposite direction. Go straight into the big city of Yichang and disappear there."

Soon, they accelerated onto a two-lane causeway that followed curves of the river. In places the canyon walls were so steep, the streamlined roadway rested on concrete pilings rising up from the roiling Yangtze.

On the outskirts of Yichang, the highway morphed into a wide city boulevard lined with trees, shops and high rise apartments.

Just when Adam thought they'd outsmarted their pursuers, a siren blared and a PAP—People's Armed Police—car appeared in the rearview mirror, coming on fast.

Getting captured was not an option. There was no way Adam was going to let Chung Qichang and his family get sliced up by organ harvesting surgeons. Having no other choice, he floored it. Luckily, he had some black-ops escape and evasion driver training. But the top-heavy, bucket-of-bolts police truck had the maneuverability of an ox cart and the stability of a round ball, nearly rolling over on the turns. However, it did have one hell of an engine. The chase was on.

Soon, a second and then a third cop car fell in behind the

first. Adam did his absolute best to shake them, dodging through traffic and accelerating to top speed wherever possible—and sometimes even when seemingly impossible and downright insane.

On corner after corner, he tapped the brakes barely enough to keep from flipping. Then, with wheels and engine screaming, he laid rubber racing to the next turn. As the chase unfolded, the poor Chung family got thrown about like pebbles in a baby's rattle. But there were no complaints, only encouragement. Little Jia yelled, "You're fantastic. You can do it."

And by golly, the cops did fall back a bit, but just slightly.

Suddenly, ahead, a police road block. A line of vehicles spanned the entire wide boulevard, blocking even the sidewalks. There was no way through.

Adam yelled, "Brace yourselves."

Then, slowing slightly, he cranked the wheel hard right. The wagon tilted onto two wheels—teetering. But, by some miracle, it rounded the turn tires down, and shot into an alley barely a foot wider than the paddy wagon itself.

With no way to miss them, garbage cans and piles of boxes went flying, then got demolished under the truck, leaving a swath of debris behind them.

Looking back, Qichang said, "Maybe that'll slow them…"

And it seemed to be working, the pursuing CPP cops were slowing.

They emerged from the alley on the next street. The street seemed clear. Oh oh, to their right, a cop car came screeching around the corner. So Adam shot off to the left.

But no matter what Adam did, the CPP cops stuck to them like glue, matching him turn for turn, speed burst for speed burst.

Like cops everywhere, if you hold them at gun point, lock

them in their own jail, bust prisoners out of said jail, and lead them on a wild chase, they take it wrong, they get upset, they think it's personal, and they get really, really pissed.

No matter what he did, Adam couldn't shake 'em. It was over.

Let's face it, what other outcome could they have expected in the totalitarian surveillance capital of the world, maybe the universe. They'd given it a valiant shot. One hell of an effort.

What a fucking shame that this precious, precocious child Jia should meet such an end.

Chung Qichang, with his phone to his ear, was talking with someone. What a time to chat! Then he started laughing, chortling like a maniac.

Had the man cracked? Just too much stress? There was only so much a human could stand. Who could blame him? With your whole family doomed to vivisection, who wouldn't go mad?

Chung Qichang yelled, "There's hope. We're in luck! Go left at the next intersection."

"What?"

No time for questions. Just do what the man says. Adam wheeled around corner after corner working deeper and deeper into Yichang, doing his absolute utmost to follow Chung's rapid-fire outpouring of directions.

Suddenly they were surrounded by a mob beating on the metal shell of their vehicle. As far as the eye could see, the wide avenue was jammed with people. Thousands upon thousands of angry, screaming people. The paddy wagon reverberated like a drum from the pounding. Then, to make matters worse, the crowd began rocking the truck from side to side.

They were likely to go over at any moment. It was either get crushed in the van or somehow get out of that paddy wagon.

Instead of death under a surgeon's knife in an organ harvest "hospital," it looked like death at the hands of a mob blind with rage. An unthinkable way to go, torn limb from limb, beaten to a pulp under a down pouring of human fists.

CHAPTER 28
CONVOY FROM HELL

"It's OK! They're our people!" Chung Qichang yelled over the din, then pushed open the doors. As soon as the crowd saw they were not in uniform and not the police, the angry faces turned to smiles and the pounding stopped. Chung Qichang ushered his family and Adam out of the vehicle, and the six of them merged into the crowd.

Looking back, Adam saw the crowd surround and hammer blows down upon the three pursuing PAP cars, beating on their roofs, windows, and hoods. The uniformed cops inside were trapped and wouldn't be chasing anyone for awhile. Chung Qichang and Adam laughed, giddy with relief.

As they moved away from the squad cars, Qichang said, "That facial recognition block is probably no longer working." Reaching into his bug-out bag, he brought out a handful of chunky, thick framed eye glasses. Everyone put them on. There was even a child-size pair for little Jia.

Qichang said, "They're called Reflectables. The rims reflect visible and infrared light."

Jia said, "They look like regular eyeglasses."

"Yes, but on security cameras, our faces will look like shining orbs."

A man materialized out of the crowd and gave Chung Qichang a big hug. They talked rapidly for a while. The man handed over a small satchel, then vanished back into the sea of people. Had to be a member of an impressive network. Maybe some sort of pro-democracy, Falun Gong movement?

Staying together, Adam and the Chungs moved with the crowd along a tree-lined boulevard, going deeper into central Yichang.

After walking with the protesters for a while, their group of six ducked into an alley and split away in a different direction.

They were moving along a lightly populated street, when Qichang checked his phone, then said, "The train for Wuhan is boarding right now."

Adam wanted to break into an all out run, but that would have drawn too much attention. So they speed walked as fast as they could toward the station.

At first it was just a low, rumbling, barely audible white noise emanating from the distance ahead of them. But the sound and vibration grew stronger—and stronger.

Then, from around a bend in the boulevard a block away, a truck popped into view. Then another truck. Then a whole convoy. A good two dozen heavy GLA trucks and armored vehicles. Loaded with soldiers. With mounted machine guns. All coming straight at them. The rumble rose to a deafening roar. The gates of the underworld, it seemed, had opened, spewing forth hell over the earth.

As the military column closed on them, the heavy-caliber machine guns on the roofs of the lead vehicles swiveled to stay zeroed in on Adam and the Chungs. How had the GLA found them so damn fast?

Caught in the open, in plain view, with nowhere to hide, they couldn't help but flatten themselves with their backs to a wall, hoping against hope they wouldn't be chopped to pieces in the next few moments by a hail of hot lead. Guessing they were doomed, Adam nonetheless said, "Steady, steady. Stay calm."

The convoy was upon them. And then, instead of stopping,

it thundered straight on past, headed in the direction of the protesters.

Shit! They're going to put down the demonstration. Those people are going to get slaughtered.

Adam yelled over the din to Chung Qichang, "Call your network. Tell 'em what's coming. They gotta scatter." And to the Chungs he shouted, "Let's catch that train."

As they speed walked faster than ever, Chang made the call and Adam overheard the words, "—another Tiananmen Square—."

Still speed walking, Qichang thumb typed for few moments on his phone. Then he said, "Got our tickets. A soft sleeper compartment all to ourselves."

Instead of moving as a group of six through the camera infested station, they filtered through in ones and twos. Whew. Barely in time. The train began moving moments after everyone reached their private compartment.

CHAPTER 29
THE SOFT SLEEPER

Despite there being six comfortable seats in the compartment, the Chung family huddled together on the floor in a corner, clutching and hugging each other, crying tears of joy and terror.

Chung Qichang was the first to calm down enough to take some deep breaths and look around. Catching Adam's eye, he said, "Time for some proper introductions. Adam, I'd like you to meet my father, Bo."

The exact mirror image of his son, with the same prominent forehead and fit, sinewy body, Bo freed an arm from the family tangle to reach out and shake hands with Adam. The father struck Adam on some intuitive level as the perfect Falun Gong man: honest, compassionate, and tolerant. But also maybe a little shy?

Adam said, "I'm honored to meet you Mr. Chung. I don't have to tell you that Qichang is extraordinary, and now I see where he gets it. You all handled yourselves with wonderful grace under pressure back there."

Qichang gestured toward the slim, older woman beside him, and said, "My mother, Mei." Mei half smiled, half grimaced as she and Adam shook hands. Like every other Chung, Mei looked quite fit, and did not seem to have an ounce of fat on her. But unlike the others, she was bent and hunched over, as though from carrying a great weight. She was also boiling with anger.

Smiling toward the lovely woman on his other side, Qichang said, "My wife, Mingshu." Mingshu wiped away tears, flashed a brilliant smile, and warmly shook Adam's hand in both of hers.

"And I'm Jia," said the child, smiling broadly.

Reaching out to shake her small hand, Adam said, "I'm so pleased and impressed to meet you all, especially you Jia. Thanks so much for your encouragement back there."

Jia's smile broadened even wider, and Adam beamed back. Here was an indigo child if there ever was one. Perceptive and deeply, naturally empathic, this young soul radiated aliveness, brilliance and warmth. In particular, Adam saw in this special kid an uncanny ability to tune in to people, instantly sense how they're feeling, and offer support.

The Chungs untangled from one another and eased into the compartment's comfortable seats. There was a collective sigh of gratitude. It was astonishing. They were still alive, and, against all odds, they still had hope—and one another.

Adam said, "Those protestors completely saved us. What were they protesting?"

Chung Qichang quipped, "A better question would be: What weren't they protesting?"

Oops, did that touch a nerve? The Chungs fell silent, eyes downcast. Even bold little Jia buried her face in her mother's lap. Her mom Mingshu stroked her back. The others instinctively reached out and touched one another, and looked to Qichang, apparently electing him to explain.

"It's a long, sad, infuriating list," Qichang said. "For a lot of them it's about the toxic pollution of the Yangtze. Killing fish and livestock. The widespread food poisoning, sickness, and allergies. The cancer clusters in villages along the river.

"For others, it's about the Three Gorges Dam, which

flooded their farms, towns and cities. For many it's about the suppression and genocide of Falun Gong, Tibetans, and the Uighurs."

The Chungs nodded in agreement, their eyes fierce.

"For almost all," Qichang continued, "it's about having no protection under the law. In communist China, your property can be taken away at any time. And you can be punished, jailed, and even executed for literally anything."

Mei, scowling, jumped in, "People get jailed for not watching the National Day Parade."

Jia explained, "That's the big parade in Tiananmen Square on October 1st every year."

"In China," Qichang said, "no one really owns anything. Even if you're a billionaire like Jack Ma—whatever you have can be taken from you."

Mei said bitterly, "It's how the government generates it's day-to-day operating funds."

Bo the father added, "Not just operating funds. They seize enough to make themselves rich."

Then little Jia cried out, "They took our farm!"

There it was. Perhaps the family's most devastating wound. The excruciating pain in the child's voice—and the agony on everyone's face—testifying to its ongoing impact on this family.

Wiping away tears himself, Qichang said, "China is a powder keg, always ready to blow. On any given day, it's estimated there are over six hundred spontaneous protests and riots, each comprised of hundreds, thousands of people."

Adam said, "I didn't know that. I rarely hear anything about these protests in the news."

"Of course not," Qichang said. "To report such things would not be harmonious. In fact, it would be considered a crime against the state, and get you a very long prison sentence."

"And very likely," Mei added, "death by organ harvest."

Adam asked, "In a totalitarian censorship state with no free speech and no free press, how do protests get organized?"

"Well, for example," Qichang said, "today's march erupted because the local government confiscated another family farm—a farm a lot like ours. The family owned and worked the place for generations. The news spread like wildfire by text, email, word of mouth. The general, constant, long-built-up anger, the simmering frustration boiled over. Exploded. Happens all the time."

Chung Qichang's phone rang. Putting it to his ear, he listened briefly, then turned ashen. "That GLA convoy opened fire on the protesters."

As rugged mountains glided past their compartment window, the Chung family sobbed, loudly at first, then quietly, hugging one another.

Mei growled, "Another Tiananmen Square. And there won't be one word about it in the news."

Qichang said through clenched teeth, "Happens all the time."

Adam couldn't help asking, "Those were friends of yours. Will this wipe out your network?"

"Believe me," Qichang said, "we treasure every participant and mourn everyone lost, but our movement spans all of China."

"Falun Gong?"

"That's part of it. But it's way bigger than even that."

Adam said, "I've got good news for you, but for now suffice it to say: I've got people in the US who will be thrilled to meet you!"

Realizing something, Qichang snapped his fingers and dug into the satchel he'd received in the protest. He handed a cell phone, ID card and money to Adam. "The phone is untraceable, and the ID card shows you're an important—and innocent—American businessman."

Looking it over, Adam said, "John Brown. I like it. My photo and everything. So, am I now in their system as John Brown?"

"If they run the card, you'll show up as John Brown, a VIP investor. But if they take your photo, and run that, then you're in trouble."

"So the surveillance cameras will still identify me as Adam Weldon?"

"I'm afraid so. You—and all of us—need to keep wearing facial recognition blockers." Qichang dug handfuls of stuff out of his bug-out bag, and passed them out. "This is an assortment of FR blockers. Cloth masks, LED masks, avant grade makeup, t-shirts with adversarial patches, head scarves with faces, etc. They make you unidentifiable to AI. Wear each device for only a few hours, then switch to another."

Chung Qichang looked out the window as the outskirts of Wuhan slid by. After a pause, he said, "One thing you never want to do is count on the CPP security people to be dumb. That's generally a losing bet."

CHAPTER 30
WUHAN

Chung Qichang pulled a small laptop out of his satchel. After a while, he said, "I tapped into Public and State Security communications. There's no mention of us Chungs, but they really really want you Adam."

The train began slowing. Bo said, "We're pulling into Wuhan station." Through the window, they saw the station platform was crowded with CPP police!

The Chungs, their mouths open wide with surprise and terror, looked at Adam, who said, "The good news is they're looking for me, not you. If I disappear, there's nothing to implicate you." Adam said.

The train came to a complete stop. Cops clamored aboard and began banging on compartment doors, yelling, "Police. Open Up." These guys were full-on storm troopers. Whenever there was a delayed response or no response, the police immediately bashed the doors open, swarming one private compartment after another.

Their own door would fly open at any moment. Sticking his head out the window, Adam saw that all the cops had boarded the train, leaving none on the platform, giving him an idea. Over the din, he said, "Use your new IDs to get to Hong Kong or to any US Embassy. Then call that number I gave you." Then to little Jia, whose eyes welled with tears, he said, "Don't worry honey. We're all going to be OK."

Next, after pulling on an FR mask, he squeezed out the window, hit the platform, and ran off into the railway station.

Great. There he was all alone in the exact dead center of the biggest, most advanced surveillance state on the planet. What was he supposed to do now?

Hmmmm. Signs pointing the way to long-term car parking. A little gift from the universe? Taking the hint, he followed the signs and soon found himself walking among rows of surprisingly fine automobiles.

One thing about a totalitarian, gangster-run state: Government crime was rampant, but civilian crime was low. Car theft was so rare, he even found an unlocked Mercedes. He hot wired the car in under five minutes, drove sedately out the exit, and headed north.

The vast smoggy metropolis of Wuhan sprawled between and around numerous lakes and rivers. As he drove through its oddly vacant streets and out along an unusually empty highway, Adam pondered his situation.

In a land with more surveillance cameras than people, it wouldn't take long for the watchers to figure out the identity of the blurry figure who climbed out of the train window in Wuhan. Soon thereafter they would track him to the Mercedes. Then, like lightning, every cop within five hundred miles would be on the lookout for both the car and the tall American. He needed to ditch the Mercedes soon. Out of sight of cameras.

Out of nowhere, sirens squealed and two sets of flashing lights popped up close behind him. Then a third cop car peeled onto the highway from the right shoulder to plant itself smack dab in front of him. Adam swerved left, then right, but the car ahead did likewise, staying directly in front of the Mercedes.

Damn it to hell! That was just too bloody fast. What in hell was going on? What was China and the world coming to? When you couldn't steal a car and have it to yourself for even twenty minutes?

The Mercedes had power and speed, but two police cars were inches from his rear bumper, and the third inches from his front. Having no other option, he pulled over. The three police vehicles boxed him in, and six armed officers surrounded his car, their hands on the butts of their pistols.

One of the dark-olive uniforms came up to his open driver's window. Adam asked, "What seems to be the problem officer?"

The cop barked, "What's wrong with you? What are you thinking? No one is allowed to just drive out of Wuhan. This city is on lockdown."

Totally surprised, but endeavoring to recover, Adam said, "Sorry, I haven't seen or heard the news. I just arrived on a train from out of town. From the train, I went straight to my car, and then drove here. I haven't had contact with a single person in Wuhan."

The cop looked unmoved, "I'll need your ID and your car registration."

Digging in the glove box, Adam breathed a sigh of relief when he found the car's registration papers, which he handed over with his new ID.

The cop glanced at the documents, then sneered, "This isn't even your car."

Doing his best to sound innocent and helpful, but like someone with some clout, Adam said, "That's correct officer. I borrowed it from one of my assistants."

"We'll see about that," the cop said as he took out his phone and photographed the ID and car registration.

The cop then studied his screen, and as he did so his facial expressions, posture, and entire manner changed.

He become apologetic, obsequious, his whole body subtly stooping and scraping with more than a little fear.

Bowing and offering the papers back to Adam with both hands, the man said, "So, so sorry to inconvenience you, sir."

Adam smiled. "No problem. Thank you officer for your excellent work. I have noted your badge number and I will put in a good word for you."

The cop beamed. A light dawned in his eyes, and he gushed, "Thank you so much, sir. You are too kind. I think we can make it up to you. Please follow us."

The six cops got back in their patrol cars, backed up a few feet, then drove around in front of the Mercedes. As soon as Adam fell in behind them, the PAP security officers fired up their lights and sirens, and led the way down the highway.

Around two bends, they came to a road block manned by thirty or so masked soldiers. When the troops saw the Mercedes getting the VIP treatment, they raised their crossbar, stood at attention, and saluted as the four-car motorcade swept through. Then, around two more bends, the same pomp and ceremony was repeated at a second barricade. Lastly, in a parting gesture befitting a commanding general, his escorts pulled over, and the six cops jumped out to send him off with not only a smart salute, but also friendly waves and big smiles. Adam waved thank you and sped off down the highway.

Fascinating. Like the world everywhere, there was one set of rules for the elite, and another for everyone else. Adam had to hand it to Chung Qichang and his buddies. If you're going to create fake IDs, you may as well make 'em VIP.

The thing was, it was only a matter of time before those cops—or their camera-watching overlords—realized their mistake. In fact, Adam half expected to see them come roaring up behind him at any moment. After a while, however, it looked like things were going to work out, at least for a while.

OK. Not bad. This fit into his plan. So far so good. When they identified him as the train jumper who stole the Mercedes, they'd think he was going north.

Now for the real real plan: To gradually, covertly, invisibly swing around toward the east and then south. The crucial part being to remain invisible. From here on out, he had to stay completely below the radar. There could be no getting his ID checked, no exposure to surveillance cameras. Nothing that would allow them to piece together his actual escape route and track him down.

Which, frankly, was going to be impossible. Cameras were everywhere. He certainly couldn't buy fuel, as every gas station would have multiple cameras. But, when you have no other options, why not attempt the impossible?

So, sticking to narrow, bumpy, winding back roads—many of them mud and gravel and rut-filled—he worked his way first east and then southeast. The gas tank had started off half full. He squeezed every possible mile out of every last gallon, every last cup, every last thimble full. Inevitably, the gas ran out. And that was okay. In fact, it was more than okay. After all, he had to ditch that wonderful car, but do it in such a way that it wouldn't come to the attention of his pursuers and give away his plan.

Running on fumes, expending his last drop of fuel, Adam parked in a sheltered spot behind a rustic cafe in a small village. When approaching the place, he had noticed a bus stop a half mile away. Telling the driver he was going to be taking the bus and would be back to pick up the Mercedes in a month, he paid the cafe owner handsomely to let him leave the car tucked away behind the cafe for the duration. Also, he wrote down the Mercedes owner's address and made a mental note to later let him know where his car was parked.

Then he started walking southeast along a dirt road. No electricity, no cameras, no internet. Excellent.

He walked many, many miles, until, suddenly, there it was. Just what he was looking for. A humble dwelling with a humble, but functioning auto. China's—and perhaps the world's—cheapest car: the Jiangnan Alto. Ten feet long and a little over four feet wide, the Alto got close to 50 miles per gallon and had four-wheel drive. Perfect for the rough mountain roads between him and freedom.

This one was old and battered, but looked operational. Brand new, it had cost $2,400 USD. This specimen was probably worth a fraction of that, and the owner would likely be thrilled to make a below-the-radar deal for enough to buy a new one.

Twenty minutes later, Adam sat folded and scrunched in his new set of wheels, rattling and bouncing southeast, and then due south.

CHAPTER 31
VILLAGE PEOPLE

Pitching and rolling along, Adam rounded a bend and suddenly found himself barreling toward a group of masked men blocking the mountain road. He slammed on his sketchy brakes, and the Alto came to a skittery halt inches from the group.

Yelling and swearing in a dialect that he couldn't entirely make out, several of the men ripped open his driver's side door and pulled him from the vehicle. As best as he could fathom, these men, all of them sinewy but muscular and wearing coarse, loose peasant garb, had been tasked by their village elders to protect their village from anyone trying to sneak in from the direction of Wuhan.

Word had spread that a deadly virus was running rampant, and these men were terrified the contagion would devastate their families, their little town. The fear in their eyes was palpable. The black death was on their doorstep, and they were desperate to stop it. For some reason—maybe because the CPP had reported that the virus was an American bioweapon—the men were convinced Adam was there to deliberately spread the virus.

These simple, remote, mountain villagers seemed to think the best way to protect themselves and their loved ones was to lynch him then and there. He counted twenty five of them. All strong, obviously hard-working, physical men. A bunch of them seized Adam and dropped a noose over his head. They threw the end of the rope over a tree limb, and holy fuck shit hell, they tied the rope to the rear of his Alto. They were going to use his own vehicle to hoist him up at the end of that rope!

These were basically good-hearted, well-meaning people. They were also fiercely patriotic and apparently accepted without question everything their government told them. Including that Americans were not to be trusted, would do them wrong, and would even sneak disease and pestilence into their nation and their village. And, by golly, they weren't gonna stand for it. They would kill the guy before he could spread his evil.

Adam was loath to do it, but this had gone far enough, and it was time to put a stop to it. Moving swiftly, he whipped his arms free, and took off the noose. Grabbing one of the men by the arms, he swung the man's whole body like a big blunt scythe to knock down the four men nearest him.

But these villagers didn't react in the way one would expect. Instead of backing away to protect themselves or attacking in ones and twos, they immediately came at him all at once, as one. They moved like a single organism, like one colossal single-minded beast with forty powerful arms and forty hard, viselike hands.

The men gripped Adam with ferocious strength and intensity. Struggle as he might, he could not get loose. The noose went back on. They tied his hands behind his back. Someone started the Alto. Without hesitation or ceremony, these people were going to do the deed. This was it. Kaput. Fini.

Suddenly, an SUV pulled up, out leapt a woman brandishing a pistol, and two shots ring out. Bang. Bang. This got everyone's attention.

"I'm from the government," she yelled. "Let him go."

The village people looked taken aback, but sullenly complied.

With her free hand, the newcomer reached into her pocket, pulled out a switchblade, deftly snapped it open with practiced ease, and cut the rope binding Adam's hands. Then she nodded toward the SUV and said, "Get in."

Adam had no idea who this woman was, but it was pretty damn clear she had been sent from heaven. So he jumped into her Chinese SUV, a Changan C375.

The woman calmly looked around, folded and pocketed her knife, holstered her pistol, and got in. As she drove them away, Adam asked, "Who are you? Who do I thank for totally saving my bacon?"

"Let's just say I'm a friend of Chung Qichang. You can call me Ling."

"So Ling, you're not from the government?"

"No way. I just said that because villagers like those people back there tend to believe and do whatever the government says."

"How'd you find me?"

"We're tracking your phone."

"It's just you guys tracking me? And not the CPP?"

"Just us good guys—I hope."

Ling handed Adam a note from Chung Qichang. "You should read this, memorize the rendezvous information, then destroy it."

Adam read the brief note, then looked up. "This says to meet him near Longhu Mountain, that's in Jiangxi province over a hundred miles from here."

Ling smiled. "Don't worry. We'll drive together."

Not bad. Miraculous, in fact. You couldn't make this stuff up. Longhu Mountain was to the south and took him closer to Hong Kong. And he'd be reuniting with the Chungs. Perfect.

CHAPTER 32
ON THE ROAD

Ling steered the Changan SUV over China's back roads with an easy nonchalance, one hand on the wheel, one out the window cupping the breeze. Although small, this firebrand exuded confidence and vitality.

"So," Adam said, "is this your full-time job? Driving around rescuing people?"

Ling laughed. "I distribute films, Westerns. Movies with cowboy heroes who fight bad guys."

"The CPP lets you do that?"

"Not under Mao. But later, for a while, yes. Although lately things have been tightening up."

"Why am I guessing there's more to your story?"

Ling flashed a toothy smile, a grin made all the more winning by uneven teeth. Turning serious, she said, "Throughout China there's tremendous hunger for change, for rule of law, for individual rights, for democracy. I travel all over distributing films. At the same time, below the radar—and the radar is intense and getting more so all the time—I build relationships, give talks, and spread word of our pro-democracy movement."

"So you don't subscribe to the Chinese philosophy of 'mei ban fa'—'nothing can be done'?"

Ling crowed, "That whole traditional Confucian attitude that says bend like a reed in the wind, never stand against it like a tree. I hate that shit!"

Adam broke into a delighted chuckle of admiration. "You're one brave soul! But throughout China? What about those villagers that came within seconds of lynching me?"

"OK, not everyone. But a growing, exploding number want property rights, want respect, and hate being ruled by a totalitarian, mafia-run government of gangsters."

"That's good to hear."

"And even those villagers," Ling said, "in their own way, operating on the best information they have, are trying to stand up against the wind. In fact, show them some cowboy movies, then let me talk to them, and they'll want individual rights, rule of law, and democracy. I've seen it a thousand times."

"I like it."

"Qichang told me what happened in Yichang. You saw those people. Hundreds of protests like that—most, thankfully, without the convoy massacre—happen every day all across China. Things are changing!"

Adam asked, "Where do you find the courage? The guts to persevere and keep going?"

"I dunno. It's just who I am, I guess," Ling said. "The source of my courage? Divine luck, maybe, and cowboy movies."

They rode in silence for a while.

Then Ling said, "The real source of my courage? America's founding documents. I absolutely love your Declaration of Independence. 'All men are created equal, … endowed by their Creator with certain unalienable Rights … among these are Life, Liberty and the pursuit of Happiness…'"

Ling flashed an earnest toothy smile, her eyes full of passion. "What could be more absolutely beautiful?"

Adam nodded, admiring this woman more and more.

Ling continued, "'Whenever any form of Government becomes destructive…it is the right of the people to alter or to abolish it, and to institute new Government, laying its foundation on such principles and organizing its powers in such form, as to them shall seem most likely to affect their safety and happiness.'"

"You memorized it. I'm humbled."

"You Americans are so, so lucky. You should be so very, very proud!"

Adam let out a deep sigh. "In America, I'm afraid our basic freedoms are under attack."

"What!? I don't like the sound of that. The principles, the freedoms cited in those documents have to be defended at all costs!"

"You got that right. But just as those documents imply, democracy is a perpetual work in progress."

Ling shook her head. "We would give anything for the freedoms your constitution guarantees. The right to think your own thoughts, the right to assemble and say whatever you want. The right to believe and worship as you choose. The right to truly own property, to have a government that doesn't seize your property whenever it wants.

"We want freedom so bad. Right now, for a while longer, we have to keep our movement hidden. But it's growing by leaps and bounds. We will not give up.

"America—you—your people fought and won your revolutionary war against the most powerful nation on earth at the time, Great Britain. That victory was a total, complete miracle. Logically, it should never have happened—but it did."

"Yeah, it did," Adam agreed. "Because of luck and unbelievable courage. Luck and courage like yours."

Ling flashed a bashful, grateful smile. "The CPP is a massive, repressive, techno-totalitarian, outlaw regime, and for that very reason it's paranoid and fragile. It seems all powerful, but it's not."

"Amen to that," Adam said.

Suddenly, Adam couldn't keep his eyes open. He hadn't slept since dragging himself out of Aiguo's ventilation system two very long days before—days packed with way too many close encounters with death. He crawled into the back of the SUV, sprawled on a thin blanket, and, despite the lack of padding and getting constantly bounced and pitched back-and-forth, he instantly fell dead asleep.

CHAPTER 33
LONGHU MOUNTAIN, JIANGXI

Adam woke and clambered forward into the shotgun seat.

Ling said, "Wow, you were out all night. How was that shut eye?"

"Aside from being stiff, groggy, starving, and mentally and emotionally pulverized, I never felt better."

Ling beamed, and they both chuckled. This was one cool woman.

"Hey," Adam asked, "how is it that you can carry a gun in Communist China? And really, how do you manage to travel all over doing what you do without attracting attention in a surveillance state?"

"It's sort of a long story. I'll explain," Ling said. "The answer to both questions has a lot to do with where I live."

"Where's that?"

"Longhu Mountain. Speaking of which, we're almost there."

Around them, a rising sun revealed high, steep-sided hills. Unlike those of Guilin, which tended to be slender towers, these hills were like scoops of ice cream—some single and some double scoops—hundreds of feet high, plopped down at ransom here and there.

"Did you know," Ling continued, "Longhu Mountain is the birthplace of tai chi and one of the four famous birthplaces of

Taoism? Both were suppressed under Mao. But now they're allowed, at least here, mainly because of the money."

"The money?"

"Tai chi tourism. Longhu is swarming with foreigners who come to learn tai chi and study Taoism. Many stay for a day or two, but some remain for months and even years living with the emonks. And believe me, it's not cheap. They all spend tons of money.

It's a golden goose—not so much for the monks—but for the CPP-connected people behind the scenes. It's a gold mine, a river of incoming foreign currency that keeps on giving."

"So how does that allow you to pack heat and carry a switchblade, and roam far and wide free as a bird?"

"I'm coming to that. You probably know our police play a very different role than American police. In China, local cops watch and monitor everyone. They check ID cards, keep track of births, changes of address, and even your thoughts. Vagabonds, people with no job, and anyone who in the cop's eyes causes disorder get arrested and sent away for years to be re-educated through hard labor.

On the upside, these local police check on and help old people and the sick. But their job is to hover and guide and create "harmony"—which, frankly, means enforcing conformity and obedience."

"Hence my question: How is it you're carrying?"

"Here on Longhu Mountain, because of all the money, and to fool the tourists into thinking China is good, the police stay hands off and keep their surveillance low-key. By living here, hidden in a sea of tourists, with the powers that be focused on the wagon loads of money rolling in, I generally manage to fly under the radar. Occasionally, though, the radar does spot me."

"What then?"

Adopting an innocent-little-me persona, Ling batted her eye

lashes, pursed her lips, and said, "Why, sir, I could never, ever do anything against the wonderful CPP."

Adam laughed, then asked, "What originally took you to Longhu Mountain?"

"My dream was to learn Kung Fu and Qigong from the masters, and that's what I did. Along the way, on the side, I built my own hut way up on the mountain."

Ling pulled up and parked at the base of a forested mountainside dotted with temples. Before getting out of the car, she unstrapped her gun and put it and other stuff into a duffel bag, which she slung over her shoulder.

Having left his Alto under less than ideal circumstances, Adam had only the clothes on his back, the combat knife, the ID, money and cell phone Qichang had given him, and the three phones—with batteries removed—from Aiguo's body-guards.

As they began walking, Ling said, "The bus rendezvous with Chung Qichang and his family isn't till tomorrow morning. The safest place to hole up in the meantime is here on the mountain. You'll blend right in. There are more foreigners—especially Americans and Germans—around here than Chinese."

"Still," Ling said as she handed him an FR blocking scarf and hat, "it's a good idea to wear these."

Stone stairs led up to a bunch of Taoist temples. This was traditional ancient China. Tile roofs up flared at the eaves. Statues of big and small walking and crouching beasts guarded entranceways and lined ridge lines and roof edges. The mountain felt alive, vibrant. Robed monks were everywhere, as were students from all over the world.

They walked side by side up a succession of stairways, through ornate gardens, and across courtyards teeming with people of all ages, sizes and nationalities meditating and practicing tai chi and Qigong.

Speaking in a low voice meant only for Adam, Ling talked as they walked. "During my years as a novice, I personally had difficulty with Taoism. One of the core teachings of Shen Dao, 'Abandon knowledge, discard self,' never made sense to me. It just wasn't in me to be detached, or calm, or embrace wu wei, non-action.

"But on the positive side, in my own way, I did learn to smile at the vicissitudes of life. Also, I learned kicking, hitting, and grabbing. And I learned to use Qigong and a special method of breathing with the lower abdomen to transform my body into armor, allowing me to withstand powerful blows, including from knives."

"Impressive."

"There really is something to it," Ling said. Then she paused to wave and flash her irresistible smile at a group of monks, who, instead of waving or smiling back, turned away. Ling frowned, but shrugged it off and said with a mischievous smile, "I learned all that and more, including that there are times when a girl wants a gun!"

At that point, Ling's normally hyper level of animation and energy seemed to double, maybe triple, as she said, "For me the key take away, the real message, the gold, was actually experiencing, etching into my bones, knowing through and through, that I—that we humans—are not just physical bodies. We are in fact powerful spirits who have physical bodies.

"Working with the breath, moving awareness around your body, you experience that we are essentially attention. You really get that we have infinite potential. Whatever we can imagine, we can create. Within us we have vast wellsprings, oceans, of energy, resilience, ideas, aliveness. All right within reach, all available to us."

Ling's insights and intensity filled Adam with profound exhilaration. Yet, at the same time, for some reason, his subliminal inner alarm kept going off. What was it?

As they walked, faces rotated toward them, eyes followed their progress. Were the watchers just curious? Probably. But something felt off. Adam met one monk's gaze, but the guy made some sort of warning gesture with his hands and quickly looked down and away. Then, moments later, another man, a narrow-faced guy who was not a monk, fixed him with a malevolent, unrelenting stare until he and Ling were out of sight.

Ling seemed aware of this, but ignored it, staying centered and focused. Apparently on a roll, she continued, "The thing is, there's a big problem. Taoism and Confucianism offer much that's valuable and beautiful. But in China today—just as they did in ancient imperial China—they serve as a soft, disarming cloak that disguises the hard, cold reality of the CPP's totalitarian, one-party, neo-fascist regime. A gangster outfit unrestrained by rule of law wielding absolute power to exploit its own people and employ every trick in the book to bully, connive, and steal its way to world domination."

Why were the monks acting so strange? Then he saw it, a tiny surveillance camera mounted high and unobtrusively on a wall.

It was easy to miss, almost impossible to spot. But once he saw one, he started seeing them everywhere. Ling's sanctuary was no more. When Adam pointed out the cameras, Ling looked crestfallen, then angry.

"Now it makes sense," she said. "My friends were trying to subtly warn us. Trying to let us know about the cameras without doing anything to call attention to you and me, attention that the cameras might pick up."

"This is bad." Ling gnashed her teeth. "Your cap and scarf blur your face for the cameras. But that very fact raises a red flag announcing, 'Hey, this guy needs to be checked out.'"

Adam said, "Also, there was a guy with a narrow face, not a monk, who looked like trouble."

"Oh, that's Fang. He is the local police chief, but he's harmless. He's been in love with me forever—a feeling I haven't encouraged, but he just won't give up. He's just jealous, seeing me with you. His real passion is collecting bribes. Oh, yeah, he is CPP. But I wouldn't worry about him."

"I wonder," Adam said. "I think the guy's trouble."

"Well, where we're headed, there are no cameras, or there better not be."

CHAPTER 34
MASTER ZHANG'S ELIXIR

"Pssst, Madam Ling."

Ling and Adam slowed their rapid pace along a temple walkway to peer into dense bushes, searching for the source of the sound, but no one was there. Then, a young boy in a small monk's robe materialized as though out of thin air.

"Master Zhang sent me. There is danger. Please follow me."

Ling looked at Adam, "It's Okay. Master Zhang is a dear friend. He's also the Tian Shi, the top Taoist priest, of Longhu. Oh, and this is novice monk Sun Changing."

Changing smiled, then took off. Darting like a deer, he led them along an unmarked route probably known only to him, pushing through impenetrable vegetation and leaping walls both low and high. The boy knew the temple and its environs like the back of his hand. Adam was pleased to see not only no people, but also zero evidence of cameras.

At length they arrived at the back entry to an ornate, magnificent structure. The door opened to reveal a robust monk who boomed, "Little Tiger."

Ling said, "Master Zhang."

They all stepped inside. The door closed. Zhang placed his palms together, Ling did likewise and, facing each other, they did a ritualistic Namaste bow. Then, with a big smile, Zhang said, "My dear Little Tiger. I see you still lack detachment, but how could I not love you."

Looking on, Adam was astonished to realize this youthful, muscular man was the 90-year-old head Taoist priest of Longhu Mountain. Talk about looking young! The man had the smooth, tight, unblemished skin of a 20-year-old and a full head of long black hair pinned into a bun with long chopsticks.

Ling introduced the two men to one another.

Master Zhang said, smiling, "Welcome, welcome. Ling's a troublemaker, but any friend of hers is a friend of mine."

Next, Zhang said, "First things first, you have pursuers. Let's throw them off the scent."

Zhang provided fresh, excellent, well-fitting cloths for them both, then he gave their old clothes to look-alike doubles. The boy Changing dressed as Ling, and a giant, powerfully built Chinese monk put on Adam's clothes and the FR blocking hat and scarf. These imposters were sent out with instructions to walk through areas with cameras and then head up to Ling's remote mountain hut.

After the departure of the decoys, Zhang led Ling and Adam up into the mountains in a different direction. At length, high up a steep slope, they came to a six-foot-diameter opening in the smooth, red, clastic rock of the mountain.

As he ushered them in, he said, "This is the sacred, secret cave once occupied by my namesake and predecessor Zhang Daoling, the first Tian Shi Taoist priest."

Zhang lit and handed out candles. The three of them passed through a short entrance passageway that opened onto a house-sized cavern. Adam and Ling breathed a sigh of relief and pleasure as they surveyed the cool, comfortable space. Wow, not only safety, but a touch of luxury! Colorful drapes softened the cave walls and ceiling, and posh pillows lined the perimeter of a polished parquet floor inlayed with a ten-foot-diameter yin-yang symbol.

"Normally only monks of the inner circle visit this sacred place," Master Zhang said. "But you are in grave danger, and, truthfully, your quest, if you succeed, will greatly benefit China and the world."

Adam was impressed, grateful and humbled—and he saw that Ling was too. This guy understood what was going on.

"In this very cave," Zhang said, "Daoling mixed the famous elixirs that awakened the dragon and the tiger."

By way of explanation, Ling said to Adam, "Hence the name Longhu. Long means dragon. Hu means tiger."

Zhang disappeared into the shadows at the back of the cave, then reappeared with two big cups on a tray. "Because you both have battles ahead—challenges of history-altering importance—I prepared these elixirs. Took me several hours—so drink up."

Unbelievable! Were they supposed to believe this was the same legendary elixir that had summoned the dragon and the tiger—and gave birth to Taoism?

"These will increase your strength and wisdom, and oneness with the Tao," Zhang said.

The potion went down like effervescent honey. Adam looked around. Well, phooey, no dragon or tiger. Or, wait a minute. What was that stirring inside him? He definitely felt something, exactly what he wasn't sure.

Ling said, "Thank you, Master Zhang. In all my years as a novice, I never dreamt of anything like this. But, how did you know to prepare this? I told no one we were coming."

"Ah, Little Tiger. We humans have many levels of awareness available to us. But very few clear themselves enough to listen and notice. The two of you have been showing up in my dreams and meditations for some time now."

As wacky as this sounded, Adam nodded, a part of him

surprised that suddenly this made sense. He noticed, too, that Ling did likewise, tears in her eyes.

Master Zhang added, his eyes twinkling, “Also, there is word of mouth, what you call the grapevine. And the fact that Qichang and I are friends.”

The three of them talked and talked. About how life on Mt. Longhu went unchanged for centuries, about the Mao crackdown, tai chi tourism, and the recent invasion of cameras, social credit scores, and increased general government monitoring.

Adam noticed that Master Zhang, although amazing in many ways, was absolutely convinced of the wisdom of his own words.

At one point Zhang said, "It took me 20 years to learn everything.”

“Everything?” Adam asked.

“Everything."

“You mean everything you consider important?”

“No, everything.”

Somehow, this didn't compute for Adam’s western brain.

At length, exhaustion and perhaps the elixir catching up, Ling fell asleep. Adam soon did likewise, plunging into a profound sleep alive with vibrant dreams. In one, he was hanging out with a powerful tiger and a massive dragon, who right before his eyes transformed into Ling and Master Zhang.

In the middle of the night, Sun Changing burst into the cavern yelling, “There is great danger! They are coming!”

Adam instantly sat up, feeling surprisingly refreshed and alert. “Who’s coming? What happened?”

Ling and Zhang also popped up as Changing’s words came rushing out, ”Eight men surrounded Madam Ling’s hut. As you instructed, Master Zhang, I hid in the bushes out of sight but within earshot. Police chief Fang showed them the way, but was not in charge."

Adam asked, "Who was in charge?"

"The leader was a man with powerful chi. You could feel it thirty feet away. His men called him Dongfeng. When they found the hut empty, they came out and Fang pointed them in the direction of this cave. They are coming here now, and I am only a few minutes ahead of them. There is very great danger!"

Ling said, "Fang shouldn't even know about this cave. I didn't know about this cave."

Adam offered, "The guy's a little more wily—and jealous—and dangerous—than you thought. We've got to get out of here."

Luckily, they had fallen asleep fully dressed. They rose. Ling strapped on her pistol. Adam slung her duffle over his shoulder. Then, after quick good byes and heartfelt thank yous to Changing and Master Zhang, they raced out of the cave.

With Dongfeng's men coming up from below, the terrain left only one way to go, the opposite direction, up over the top of the mountain. The trouble was, going up over the mountain took them to the edge of a sheer precipice. The vertical cliff itself was no problem, the issue was the sudden stop at the bottom. Four or five hundred feet below them a river glistened in the moonlight. Sure, they could jump, and they'd be fine during the descent. But impact with the water would rupture every organ and break every bone in their bodies. Not only would that be less than ideal, Adam hated it when that happened.

Ling, bless her cowboy loving heart, pulled a rope and a cord out of her duffle. She lassoed a smooth boulder, tied the cord to the small running loop in the lasso, and dropped the rope and cord down the cliff face. Adam wound the rope around one leg to create friction, then let himself down hand over hand. Ling looped her gun belt twice around the rope to create a friction break, and followed. They belayed down and down fifty, one-hundred, one-hundred-fifty feet.

Oh oh. What seemed at first like a good idea, wasn't. Looking down through the gloomy night, it became clear the rope was not long enough. There was simply no way it was going to get them to river level. They were screwed.

Adam stopped.

Ling said, "Trust me. Just keep going. Fast."

Adam did just that. Was it the elixir? Or was it a deep, accurate intuition that he could trust this woman? No way to know. Probably both. Adam and Ling slid on down the rope, on down the sheer vertical face.

All too soon, the end of the rope looked to be only thirty feet away and was coming up fast. The end dangled in mid air hundreds of feet above the water. Leaving them with what choice? A death plunge?

Suddenly, an arm's length from the bitter end, they came level with a natural, horizontal ledge cut into the cliff face. A shelf dotted with what seemed to be coffins! Ok, they could live with coffins.

But the cliff was undercut and they were dangling a good 15 feet out from the ledge. Ling belayed down beside him. Together, just like you would get a child's swing going, they rhythmically shifted their weight to swing out from the cliff and then back in, going further and further with each swing, until they caught the shelf edge with their toes. Suspended between rope and ledge, they struggled to get traction with their feet. Ever so slowly they toed, inched and clawed their way, gradually shifting their weight in over the ledge. Once they were both on solid rock, Adam pulled on the cord, which drew down the running loop of the lasso, until the cord and entire rope dropped down and he coiled them up.

Just in time. The sound of voices carried down from the top

of the cliff. Angry, frustrated men. Among them, Dongfeng's voice ranted loudest, simmering with frustration. Was there something about the mountain that lended to amazing acoustics. Or had the elixir enhanced their hearing?

They crawled in behind a casket, and lay there panting, catching their breath. After a while the voices went away.

Ling said, "These caskets were placed here by the Guyue people. I'm going to say a prayer asking forgiveness for our intrusion."

"Given that we had no other choice," Adam said, "I think they'll be OK with it."

Later, still in the dark of night, the unique acoustics of the mountain again brought a sound to them. This time it floated up from the river: three faint but unmistakable tones, the chimes of a meditation bell.

Ling said, "It's time."

The only place to tie the rope was around a coffin. They picked the one that looked the heaviest. But was it heavy enough? Adam found some big rocks and placed them in front of the casket to decrease the chances of it sliding off the narrow cliff, sending the sarcophagus into the river and the two of them to their deaths.

Again they headed down the rope. Belaying down and down and down. What an extraordinary person Ling was! What a great soul with whom to share an elixir and with whom to escape death!

At river level, the vertical cliff dropped straight into the water with no beach or ledge. But what do you know!

There, on a bamboo raft, was Master Zhang. They eased aboard, and again pulled the cord to bring down the rope. Then they were off, gliding through the night on the smooth, wide, meandering river shimmering in the moonlight, fantastical bulbous mountains looming around them.

"Hey," Adam asked, "you got any more of that elixir?"

CHAPTER 35
GHOST CITY

Chung Qichang's plan made sense, but would it get them killed?

China's train, plane, and highway systems were world class, but Qichang ruled them out because they would be under heavy surveillance. On the other hand, the vast network of slow, crowded rural buses, were likely to be below the radar. Pretty much every bus had at least one facial recognition camera, and the police did spot checks, but didn't this offer the best chance of them slipping through? The obvious question, though, was: wouldn't the shrewd Gong Dongfeng anticipate this and take counter measures?

The more Adam thought about it, however, the more the plan grew on him. Countless buses, jam packed with the rustic poor and the occasional low-budget adventure traveler, lumbered along a nearly infinite number of back roads and byways, stopping at every village, crossroad, and wide spot. Going anywhere far took forever, but so what. For Dongfeng and his men it would be like searching for a handful of needles in a field of haystacks.

If their facial recognition blockers failed, they would be cooked. If they ran out of luck, they would be even more cooked. And any endeavor where failure means getting marched to an involuntary organ harvest party is kind of a worst case situation. Still, back country buses looked like their best shot.

So, where was the bus stop? Adam and Ling had followed Chung Qichang's directions, and were standing out in the broad daylight of early morning on an empty stretch of road. A few humble dwellings clustered nearby, but there was no sign or indication of a bus stop.

Adam chuckled and asked, "What kind of a bus system is this?"

"One that's so slow, crowded and haphazard," Ling said, "no one would ever think we'd use it."

"So no bus stop's a good thing?"

But, what'ya know, a bus pulled up a few feet away right on time. As they squeezed aboard, they found the entry stairs and aisle packed belly button to backbone and every seat taken.

Where were the Chungs? As they slowly worked their way along the aisle, still no familiar faces could be seen. Was this the wrong bus? Finally, near the back, there they were.

As Adam and Ling drew close, two guys sitting next to the Chungs stood up and gestured for Adam and Ling to take their seats. It turned out that, by being the first to board earlier that morning, the Chungs had claimed two extra seats, but had agreed to let these men sit in them until Adam and Ling climbed aboard.

Little Jia jumped up on her seat to give Adam a big hug. The others were also clearly relieved to see them, but their smiles and warm greetings were brief. An undercurrent of fear and overwhelm gripped the group. Mei and Bo, Qichang's mom and dad, clung to one another with trembling arms. Mingshu, Qichang's wife, sat teary-eyed with knees pulled up to her chest, her shaking arms encircling her knees.

As Adam settled into the seat next to Chung Qichang, he said, "It's great to see you! Ling and Master Zhang are incredible. They—and you—totally saved my bacon."

Qichang nodded and smiled shyly.

Adam went on, "Back in Guilin, you did a hell of a lot more in your windowless office than just Falun Gong exercises. You inspired one hell of a movement."

Qichang replied, "I just play a part. The movement is way bigger than me. Thousands of people like Little Tiger—"

"You call her Little Tiger too?"

"Her codename. Most of us use codenames."

"So, how did you know to save a seat for Little Tiger? How did you know her cover would get blown?"

Qichang said, "It was bound to happen sooner or later. She volunteered to help you knowing it was likely. So we took the precaution of grabbing seats for both of you."

As they talked, Adam's respect and admiration for Ling, Qichang, Master Zhang, and their compatriots soared higher than ever. What extraordinary people!

At one point, Adam asked, "What's the story on the Wuhan virus COVID-19?"

"Well, for one thing it didn't start in that wet market. The virus derives from Horseshoe bats—and no such critters are sold in that market. The nearest Horseshoe bats are found a thousand miles away in the far south of China. It's essentially a bio-weapon that got loose, probably by accident."

As the day and night and next day wore on, as they worked their way ever southward, they changed buses a number of times to avoid camera-dense city terminals and stay on remote, little-traveled backroads. The succession of buses and countless rural miles were becoming a blur when suddenly the squawk of a police siren sounded close behind their umpteenth bus.

Adam, instantly on high alert, jumped up and forced his way to the front of the bus as the driver pulled over. The instant the bus stopped, Adam was out the door headed for the police vehicle. How in hell do you defeat a police spot check of a bus?

Two cops, both looking well-fed and a little portly, were just getting out of their paddy wagon-type truck, which—hmmm!—was just like the one in Yichang. Adam flashed his ID, giving them just enough time to see that he was a VIP, but not enough to register details. In an authoritative but friendly manner, as though confiding with allies, he said it was very important that he talk to them in private immediately. Pulling open the rear door of their vehicle, he climbed in, motioning for them to follow. Surprised but perhaps bowled over by his manner, the two cops looked at each other, shrugged, and joined him in the vehicle.

The moment Adam had the pair of officers sitting in front of him within arms reach, he reached out with lightning speed and slammed their heads together, knocking them out cold. He handcuffed the unconscious men to the bench frame, gagged them, and smashed the vehicle radio. He put their IDs and money in his pocket, and tucked their hand guns under his shirt at the small of his back. One of the officers had a compact back-up pistol in an ankle holster, which he transferred to his own ankle. Last, he gathered up their phones, keys, and comm radios. As he stepped out of the paddy wagon, he threw these into the back of a passing truck going north.

Before returning to the bus, he checked the sight lines and was glad to see that none of what just happened had been visible to anyone in the bus.

Adam climbed back aboard, flashed his VIP ID, and said to the driver, "Everything's fine. It's OK to head on down the road." The driver was probably both confused and intimidated, but did as directed. As Adam returned to his seat, he noticed a GLA soldier eye him suspiciously from the back row. Oh oh, a little too much interest.

Moments later, as the bus changed into a low gear to grind up a slope, the fit, lethal-looking army guy came up the aisle, snapped several photos of Adam and his group, and then returned to his seat. Not good. Probably part of the new 'see something, say something' paradigm that urged people to spy on their neighbors for social credit points.

Ling popped up, followed the guy, and was on him, pouring on the charm, before he could upload, send, or even look at the photos.

At first, face to face with Ling, he smiled broadly and seemed flattered and excited, then, when Adam looked back a short time later, the guy's Bruce Lee body was slumped down, apparently asleep. Ling returned to her seat with the guy's cell phone in her brave, ingenious, dangerous little hands.

Had this little drama attracted the attention of the other passengers? Looking around, Adam saw everyone in the vicinity sort of shut down and draw into themselves. On rare occasions, the societal cancer of 'mei banfa'—no solution, nothing can be done, don't care, look the other way—was just what you needed.

It was time to change buses ASAP.

Several buses and many hours later, in the middle of the night, after so many successes, so many narrow and, let's face it, heroic escapes, Adam woke up with a start. They'd blown it. Too many days of mounting fatigue and sheer, utter, total exhaustion had finally caught up with them. They'd all fallen asleep and woke up to find the bus deep in a city, a huge metropolis no doubt loaded with cameras and alert police. Skyscrapers, apartment complexes and office buildings towered into the night sky. The bus's headlights lit up wide boulevards, broad plazas, artificial lakes, and spacious amphitheaters big enough to hold thousands upon thousands.

But something was off. Literally, the lights were off. In the whole immense place, there were less than a half dozen pin points of light scattered through a never-ending darkness. This huge urban setting was empty. Block after block, mile after mile, hardly a soul was visible. The bus pulled into at a brand new, beautifully-designed bus station that was completely devoid of people and where, naturally, not a single soul got on or off.

"It's a ghost city," Qichang said, "Vacant cities like this were built all over China—mostly with US pension funds. They're all empty. The apartments are priced too high. No one can afford them. The companies that own these empty buildings are essentially bankrupt, which means their US investors stand to lose most of their investment."

"What's going to happen?"

"The CPP is putting off the day of reckoning. But someday soon bankruptcies will kick in. The buildings will lose 80% of their value. It'll be a shock to the Chinese economy, but they'll recover. The good news is 350 million Chinese will then be able to afford a miraculous housing upgrade. The bad news is it will mostly be at the expense of US pension funds, mismanaged funds that working Americans depend on in their old age. The CPP pulled a fast one, but it would not have been possible without the complicity and corruption of Wall Street."

CHAPTER 36
DONGFENG'S REPORT TO SUPREME LEADER

Great, great sir,

Per your wise order that I always report to you the unvarnished truth, I must admit the tall gweilo and Chung Qichang have proven quite resourceful and elusive. But they remain mice in our maze with no possibility of escape. We have picked up their trail and are closing in. All will be put right soon. It won't be long now!

Thank you so much for the trust you place in me. I will not let you down.

Your true loyal servant, Gong Dongfeng

CHAPTER 37
TYPHOON RESTAURANT, WUZHOU, GUANGXI

At length, their seemingly random, circuitous, backroad itinerary brought them, by design, to Wuzhou, a city in southeastern China on the Xi River. Entering an actual city seemed insane, but it had to happen eventually.

In an attempt to thwart the city's ubiquitous surveillance cameras, they donned an all new set of FR blockers. Wraps and scarves of silver-plated fabrics that reflected thermal radiation, fashionable camouflage make up, an electronic cloaking device that scrambled pixels, and clothing covered with various facial images. Anything to foil AI facial recognition.

But it wasn't just the cameras that were the problem. Top priority arrest warrants, they knew from Qichang's online sleuthing, had been issued by the Ministry of Public Security for all seven of them. Every cop in China had their photos and was actively looking for them.

The Ministry had even taken the extraordinary step of promising a promotion to any police officer who helped capture them. To come within sight of a cop spelled danger. But of course staying out of sight of all cops was going to be impossible.

Their most immediate problem, however, was hunger. Everyone was starving. As they entered central Wuzhou, Ling sweet talked the smiling, head-bobbing driver into stopping directly in front of a restaurant named the Typhoon. Adam and the others peered out of the bus's windows in every direction. The coast looked clear. They stepped off the bus one and two at a time, and trickled into the Typhoon, which consisted of a single large room with three walls and rollup doors across the front, all open. Fortunately, there was an empty table way in the back.

Adam sat with his back to a rear corner, where he was partially hidden but could see the street. Ling sat beside him also with her back to the rear wall.

As soon as the seven of them were seated at their round table, the Chungs asked the chef to come out from the kitchen. There was the usual rapid-fire conversation with the chef during which a number of wriggling fish were presented for inspection, approved, and sent to the kitchen.

Adam asked, "Why always the live fish?"

Qichang replied, "In China, it's one of the few ways to guarantee food is fresh and healthy, and not spoiled."

Mei, Qichang's mom, said, "So much food in China is polluted and toxic, coated in pesticides, mixed with plastic. There is much cancer, allergies."

Jia said, "Any one who can manage it only eats imported food. My mom only lets me eat food from outside China."

At this, Jia's mom, Mingshu, made a shushing sound and looked around as if her daughter's words would get them in trouble.

Before long a huge bowl was carried out and placed in the center of their table and a bowl of rice appeared beside it. They all dug in. Everyone ate directly from the big bowl. Each morsel of fish or vegetable was plucked up by chopsticks, and as it moved to the mouth a small rice bowl was held under it to catch any drippings.

Adam marveled at the brilliance and tender humanity implicit in this way of communal eating. By keeping all of the food together in the main bowl, and not dividing it up on individual plates, it created, if not the reality, at least the face-saving appearance of abundance. It also allowed each individual, in a sense, to voluntarily choose to eat less in order to leave more for their loved ones.

Struck by a thought, Adam asked, "What would happen if one of us ate more that his or her share?"

Interestingly, the very idea that someone might eat more than their share was such a foreign notion, no one even understood the question. When Adam finally managed to explain the concept, everyone said they would simply stop eating and just look at the person. What a truly amazing example of human grace, ingenuity, and adaptability. What an elegant, subtle, yet powerful way for so many people to get by, so often, for so long, on barely enough or not nearly enough food. Adam teared up, but wiped his face dry, hoping no one noticed.

Adam kept one eye on the street, watching for any sign of impending trouble. To all appearances, so far so good. But, on some gut level, he sensed danger coming their way. Still, he said nothing. The meal and momentary escape from crushing worry were visibly reviving the Chungs. He wanted them to be able to bask in this brief sanctuary, this feeling of relaxation and safety, for as long as possible. Even if it was an illusion.

As the meal progressed, Adam noticed that occasionally someone would pick up an especially tempting tidbit with their chopsticks and drop it into someone else's small bowl. What a sweet custom. With his chopsticks, Adam picked up a delicious-looking chunk of fish and dropped it into Mei's bowl. Everyone—except Adam—burst out laughing. What was it that he didn't understand?

Jia came to his rescue, saying, "Mei does not eat fish. We

laughed seeing that you meant to do something nice, but, in fact, you pretty much don't understand anything."

At the end of the meal, Qichang and his father Bo belched with gusto. Not only did they make no effort to suppress these eruptions, if anything they proudly increased the volume. Very likely, this indicated praise for the chef. The longer and louder the belch, the greater the praise.

No sooner had belches celebrated the end of the meal, than two PAP officers strolled by the restaurant. Although outwardly nonchalant, they peered into the restaurant a little too long, with a little too much intensity. Had a camera ID'd them and the AI overlord already sent cops?

Adam and Ling exchanged glances.

Adam spoke quietly to Ling, "I think we've been made. I'm going to take the Chungs out through the back. I'm thinking we're going to be slowed down a little. See if you can slip out and get to the ferry. Don't let the ferry leave without us."

Ling grabbed her duffel and was gone in an instant. Seeing her go left Adam with a momentary pang of loss. He hoped to God this would not be the last time he saw this fearless soul.

Adam slapped down money to cover the meal, then hustled the Chungs out the back. They headed along an alley toward the next street over. So far so good. But just as they emerged from the alley, Adam felt a gun jam into his back. Three very fit, competent-looking PAP cops, all with guns drawn, had them surrounded. With so many Chungs around, it was too dangerous to make a move.

CHAPTER 38
PAP OFFICERS BOHAI, CAO, DA AND ZHULIANG

Adam learned later that the AI brain of Wuzhou's IJOP—Integrated Joint Operations Platform—a component of China's nationwide surveillance system developed with the help of American big tech, had alerted the nearest People's Armed Police station to check on Typhoon restaurant.

The IJOP continuously gathered and analyzed data from the region's vast network of cameras and intrusive mobile spyware built into every citizen's phone, and sent a steady stream of "push notifications" telling the PAP to investigate individuals and places. But this alert had been different. It was not the usual witch hunt. The three officers in the duty room, Cao, Bohai, and Da, sensed this one just might be their golden opportunity to make a name for themselves. This was their chance to not only impress people far above them in the People's Armed Police, the Global Liberation Army, and Communist People's Party hierarchies. Best of all, with this bust, they would leapfrog over their troglodyte boss Zhuliang who consistently claimed credit for their good work and gave them none.

*   *   *

The three gendarmes marched Adam and the Chungs back into the alley and ordered them to lean spread eagled against the wall. These guys knew what they were doing. They'd set up their ambush in a clever location, and had seemed to pop out of nowhere. They could see who was a threat and who was not, and kept their weapons zeroed in on Adam.

As the police began handcuffing her family, Jia broke down completely a little ways away. Utterly devastated, the fragile girl wept and blubbered inconsolably, tiny and helpless. The cops turned their backs and ignored her.

Adam was surprised by Jia's infantile regression. But who could blame her? The kid had been through so much in her young life. The mass arrest of her entire family, he guessed, was the final straw. Especially with an organ harvest no doubt coming soon.

Adam got handcuffed and thoroughly searched. They seized the guns and the knife. Having his arms pinned behind him was bad, but having no weapon was worse. These guys pissed him off.

When the handcuff guy came to Mei, the cantankerous older woman pulled her hands from the cop's grasp, turned around, and slapped him hard across the face. Totally surprised, the man did not strike back. Instead, perhaps because in Chinese culture great deference is paid to older people, he withdrew a step and rubbed his face.

"Come on, Da. Get on with it," barked one of the other cops.

This time, Da swiftly and deftly grabbed both of Mei's wrists and cuffed them behind her back. Even as he did this, though, he held her gently.

When it was Qichang's father's turn to be handcuffed, something in the elderly man exploded and he threw two rapid Kung-Fu punches. But Da, with lightning speed, blocked the blows, hurled the old guy to the ground, cuffed him, pulled him to his feet, and slammed him against the wall.

Of course, if Adam tried that, he'd be riddled with bullets. It showed in their eyes. Wariness—of him. Itchy, itchy trigger fingers for the tall dangerous gweilo.

Standing well back with guns drawn, the hyper alert PAP operatives marched Adam and the Chungs over to and into a nearby paddy wagon. Without leaving the slightest opening for Adam to make a move, the officers locked each of them to stout metal rings welded to steel benches lining the walls of the vehicle. For good measure, being no fools, they also put leg irons and extra handcuffs on Adam.

Once Adam and the Chungs were immobilized, the three cops breathed a sigh of relief and visibly relaxed.

Da said, "Can you believe it, Bohai? We did it. This is big."

"Oh yeah," Bohai said, holding up his phone. "These are the fugitives in all the bulletins. Their photos are right here on my screen."

Da said, "I can't wait to see Zhuliang's face when he realizes we're going to be promoted over him!"

"That bastard. Always grinding us, tormenting us, holding us back," Bohai said. "This is gonna be so, so, so great!"

The third cop asked, "Where's that kid? We must take her too."

Oh oh. Adam was hoping that at least Jia would get away. He'd been in many a tough spot, but this time it just didn't look like there was going to be any escape. An enormous sadness settled upon him—for the Chungs, for himself, for Tripnee and everyone back home, for the world. But at least Ling and, hopefully, Jia would have a chance to live!

Also, dammit to hell, it wasn't over 'til it was over. Shaking himself, he pulled his attention back into the present. His senses sharpened. It was show time. His wits, his survival instincts kicked in. He took in every tiny thing, every detail around him.

The weeping of the Chungs. The unyielding steel of the bench under him. The tightness of his wrist and ankle irons. The locked heavy mesh door between him and the cops. The interactions of the cops and their strange obsession with someone named Zhuliang. Hmmm. That might be helpful somehow. Survival looked impossible. But you never knew what minuscule opening, what trifling detail might change that. No matter what, he'd go down fighting, searching for a way, any way for his friends and himself to live!

While the other two cops went out to find Jia, Bohai sat in the front of the truck laughing and chuckling to himself, muttering, "Zhuliang, Zhuliang. Oh, how I'm gonna walk on you, walk on you, walk on you."

After a while, the rear doors opened, Da lifted in a crumpled, crying Jia, and the doors closed. Adam's heart sank further, and the Chungs's sobbing increased.

As Da and the third officer climbed into the front seat, the third guy said, "With all these prisoners, we should call for back up."

"No way, Cao," Bohai said. "Zhuliang is not beating us out of this promotion!"

"Bad idea," Da said.

Bohai said, "The three of us can easily handle this. We are not calling for back up. Our prisoners are chained up and really there's only one who is dangerous, and we've got him double cuffed and ankle cuffed."

Da, sitting in the driver's seat, said, "Hey, you drove last Cao. Where are the keys?"

"I left them in the ignition."

The three searched their pockets and around the driver's seat, but found no keys.

"I hate to say it," Cao said, "but now we really have to call for back up—at least a second truck."

"Not so fast," Da said.

"No way," Bohai said. "This big guy and the others are totally locked down. Two of us will guard them while you, Da, go back to the station to get the duplicate keys. I don't have to tell you, say nothing to Zhuliang."

Without interrupting her wailing, Jia, who was curled in fetal position around Adam's feet, looked straight up at him for a fleeting moment and gave him a big wink. Ha! Adam knew it! There was more to this extraordinary young soul than met the eye.

Even as her bawling continued, he felt his ankle irons being unlocked. The clever little performer had managed to steal the cops' keys while their backs were turned. Absolutely an Oscar-worthy performance.

Jia left the unlocked shackles in place, looking secure but in fact ready to be shucked off with a shake of his legs. A moment later, he felt the consummate young actress press keys into his hands at his back. Working by feel, he unlocked the two sets of handcuffs binding his wrists.

With Da gone, Bohai and Cao faced forward in the front seats of the paddy wagon, but glanced back frequently to check on their prisoners. Unlocking the mesh door between him and the cops without being noticed was not going to be easy. Fortunately, Adam sat within reach of the door, and he'd been studying the timing of the cops's backward glances. On average one or the other glanced back about every ten seconds. A damned tight window to unlock the door and get the jump on them. But what the hell. There's no time like the present.

As quietly as he could manage, Adam placed his handcuffs and shackles on the floor. At the same time, Qichang, by prior arrangement, signaled his family to keep up their sobbing, lest a sudden silence cause a glance backward.

Oooops! Some subtle inadvertent change in the keening caused Bohai to look back. But the instant the cop's head began to turn, Adam thrust his arms back behind him as though he was still handcuffed. Thank God the policeman did not look down to see the cuffs and shackles, but simply glanced around at everyone's upper body, then turned back around.

Adam leapt into action. The keys unlocked the mesh door. Whipping it open, he sprang forward, his fists already in motion. But the cops were fast. Their pistols came out. Barrels swung up. In half a heart beat, they were gonna blast him dead. Thing was, Adam was faster—and more motivated. He grabbed both guns, one in each hand. The detectives were strong. But Adam was stronger. Holding the gun barrels gave him leverage. He wrenched and twisted the weapons. The guns fired repeatedly. The truck shook. Deafening shot after shot penetrated the roof. Bohai and Cao howled with pain, their trigger fingers mangled. Adam yanked both guns free. Gripping the red-hot barrels, he bashed the cops with the butts. But the PAP men fought back, their fists pummeling him, their fingers gauging his eyes.

Time for a double knockout. With lightning speed, Adam simultaneously swung at the temples of both men. Cao had his arms extended to gouge out Adam's eyes, leaving the him wide open, and got knocked out cold. Bohai got an arm up to cushion the blow, so, instead of getting laid out unconscious, he merely got stunned silly for a few heartbeats.

In the split second lull, Adam grabbed the two guns by their handles, and leveled a pistol at each cop. "Hands up or I shoot."

Bohai's eyes were wild, searching for an opening. But seeing none, he slowly raised his hands. Cao gradually came to, and did likewise.

Had the noise and ruckus drawn attention or raised an alarm? The gun shots had been partially muffled by the truck, but had to be loud enough to be heard for at least a block or so. But there was no crowd. Instead, passersby looked down and away, and quickened their pace to hurry on by. Good old 'mei banfa' in action: nothing to see here, nothing to be done.

The Chungs could hardly believe their sudden good fortune.

Jia grabbed the keys and started unlocking everyone's hand cuffs. Qichang and the others said over and over, "Thank you. Oh, thank you, thank you, thank you."

Suddenly, without warning, the rear doors of the paddy wagon flew open and a deep, gruff voice yelled, "Drop your weapons or I shoot!"

With himself and the Chungs fully exposed, Adam had no choice but to lower the pistols to the truck's floor.

A look of utter surprise and relief came over Bohai, as he said, "Zhuliang?"

The gravelly voice of Zhuliang barked, "I figured something was up when you insubordinate idiots snuck out of the station in such a rush."

Cao looked mortified, and Bohai's voice took on a note of anguish. "Sir, we can explain."

"Explain that you pig-headed fools, acting on your own, without your commander's permission, totally botched the biggest arrest in Wuzhou history?"

"But sir—"

"And had to be rescued by that same commanding officer!?"

Bohai—and Cao too—sputtered and almost wept. While Adam and the Chungs, truth be told, pretty much did the same.

Bang!

Zhuliang's gun flew out of his hand. "Ooww!"

Ling walked out of the alley, her gun aimed straight at Zhuliang, who clutched his bleeding hand. "Freeze right where you are. Move and you're dead. What were you saying about rescuing your incompetent men?"

Grinning, Adam scooped up the two pistols and, with a mischievous wink, aimed them again at Bohai and Cao.

CHAPTER 39
OVERNIGHT SLEEPER FERRY

Jia resumed unlocking handcuffs. Adam and Ling marched a very unhappy Zhuliang, Bohai and Cao into the alley, where they handcuffed them to a steel fire escape and relieved them of all keys, weapons, cell phones, IDs, and money. Then, Adam, Ling, and the Chungs raced away in the paddy wagon.

A short, hair-raising ride later, they screeched to a stop on the Wuzhou riverfront wharf where a small, weather-beaten ship with a jillion portholes was just casting off. The gang plank had been pulled in. But when the deck crew saw them, the plank was re-extended and they sprinted aboard. Whew, a minute later and they would have missed the boat. Gotta stop lollygagging!

This low-budget, Wuzhou-to-Guangzhou, overnight sleeper ferry was part of China's peasant transportation system. Built for function not beauty, but beautiful in its functionality, the creaky old craft had no seats in the normal sense, only ten layers, or decks, of flat, crawl-in berths. The ten decks ran from bow to stern along either side of the vessel, leaving a ten-foot-wide, forty-foot-tall canyon-like atrium of open space in between.

Ling pointed the way to their above-the-waterline berths. Before settling in, Adam walked the entire ship, scoping it out, weighing their next options.

Given Wuzhou's ubiquitous AI-controlled surveillance

cameras—not to mention the location of the abandoned paddy wagon on the wharf and all of the witnesses who saw them embark—it was only a matter of time before the People's Armed Police figured out they were escaping aboard the ferry and prepared a welcoming party at its next and only stop: Guangzhou.

Another problem was that either the PAP or the Chinese Coast Guard might order the ferry to simply stop dead in the water or divert to some nearby port where they would be waiting with weapons locked and loaded. To head off this possibility, Adam asked Qichang to hack into and disable the ship's incoming communications.

"And while you're at it," Adam added, "keep on monitoring PAP and Coast Guard communications in the area."

"I'll do my best," Qichang said, fingering his laptop. "Could be sketchy on this old boat."

Thing was, at least for the time being, it looked like their best bet was to stay put. Guangzhou, after all, was close to Hong Kong. The longer they could stay on the ferry, the closer they'd be to freedom. Just so long as they didn't stay too long and get caught, then tortured, then sliced up.

Adam also asked Qichang, "Are there any of your pro-democracy people around here who could help us?"

"Yes, they're pretty much everywhere. But, involving them in this situation, with the PAP hot on our tail, would put them in too much danger. We're going to have to get out of this one ourselves."

"I understand," Adam said.

Adam slid into his port-side, flat-as-a-board, 3- by 7-foot space. After being scrunched for days in bus seats, it was a luxury to simply stretch out flat. Although he couldn't see anyone on his side of the boat, looking across the center atrium gave him an intimate view into the starboard-side berths.

Couples and families had pulled up the divider boards separating their rectangles to create spacious "living rooms" where they lounged together, massaged one another's feet, shared back rubs, and slept together in piles, touching and hugging. Clearly, these families shared a special, physical closeness.

Each above-the-waterline berth had its own porthole. Adam opened his and shimmied up to hang his head out. Mesmerized, as day faded to night, he watched China and the world glide past. Their desperate situation had his gut clenched in a knot. But he was awe-struck. He also felt alive—really alive.

Warm, humid, soot-filled air flowed over—and through—him. It was like breathing airborne powdered Jell-O. Nonetheless, as the hours and miles flowed by, he marveled at the sights, sounds, and smells of this vibrant and troubled land. The ship's crew skillfully navigated narrow, rocky gorges and powered across wide valleys. Cormorant fishermen on bamboo rafts glided by in the dark. Dwellings of every description, villages, and factories—some spewing phosphorescent toxins, some not—slid by. Shadowy boats of every size and shape passed in the inky blackness. Despite all its turmoil, what a remarkable place!

A couple of times Adam tucked back into the vessel and drifted off to sleep—only to awaken after an hour or two and slide his head back out to again immerse himself in the vibrant, other-worldly passing scene.

At one point, in the dim glow of the ship's interior night lights, Adam noticed a GLA soldier in a starboard berth looking back at him a little too intently. Was this guy going to be a problem? Sure enough, the man slid out of his berth and came around intent on a confrontation. "There's an arrest warrant out for someone who looks like you. Who are you? Where are you going?"

Oh oh. Up close, this guy moved with the self-assurance of someone who knew how to handle himself in a fight. Also, he wore an officer's uniform.

Adam replied, "I can explain everything. How about we go outside so we don't disturb others?"

The GLA officer nodded, stepped back, and gestured for Adam to slide out of his berth. Rising, Adam was surprised to find the two of them were the same height. Turning, he led the way toward the ship's stern.

Out on the ship's almost water-level stern deck, Adam stopped next to a stack of life rafts. Turning, he found the GLA man aiming a pistol straight at him, its muzzle inches from his chest.

This was serious. Adam's instinct for improvisation plus his Navy SEAL Krav Maga training kicked in. First, he bowed in a trembling, supplicating manner and raised his hands in a pleading, palms-out, please-don't-shoot gesture. Next, in a flash of speed, he knocked the barrel left, closed his hands on the man's gun hand, and snapped the guy's wrist. Then, before the man could even cry out, Adam kneed him in the groin and knocked him out cold with an elbow to the side of the head.

Adam pulled a life raft off a stack and balanced it on the edge of the poop deck. After relieving the unconscious man of his cell phone and gun, Adam dropped his limp body into the raft and dropped it off the stern. Sparing the man's life could conceivably come back to bite them. But Adam couldn't help but feel the guy was just trying to survive in an authoritarian system not of his making.

Adam returned to his berth, and resumed alternating between sleeping and sticking his head out to take in the sights and sounds of China by night.

Some hours later, he felt someone tap his foot. Adam pulled his head in from the porthole to find Chung Qichang hunkered down peering into his berth. "PAP and Chinese Coast Guard boats are swarming toward us. They'll be here any minute."

Adam nodded, not surprised. "Round up everyone, and meet me on the poop deck."

It was time for plan B. Adam raced back to the ferry's stern. As well as the stacks of life rafts, the poop deck had a beat-up power launch on davits. Gotta lower that sucker in the water, load up his motley group, and get the hell out of there.

Ling and the Chungs rushed up. Adam reached for the winch control to lower the motor launch, but froze at the sound of approaching boats. Some kind of high tech speedboats were coming in quiet and fast, their shapes suddenly visible in the gloomy mist.

Damn it. Damn it. Damn it. Their escape cut off, Adam, Ling and the Chungs, holding their breath, not moving a muscle, scrunched down and compressed themselves into the shadowy darkness behind the stacks of life rafts. Mei and Mingshu, their cheeks glistening with unstoppable silent tears, buried their faces in their hands.

Two small, swift hydrofoil patrol boats, their engines off, glided in. Adept men stepped onto the poop deck and secured mooring lines. Peering out through a gap in the raft stack before him, Adam counted eighteen men.

A commanding whisper emanated from the darkness on the other side of Adam's raft-stack hiding place. It was so close he could reach out and touch the source. Son of a gun. It was the gravelly voice of the Wuzhou PAP commander Zhuliang. As the man spoke, Adam caught a glimpse of his bandaged right hand.

"Men, this is a major major bust. These fugitives are armed and dangerous enemies of China. Go with guns drawn. You know their photos. Shoot first, ask questions later."

A whispered question came from one of the men. “What about innocent bystanders?”

“On a boat like this, don't worry about collateral damage. It's to be expected.The main thing—the only important thing: Don’t let any of these violators get away. We are not going to let them escape or embarrass us a second time.”

Zhuliang sent teams of men to different areas of the ferry, then said, “Ming and Chen, you guard the boats. Be alert. Don’t fucking blow it.”

Ming and Chen whispered, “Yes, sir. Shoot first, question later.” “You got it sir. Shoot the bastards.”

After sending most of the men off, the PAP commander hissed,

“Bohai, Cao, and Da, a word.”

“OK, you bozos, like I said, I’ll share credit with you, but only if you don't botch this up. Don't be fools. Your reputations, your careers, the reputations of your families are all on the line. And more important, my reputation, my career, my family are on the line. The bastards are on this ship. Get them. And don’t let them handcuff you and don't let them escape.”

Bohai, Da and Cao could be heard kowtowing to their boss.

“Yes sir.” “Yes sir.” “We understand sir.” “Everything is on the line.”

Zhuliang’s voice picked up intensity as he continued, “The Chinese Coast Guard fleet and more PAP boats will be here any minute. We've got to capture these prisoners before they get here.”

“Yes sir.” “Right you are, sir.” “We’ll get it done.”

As the four of them headed into the ferry, Zhuliang concluded, “Failure ain’t no option.”

His three lieutenants chorused, “We get it. We get it.”

These four PAP officers were desperately trying to redeem themselves—and save their careers and maybe their lives.

They'd grabbed fourteen PAP foot soldiers and two hydrofoil patrol boats, and chased the ferry all the way down river through the night. In their outfit, the consequences of failure in a major bust were apparently too terrible to contemplate and were driving them to desperate measures.

The poop deck was quiet. The perfect escape craft bobbed in the water a few feet away. But the two guards were on high alert with weapons drawn. How were they going to get past those trigger-happy characters without raising an alarm that would bring sixteen armed men running?

Adam whispered an idea into Qichang's ear. Qichang swallowed, trembled, then nodded. He crept silently to the hatchway door going into the ship, then stood up, making it look like he had just popped out of the doorway. He said in an urgent whisper, "Ming and Chen, come quick. Zhuliang needs you. He's up on the bridge."

Then, before the two men could get a good look at him, Qichang ducked through the doorway into the ship. Ming and Chen jumped from the boats onto the ferry's deck and disappeared into the ship, racing after Qichang.

Adam hustled the Chungs aboard the larger speedboat, and at the same time loaded a pair of oars. Moments later Qichang raced back out of the hatchway and leapt aboard. Adam and Ling cast off both PAP boats. Taking the smaller one in tow, Adam began rowing away.

They'd only gone a few yards when the ferry engines suddenly stopped. In the silence, they heard boats approaching. Had to be a dozen or more coming in fast. From multiple directions.

Which way to row? How to avoid them? No way to know.

Picking a direction at random, as quietly as possible, straining with all his might, Adam pulled like a crazy man on the oars. Thankfully, there was fog. But it was not thick enough, and they were too damn close. It would be a miracle if the incoming boats didn't bump right into them. A single searchlight could sweep the area and pick them out of the darkness. Sensing the extreme danger, the Chung family sat stone silent. Ling and Qichang fingered automatic weapons found onboard. Adam rowed and rowed.

The CPP boats converged on the ferry in stealth mode, with engines quiet and lights out. One passed within fifty yards.

The small but athletic Ling found an extra pair of oars. Putting down her machine gun, she began rowing with Adam, silently matching him stroke for stroke. Wow. So much strength and energy in a small package. Was Ling still flying high on the elixir? Adam felt the difference. Their speed doubled. But they had a long way to go before they'd disappear into the misty night.

In the silence, a familiar voice carried over the water. Although they could not make out the words, it was Dongfeng, no doubt berating Zhuliang and his men. Adam almost felt sorry for these outmatched PAP cops. Like the GLA officer floating in the skiff somewhere back upriver, they were essentially just trying to survive in a tyrannical system.

As luck—and the elixir—would have it, the fog grew thicker, more opaque. In the time it took Dongfeng to vent his disgust and outrage, Adam and Ling were able to pull away and vanish.

CHAPTER 40
GOOD LUCK PIG

They had traveled most of the night on the ferry. Hong Kong had to be within reach. As he and Ling rowed through the foggy blackness—keeping up a strong, silent rhythm—Adam reflected on the vibrant city that until recently had been the free-wheeling financial powerhouse of Asia. The place had once overflowed with enterprise, glamour, and what locals called "the smell of money."

But no more. The CPP had reneged on its treaty with Britain promising one country/two systems, and it now engaged in aggressive, ever-escalating encroachment. Now, at the whim of the CPP, anyone could be extradited for anything. The CPP disqualified candidates for municipal office at will, and only CPP party loyalists were allowed to have a voice or wield power. People could even be—and were—thrown in jail simply for selling books.

To protest their loss of freedom, the distraught population poured into the streets by the millions waving American flags only to be brutally beaten down by police and CPP-backed triad ruffians. The ubiquitous American flags said it all. These people craved freedom—the very freedom that Americans took for granted.

In thinking over the whole situation, one thing that absolutely made no sense to Adam was how protesters in the

US burned American flags while waving flags of Communist China.

Adam hoped and prayed that Hong Kong still had enough freedom—or slippage—or wiggle room—for his little posse to sneak in, board a plane, and fly out.

Chung Qichang, his open laptop in his hands, interrupted Adam's anxious musings. "Good news! We're close to Guangzhou. A bunch of river deltas intertwine around here, creating multiple channels. Not bad for hiding, evading, and sneaking toward Hong Kong.

"Hong Kong proper is about 100 miles, and the airport on Chek Lap Kok Island is on the near side—only about 80 miles.

"The thing is they know our boats. The closer we get to Hong Kong and that airport, the more difficult it will be to slip through."

"The CPP is relentless," Ling said. "They'll be out in force with orders to shoot first and ask questions later."

Shaking and crying, Qichang's mother Mei blurted out, "They'll see us. We're done for."

Bo and tiny Jia, themselves fighting back tears, hugged Mei and stroked her back and shoulders.

Jia said, "It's a miracle we've made it this far. There's got to be a way. I'm betting Adam, Ling, and Qichang—and all of us—figure out a way through this. We just have to hold it together a little longer."

There was your miracle. These words, utterly remarkable coming from someone so young, calmed and steeled the group.

They were now miles away from where they'd left the ferry. The faintest early glow of dawn showed the fog beginning to lift around them.

"These boats," Adam said, "are too small to show up on radar—even when speeding along on their hydrofoils. But once the sun's up and the fog's gone, we'll be easy-to-spot sitting ducks."

"So what are we going to do?" Mei asked, her lips quivering.

Adam said, "I've got a half-baked idea," and outlined his proposal. At first, there were skeptical looks and heads shook. Then, as they discussed and refined the plan, smiles gradually appeared and heads nodded in the affirmative.

It was time to act. Ling jumped into the second smaller hydrofoil boat. Had she ever driven one? "No," she said, "but how hard could it be?"

Adam fired up the engine of the larger vessel, put the craft in motion, and soon had it up on its hydrofoils. Qichang sat at his elbow reading computer maps, pointing out the way. They raced through the delta channels, gliding along at forty-five knots—with Ling following close behind, laughing.

The first order of business was to find either a sleepy marina or some isolated smallish boat at anchor before sunrise, while it was still twilight. The minutes—and the miles—ticked by. But they found no solo boats at anchor and every harbor they came to was already a beehive of activity this early in the morning. Too many people around to secretly beg, borrow or buy a boat.

"The maps show no marinas for several miles," Qichang said. "We're running out of twilight."

"We can still pull this off. There's still a little time," Adam said, going full throttle. "But none to spare."

Suddenly, in the middle of nowhere, it happened. Slam! Bam! Splat! Adam's boat came to an abrupt stop. The bow dove into the waves. Everyone aboard was thrown violently forward. Poor Mingshu flew clear overboard.

Mei, her fists pounding the air, screamed, "I knew it! I knew it! We'll never get to Hong Kong or America!"

"Hold on," Adam said. "It ain't over 'til it's over."

Jia, despite having just received a big black eye in the crash, agreed. "Adam's right, grandma," she said. "As long as we're alive, there's hope."

There were bangs and bruises, but no serious injuries. After Adam and Qichang pulled Mingshu back in, Adam checked the boat. "You won't believe it," he said. "We hit a floating pig carcass. Broke the hydrofoil."

"That's China for you," Mei said. "There was a huge pig die off upriver. The farmers dumped the corpses right into the river. Of course they washed down this far. Of course!"

As they transferred everyone to Ling's boat, Jia pointed into a side bay and said, "Hey, what's that?"

Almost entirely hidden far up the curved, sickle-shaped inlet, an old Chinese junk sat at anchor. They motored toward it.

About fifty feet in length, the thing looked at first like an old hulk.

They hailed the vessel, but got no response. Climbing aboard, they found it unoccupied—and, to their surprise, it seemed to have everything needed to function.

Adam had passed many a day with BC sailing BC's Chinese junk in and around San Francisco Bay. He knew what to look for, and he smiled at what he saw. The fully battened sails seemed to be in order. The ship's wheel moved the rudder from side to side. And the engine even started. Although this ancient-looking, classic old ship had seen better days, she still had some life left in her old bones. In a way, this was the perfect incognito vessel for the next leg of the plan. What an absolute gift from heaven.

Jia said, "If it hadn't been for that pig, we would've gone right past this inlet, and never would've found this boat. Thank you, pig!"

CHAPTER 41
APPROACHING HONG KONG HARBOR

In the scant remaining twilight, they pulled up the junk's anchor, took the PAP hydrofoil boats in tow, and motored out of the small crescent-shaped bay.

Soon, the channel spilled out onto a broad estuary which, to the south, gave out on the open water of the South China Sea.

It was high time to get rid of the PAP boats. First, they put aboard the smaller one—the one with the intact hydrofoil—a bunch of their turned-on cell phones. Then they pointed it due south, lashed the wheel, pushed the throttle to max, and let her rip.

As it raced away into the distance, Adam said, "Might hit an island, but it also has a good chance of making it out into the deep, into the South China Sea. Either way, it might lure the CPP into a chase—a wild goose chase—which would draw off boats and make it easier for us to reach Hong Kong."

Ling asked, "And the other boat, the broken one?"

"We'll sink it right here. As long as at least one of the boats is missing, they'll keep searching for it—hopefully as their primary focus."

Adam opened the boat's transom drain plugs—and watched water trickle in. Too slow. Bo found an ax and handed it down. With it, Adam chopped a hole in the boat's bottom. The sea surged in, and Adam jumped back aboard the junk. As the first rays of sun burst over the eastern horizon, the PAP patrol boat disappeared below the waves.

A light but steady breeze eased out of the east. They hoisted the ship's two battened sails—the foresail and main—each on its own mast—and settled into an entirely new, different mode of travel. Rolling gently in the wind and swells, the battered Chinese junk lulled along at three knots.

"Hey, look what we found." Ling and Mingshu came up on deck with armloads of rough peasant clothing and conical Asian hats. The stuff got passed out, and soon they looked, at least from a distance, more like the crew of semi-derelict junk. Mingshu had also found needle and thread, and with impressive speed altered a shirt and pair of pants to fit Adam. To conceal his height, Adam plopped down on a bench on the high poop deck, and to hide his pale skin, he put on one of the wide-brimmed bamboo hats. Meanwhile, Ling took the wheel.

Adam knew better than to do it, but he couldn't help feeling an upwelling optimism. The worst had to be behind them. They were, what, maybe thirty miles from Hong Kong? The CPP would be doing everything they could to find them. But Hong Kong was one of the busiest harbors in the world and already, in every direction, more and more boats big and small were popping into view. There was no way they could check every boat. The key was—as they had done—to have gotten rid of the PAP patrol boats. Now, in this old junk, they were, they had to be, the very definition of incognito. Right?

Adam had no sooner indulged in this brief euphoria, than a CPP search plane came by flying low and slow, clearly checking out one boat after another. The plane sent Mei into a fist-shaking, sobbing fit.

Qichang whispered to Adam, "We've got to do something to distract Mei. In our family, we're used to this. The key to calming her is to give her something else to think about. I know it sounds crazy, but talking about interesting things, especially about history, works the best."

"Or give her a job?" offered Adam. "Hey, Mei, I need you to find out who owns this boat. Later, when this is over and we're safe in America, I want to tell 'em where to find their boat. Also, I'll pay them enough to fix her up like new—or buy a brand new boat."

This worked wonders. Now that she had something to focus on, Mei calmed down and went below on a mission to identify the owners. Qichang flashed a big smile and gave Adam a thumbs up.

The closer they got to Hong Kong, sure enough, the more boats materialized around them. But at the same time, the closer they got, the more patrol boats and search planes they saw prowling around in the distance. It was hard to tell from a long way off, but it looked like the PAP and Chinese Coast Guard were stopping and boarding boats at random. Thank God they were off in the distance!

Oh oh! A Coast Guard cutter headed straight toward them. Was it coming along side to board?

At that moment, Mei climbed out of a hatch and, without looking around, stepped over to Adam to hand him an ID card and boat registration papers. Then, she saw the cutter closing in. Her body convulsed, she started sobbing, and she nearly screamed.

Qichang quickly stepped between his mother and the approaching boat, screening her from view.

"Don't worry, mom," he said, "Everything's OK."

"Qichang," Adam said, "maybe you should take Mei back below."

Mei shrieked, "No way! I get seasick down there!"

Remembering what Qichang had said about calming his mother, Adam said, "Mei, how about an interesting tidbit—"

The transformation in Mei was hard to believe, but real. She sat down next to Adam and said, "Yes, tell me."

"Did you know the design of Chinese junks has remained basically the same for thousands of years? Why do you suppose that is?"

With one eye on Mei and the other on the fast approaching CPP boat, Adam said, "Have you noticed that Chinese junks all have battened sails, multiple watertight compartments, and how the stern—the back—is higher than the bow—the front?"

Adam was relieved to see Mei looking straight at him, nod, and ask, "Why is that?"

"It's all about surviving typhoons."

The CPP boat was close enough to make out individual members of its crew, which meant they could see his crew as well.

Adam continued, "In a typhoon, all hell breaks loose. Wind and waves rip away sails and rigging, people get washed overboard, and ships fill with water, capsize, sink."

The CPP cutter, now only a hundred feet away, bristled with weapons—including two heavy-duty, belt-fed, mounted machine guns—all aimed at the junk. Mei, thank the universe, remained, for the moment, focused on Adam, and he had to keep it that way. "Junks are ingenious," he said to her. "With multiple watertight compartments, even if one or two or even three flood, the boat still has buoyancy and stays afloat."

The patrol boat started to circle the junk, and a load speaker boomed, "Prepare to be boarded. We're coming alongside."

With the cutter in his peripheral vision, Adam kept his main focus on Mei. "Battened sails don't need stays or spars, so in a typhoon only bare masts are left up, leaving nothing for the wind to tear away."

As the seventy-foot cutter came along side, several crew were moments away from clamping onto the junk with grappling hooks. But before they threw the hooks, a uniformed sailor emerged from the boat's radio shack—identified by its big antenna—and ran to his captain—clearly older than the others and wearing a captain's hat and uniform. Hurried words were exchanged, and suddenly the cutter wheeled away and accelerated toward the south. Had the hydrofoil been spotted and the cutter ordered to pursue it?

"Best of all," Adam said to Mei, "the high stern superstructure acts like the feather of an arrow and keeps the bow pointed into the wind and waves. This minimizes the chances of capsize and allows the crew to ride out the storm safely below deck."

Still looking at him intently, Mei said, "So interesting. I love learning new things."

As the CPP boat raced away, becoming small in the distance, Adam, Ling and the Chungs—everyone, that is, except Mei, who was already relaxed—breathed a collective sigh of relief.

"Whoopee!" Ling shouted. "Hallelujah! That's as bloody close as I ever want to cut it. I think what saved us was how calm we all were, especially you two, Adam and Mei. You sat there casually chatting the whole time, paying no attention to them. Absolutely great body language proclaiming we're totally at ease, with nothing to hide. On some subliminal level, that's what saved us."

CHAPTER 42
HONG KONG AIRPORT

The Hong Kong Special Administrative Region of China includes Hong Kong Island itself and also the New Territories peninsula plus a slew of nearby islands. Victoria harbor—the waterway between Hong Kong Island and the New Territories—would be thick not just with commercial and private boats, but also with PAP and Chinese Coast Guard patrol boats.

Fortunately, their long-sought destination—Chek Lap Kok Airport—was well east of and much closer than the main harbor. Built on a flat pancake of reclaimed land, the airport was adjacent to the north side of mountainous Lantau Island.

Unfortunately, as they drew near, Adam saw that the Chinese Coast Guard had thrown a tight blockade of patrol boats around the airport.

Where to go? Wracking his brain, thinking back to an earlier visit, Adam remembered a little fishing village also on the north side of Lantau Island, east of the airport. What the heck was the name of that place? Oh yeah, it came back to him: Tai O.

Wedged into a small bay at the foot of Lantau's steep, mountainous shoreline and built on stilts over the water, Tai O was an oddball, out-of-the-way place that might be just what they needed. It was, he hoped, far enough out-of-the-way to escape scrutiny, but close enough that a short taxi or bus ride would get them to the airport. Home of the Tonka people, the village's maze of narrow waterways and flow of tourists offered a setting where they might be able to inconspicuously transition from water to land, from escapees into normal travelers.

As they sailed toward Tai O, Adam, for the umpteenth time, pondered the risks ahead. The CPP had egregiously violated the one-country/two-systems treaty with Britain, and was rapidly imposing its system of total surveillance, social credit and oppressive control in Hong Kong. He sensed freedoms were disappearing fast. Was this once vibrant city already too locked down for them to slip through, board a plane, and fly away? Only one way to find out.

They dropped anchor in a sheltered cove a quarter mile from Tai O. Got to get off the junk before a patrol boat happens by. To better blend in once on land, they changed back into their regular clothes. Adam hailed a fisherman on a passing sampan and negotiated a ride ashore for them all.

The wooden, flat-bottomed, thirty-foot sampan, with its low bamboo hoop shelter amidships, was the live-aboard home of the man, his wife and two infants. As Adam, Ling and the Chungs climbed down from the junk and stepped aboard, the boat handled everyone's weight with surprising ease. With a single sculling oar, the small, gaunt man expertly sent them gliding toward Tai O.

From a distance, the place looked like an impenetrable forest of bamboo poles jutting straight up out of the bay—a towering forest with a thatched-hut village perched on its top high above the water. As they drew near, Adam saw narrow openings. Their boatman took them into one of these slots and propelled them with surprising speed through tight, twisting passageways.

As their boat squeezed along, Qichang passed out a fresh new set of facial recognition blockers: LED goggles; privacy visors that made the user no longer scan as human; head scarves and t-shirts covered with faces designed to thwart the algorithm; and wearables that made a person virtually invisible to automatic surveillance cameras. Would the stuff work? Again, only one way to find out.

Adam was glad to catch glimpses of other sampans loaded with tourists. At length, they glided up to a floating dock crowded with tourists climbing on and off sampans, beginning and ending guided tours of the stilt village. Perfect. As they climbed a ladder up to the village level, they blended in seamlessly. He hoped.

A network of bamboo walkways took them to land, where they found buses and taxis. Splitting up into ones and twos, they fanned out and climbed aboard various vehicles for what would either be a short ride to the airport or a terrible living nightmare ending in death by involuntary organ harvest.

Enroute to the airport, Qichang booked tickets online for a non-stop flight to San Francisco leaving in less than an hour. To Adam's surprise, they actually made it to the airport and passed through security without incident. Whew. Almost unbelievable.

But at that moment the plane was already boarding. With a thick sprinkling of police throughout the airport, it was not a good idea to call attention to themselves by running headlong through the place. So they set off on a fast walk toward their departure gate.

Who knew? Maybe they were actually going to pull this off.

As they speed walked, Qichang fell in beside Adam and said with suppressed emotion, "Adam, you, you've got the most amazing powerful chi and oneness with the Tao. You've achieved the impossible—often by doing the right thing, by doing what your president Lincoln described as 'acting out of the better angels of your nature.'"

Adam said, "You, too, my friend. You—"

"Let me finish," Qichang interrupted. "I want you to truly take in how grateful we are and how amazing you are. I would've been tempted to kill the Wuzhou PAP cops. But by letting them live, they came back to provide us with the speedboats! And finding the junk because the pig stopped us. That was your karma, your wonderous karma."

"It wasn't just me, that's our karma—"

"Shush, it's you. What you did calming Mei! Let's face it, that was superhuman—and totally saved us."

Qichang, with tears welling in his eyes, reached up to put a hand on Adam's shoulder, "You create good karma. Your example teaches me how to be more at one with the Tao."

Not knowing how to handle such a sweet compliment, and pretty sure he didn't fully deserve it, Adam smiled with genuine delight and said, "Thank you my friend. But really, it was not just me, it was all of us. Your family, Jia, Ling, you. It took all of us to pull this off. And I hate to remind you, we're not quite out of here yet."

"OK, true. But you valued and believed in me—in us. You gave us courage. You made it happen. Take it in, own it. You're great!"

Adam felt a little sheepish. "Do you know what the Zen Buddhist said to the hot dog vendor?"

Chung Qichang looked bewildered. "No, what?"

"Make me one with everything."

CHAPTER 43
BOARDING THE PLANE

They reached the departure gate as the last passengers were filing aboard. For some intuitive reason, Adam sent Ling onto the plane first. Next was little Jia, then her grandparents Mei and Bo, her mother Mingshu, and then Qichang. Bringing up the rear, Adam let out a sigh of relief once they had all stepped aboard. And just in time. They'd no sooner entered, when the crew began closing the door behind them.

Such a beautiful, beautiful door! Closing. Ending their ordeal. Protecting them from the hounds of hell.

The door was mere inches from sealing tight when Adam heard running feet and a commotion on the boarding ramp. Abruptly, a half dozen hands gripped the door's edge, preventing it from closing, prying it open.

Dammit to hell! There stood Gong Dongfeng, with a squad of enormous soldiers—giants all bigger than Adam—right behind him.

Seeing Dongfeng, Mei screamed.

Taking in what was happening, the American pilot stepped into the center of the entryway, blocking their way. "This airplane is US sovereign territory," he declared. "This crew and these passengers are under United States protection. You are not coming on this plane—"

Without hesitation, Dongfeng spun to deliver a roundhouse

kick straight into the pilot's chest, knocking him down. Dongfeng then stepped aside to let his bio-enhanced super soldiers charge onto the plane.

Then it was Adam who blocked their way. The lead soldier aimed a straight-fingered thrust at his eyes. Adam blocked the jab with his left arm, and slammed the side of his right hand down on the man's carotid at the base of the neck, dropping him in his tracks. But in the same instant, four soldiers en masse swarmed Adam, grabbing and pinning his arms. Dongfeng and the other three soldiers swept past, racing to grab the Chungs and Ling.

Sizing up the situation, Adam saw a way to save his companions. First, he whispered to the pilot who was just getting back up, "As soon as these goons and I are off this plane, take off fast."

The pilot met his eye and nodded.

Then, summoning all his strength and speed, Adam wrenched his arms free. Using blows to stun rather than kill, he brought an elbow up under the chin of one man, kneed a second in the groin, and toppled the other two over the body of the first guy he'd put down.

Knowing he was the person Dongfeng wanted most, the known spy, the man who knew America's plans, Adam sprinted out the plane door and up the boarding ramp. Sure enough, Dongfeng chased after him, calling for his men to do likewise.

Adam tore through the airport, dodging through the throngs of people like a broken-field half back. Glancing back, he saw the soldiers falling behind, getting slowed down by the crowds. But, oh oh, he glimpsed Dongfeng talking into a throat mic. No doubt the spymaster was calling upon the airport police to lock down the terminal and encircle him.

Adam did not let up, did not miss a stride. Bobbing and weaving through the masses of people, he led his pursuers on a long, wild chase. All the while, though, he knew it was a lost cause. Try as he might, even if he got out of the airport, he could not escape this time.

But he had to distract Dongfeng and his men as long as possible, hopefully long enough for the pilot to get the plane in the air and his friends to safety.

The question was, once Dongfeng captured Adam, would they torture him to death? Extracting everything he knew in the process?

CHAPTER 44
HERE WE GO AGAIN

Maybe it was tasers or knockout darts. Adam didn't know. One minute he was running through the airport. The next he was strapped to a chair, his arms and legs bound tight, looking at a blurry Gong Dongfeng.

The room was small and windowless. Between them was a table. At least this time he wasn't in a yellow jump suit, but his pockets felt empty. As his eyes focused, he saw the contents of his pockets spread out on the table.

Dongfeng said, "So, Adam, we've been here before."

Adam thought to himself, Was it Yogi Berra who said, 'It's déjà vu all over again'? Except this time Adam had a plan.

"You've caused us quite a bit of trouble," Dongfeng said. "All for nothing, however. Except that now our patience has run out. You will cooperate completely, or regret it immediately. Also, I guarantee: you will not escape a second time."

"My friends?"

"Gone, I'm afraid. Escaped on the plane."

Adam breathed a profound sigh of relief. The Chungs and Ling were free!

Dongfeng leaned back in his chair and splayed his feet on the table. "Their escape puts you in deep trouble. Much deeper than before. If you do not cooperate, your pain and suffering will surpass anything you can imagine."

What do you say to a guy who is going to torture you to death?

Dongfeng sat up and leaned forward, looking somber. "Once again you have a choice. I recommend, for your sake, that you talk freely—tell us everything. Seriously, Adam, talk and you'll be okay. Otherwise you're in for real, actual, living hell. If you resist, the pain will be unbearable and you'll end up telling us everything anyway. The problem is, with the second option, your body, psyche, spirit, and mind will be damaged beyond repair. Forever. For nothing."

As Dongfeng spoke, instead of gloating in triumph, he seemed genuinely sad and sympathetic. Was there hope for this guy yet?

Adam said, "I have crucial information that you yourself need. You won't like it, but you need to hear it."

Dongfeng looked skeptical. "Sounds like a trick. I'm warning you—"

"No tricks, just the truth. Facts that any man in your position would want to know. Absolutely needs to know."

"What?"

"Aiguo knows about you and Roe Rosen—"

"He knows what exactly?"

"He knows everything—he's seen videos of you and Rosen in her bedroom."

Dongfeng grimaced. Got his attention.

"The fact is you're on his kill list. And his grandfather won't stop him, at least not for long. Old man Xu has already given Aiguo permission to kill you."

"Nice try, but that's bullshit."

"It's true."

"Xu'd never do that."

"I have proof."

"No way! I'm too valuable."

"Yes, you are—and hats off to you. You're ten times—a hundred times—the man Aiguo is. If there were any justice—any real wisdom—they'd give Aiguo's rank and position to you in a heartbeat."

This seemed to resonate with Dongfeng, who cocked his head, almost nodding.

Adam continued, "But wake up—admit it—you're not in a meritocracy where competence is rewarded. You see it every day—the CPP is corrupt—and rewards people not on merit, but on their connections, their family name."

Dongfeng looked shaken for a moment. But the man was wary by nature, and pulled back. "Very clever Adam. I have to hand it to you. You're a psyops master. You had me going. But I'm Chinese and no matter what I'm loyal to China."

"I understand," Adam said. "But, if I were you, I would at least want to see the evidence. To know the details, to know who said what about you. A video on my phone says it all. You have to see it."

Adam told Dongfeng the password. Opening the phone, Dongfeng played the recording of Aiguo's video conversation with the most powerful man in China, his grandfather Xu. At first, Dongfeng listened with his usual nonchalance. But as the video played, he grew more and more riveted. By the end, he listened with rapt attention, hunched and tense, his hands and lips trembling.

Then came grandfather Xu's devastating final words to Aiguo:

"Okay, my little Chickpea, I see I've gotten your attention. You will not kill Gong Dongfeng—at least not yet. Yes, he overstepped and does not know his place. He should not have trespassed on your plaything. But right now we need Dongfeng. We need him to deal with the American, find out what the

Americans are doing, and stop them. Afterwards, when this is over, then you can kill Gong Dongfeng."

Dongfeng was no fool. Quite the opposite. This master spy was sharp, able to swiftly and accurately assess a situation, and adjust accordingly.

His whole position in life was not what he'd thought. His talents were only marginally appreciated. His loyalty to the elder Xu was not reciprocated. He had dedicated himself to advancing an entire system that considered him second or third class, a permanent underling, sub-human. A system in which he had the status of a bug, a bug that could be snuffed out on a whim. It was time for big changes.

Still, at the same time, the guy was only human. As the magnitude of what he needed to do sunk in, this normally super cool operator shook with emotion and poured with sweat.

CHAPTER 45
FLYING DRUNK

Adam and Dongfeng sat side-by-side in first class, flying non-stop from Hong Kong to San Francisco. Dongfeng looked stricken, in a state of shock, no doubt struggling to adjust to his new circumstances. For his whole life, the guy had maneuvered and climbed his way up in a totalitarian system where independent thought was not tolerated.

Now, to literally save his life, Gong Dongfeng had crossed over to the other side, the side of his longstanding enemy. The transition, to say the least, had to be jarring. The man's universe had turned upside down, and he would have to re-examine and re-fashion his entire world view.

Adam asked the graceful, svelte Greek flight attendant—whose eyes seemed to light up whenever she looked at the two of them—to bring two margaritas. Dongfeng was a potential treasure trove of valuable intel, and Adam wanted to seize the opportunity to learn all he could. But he also felt like celebrating. He was out of imminent physical danger for the first time in what felt like a very long time. Finally, on this thirteen-hour flight, he could relax, glory in simply being alive, and also celebrate the emancipation of this interesting human being sitting next to him.

At the same time, he had to be careful with Dongfeng. To have played all the roles he'd played, this master spy had to be a consummate actor. Enjoy, drink up, but stay sharp and don't take anything at face value.

The margaritas arrived. At first, Dongfeng spoke warily. But as time passed and the drinks kept coming, he became more and more loose and open. The Chinese spy master seemed to gradually realize he could say what he really thought—and found himself loving it.

They discussed things that Dongfeng confessed he had rarely even let himself think about. For example, could a person break from the CPP regime and still remain loyal to China? Once the question was posed, the answer was obvious: "Yes, absolutely. In fact, this's exactly what China needs to evolve, to fully take its place in the family of civilized nations.

"At present," Dongfeng said, "China is a gangster-run state, where success and survival depend on how connected you are and how well you kiss up to and pay off the all-powerful CPP oligarchy."

After a while, Dongfeng's realizations came in a flood. "Instead of gangster cronyism, China needs consistent, even-handed rule of law. Stop slave labor. Stop disappearing people. Stop involuntary organ harvesting. Stop taking away people's property. Stop silencing differing opinions. And for everyone's sake, stop surveilling people 24/7—and do away with social credit scores."

Adam, who was also enjoying the margaritas, fully agreed and went even further. "They need honest, wide-open elections, and freedom of speech, religion, assembly, and the right to bear arms."

On this last point, Dongfeng disagreed. "Don't get me wrong," he said. "I admire the Second Amendment for America. After all, in the U.S, where gun ownership is highest, crime is low. But in China this would never fly."

How in hell were such sweeping changes to be brought about?

"It's got to be done without civil war," Dongfeng said. "If 1.4 billion Chinese fight each other, the chaos and trauma would know no bounds. Blood would flow like a river."

"There's got to be a way," Adam said, "to bring about change without war. Gradually over time."

"You Westerners are such idealists."

A little later Dongfeng tensed, his eyes hard, glaring. "Hegemon. You know the concept? It's the key to understanding China. The imperial emperors of China were absolute hegemons. They literally owned and controlled everything under the sun—including the people. No one other than the hegemon had any rights whatsoever."

Adam nodded. "I've read about it. There was a time when European monarchs were also hegemons. But in Europe things like the Magna Carta, the Renaissance, Christianity, the Enlightenment, and the ongoing struggles between the various monarchs led to a gradual recognition of individual rights and a sharing of power."

"In China there was nothing like that," Dongfeng said. "The emperor remained the thousand-percent ruler, controller, and owner of everything.

"Instead of a governing class with hereditary rights, the empire was administered by people selected by competitive exam—exams based on Confucius, who extolled the virtues of harmoniously accepting one's place. From the hegemon's point of view, this had big advantages:

"It gave the empire the appearance of an egalitarian meritocracy run by its smartest people in accordance with Confucian principles. But, importantly and tellingly, this system also nipped in the bud the emergence of any upwardly mobile class—or any guilds or organizations—that might someday demand to share power. This completely stopped the gradual process of recognizing individual rights that happened in the West.

"Mao followed in the same mindset, and now the CPP acts exactly like a hegemon. They feign wisdom and pretend to care about harmony, but their abuse of their own people and aggressive actions scream otherwise. Only the Communist People's Party—the CPP—matters. No one has any rights but them. Rules and norms don't apply to them. Everything belongs to them. They're 100% convinced they're superior and destined to rule the world.

"When you're above the rules and clearly superior, it's okay to lie, bully other nations, break promises, violate treaties, and—in short—act like a rogue nation."

Dongfeng swallowed the last of his drink, his fist tight on the glass. "The CPP aims for global domination, make no mistake. They're the new Nazis. Except now it's called middle kingdom complex."

Adam had to agree—and was surprised by the speed and intensity of Donfeng's conversion to a pro-Western point of view.

The man went on, really getting into it. "Can you believe it? They seize Tibet. Persecute and organ harvest Uighurs and Falun Gong. Suppress Hong Kong. Grab islands owned by Japan, Indonesia, the Philippines. Claim ownership of the entire South China Sea. Skirmish with India. Threaten Taiwan. Bully Australia. Only a hegemon would do that."

Dongfeng was right, of course, but was the guy for real? Adam had never seen anyone change so rapidly, so completely. But who knew the truth better than this CPP black-ops veteran? Still, he wondered at the transformation. Was it the margaritas or Dongfeng's true nimble spirit—or something else? Hmmm, how to draw the man out?

Adam asked, "How'd you get started working for the CPP?"

Dongfeng sure as hell did not disappoint. Smiling wistfully, the older man said, "I graduated from the People's Public Security University of China, the CPPSU, Tuanhe campus. I was the first man in my entire class to earn the rank of sergeant. The prestigious, much-feared Ministry of State Security recruited me and assigned me to a special, elite division tasked with bringing down America and putting China on top.

"Of course, we knew we couldn't win an outright war. But as Sun Tzu said, 'Supreme excellence in war consists in breaking the enemy's will without fighting.' So we devised a strategy called unrestricted warfare."

CHAPTER 46
FLYING WASTED

Dongfeng's eyes blazed. "Guns and bombs were off the table. But we were determined to use anything and everything else to catch up to and surpass America. We were on fire.

"There was nothing we didn't do. We did it all. Cyber and IT theft like you wouldn't believe. We ripped off whole libraries of corporate, scientific and military secrets—the biggest theft in world history. We ran spy rings in Silicon Valley and other tech hubs. We compromised, entrapped and turned senators, congressman and state officials. We paid off top Ivy League professors in an ongoing program of intellectual theft. In one operation we stole the entire US federal employee database.

"If it hurt America, we did it. Predatory trade practices. Forced tech transfer. Dumping. Patent infringement and reverse engineering. Counterfeiting. Currency manipulation. Flooding the US with super cheap meth and fentanyl."

"All of this was huge," Dongfeng continued, "but your economy, frankly, was so strong, so fucking vibrant, even all that wasn't going to be enough to make China dominant.

"That's when the ministry reassigned me to a top-top-secret team. There were many other such teams, most worked on brainwashing the American public.

"My team—which I eventually led—was specifically tasked with weakening, demoralizing, and dividing America through disharmony. All with the ultimate, single-minded goal: drop America to its knees, and finally put China back on top, dominating the world.

"But we had a huge, colossal bitch dog of a problem. To weaken America from within, we needed to exploit fault lines, existing divisions in your society. But our research—damn fine, super thorough research—showed the United States is one of the least racist, most diverse, and most open, egalitarian and accepting nations on earth. Sure, as in any country there are some racists, but the vast majority of Americans are not racist. Frankly, the evidence was overwhelming—and depressed us no end.

"Hell, there were hardly any Nazi or white supremacist rallies, and the ones there were generally had no more than a couple dozen participants. The vast, vast majority of whites, blacks, browns, and Asians find common ground, don't hate, don't judge or condemn others, and get along with one another just fine.

"It wasn't just depressing, it was frustrating, infuriating. For a long time we just pulled our hair out. We were stumped. How the hell were we going to divide and conquer?

"Then, finally, we found ACAB—All Cops Are Bastards, FH—Freedom Highway, and CRT—Critical Race Theory. These were tiny, fringe ideas with no adherents, but they were beautiful. They ignored—and still ignore—all the positives in America and see everything through a negative lens.

"Funding these groups was the best money we ever spent. They're blind to the amazing positives of America and focus entirely on the negative. Best of all, they see racism and white supremacy everywhere.

"ACAB and the others are beautiful. Man o man, do they foment racial tension, division, hatred. It's wonderful. Their marches and protests are tinderboxes. Send in a few agents provocateur with bricks and fire accelerants, and you've got full-on riots rampant with looting, smashing, burning and widespread violence—people whaling on each other, beating each other up, burning down their own neighborhoods. What a propaganda gift to the CPP!

Dongfeng threw back the remains of his latest margarita. "I know, I know, I'm twisted. But when it comes to sparking riots, I can't help it. I'm a connoisseur."

The flight attendant started to look worried about the river of alcohol flowing into the men. But something—was it their alpha male 'everything's-OK' vibe?—kept the drinks coming. She placed fresh margaritas before them, the rims perfectly salted. Then, after lingering over them a little longer than necessary, she withdrew, her perfume hanging the air.

"I admit it," Dongfeng went on. "It's refreshing to talk about it. Shit, I love telling you about it. These groups take small problems and exaggerate the hell out of 'em. And the solutions they propose only make things worse. They're wonderful, I'm telling you. They were so great for my team. Got me promoted again and again.

"Of course, a secret to surviving in any bureaucracy—in the East or West—is to give your superiors credit for all good ideas. Telling your boss the good ideas originated with them is the fastest way to advancement.

"Anyway, the more we poured money into ACAB and the others, the more their influence grew. Like throwing gas on fire. The best money we ever spent. As they say in English—'We got a bang for our bucks.'"

This was extraordinary, revealing stuff straight from the horse's mouth. To encourage Dongfeng to continue, Adam said, "Sometimes it feels like America is tearing itself apart. Are you saying the CPP is behind all the division and strife? That would take a lot more than funding a few fringe groups. How does the CPP pull it all off?"

Dongfeng leaned back, knocked back another big gulp of margarita, and said, "It goes back to the concept of hegemon. For centuries the Chinese emperors treated the rest of the world like barbarians. They intimidated those they could, and bribed the rest. The CPP does the same. Intimidate and bribe.

"With very few exceptions, your elites act exactly like barbarians. They compromise themselves and do the CPP's bidding for fame, flattery, sex, and money—mostly money. US elites who sell out—in true barbarian fashion—become vastly more wealthy than they ever could staying loyal to their own country.

"Some of the selling out is more or less out in the open. US CEO's moving factories to China. NBA players criticizing America while remaining silent about China's genocide, slave labor, and suppression of human rights. Hollywood censoring its own movies to please the CPP, because getting into China doubles a film's box office.

"But much of the influence is hidden. Such as senators and Congress members exchanging votes and national secrets for honey-pot sex, campaign donations, shady billion-dollar business deals with family members, and—very popular—giant deposits straight into secret bank accounts.

"You wouldn't believe how deep and how far this goes. It'd blow your mind. Suffice it to say, the CPP has tremendous influence over the US government, media, academia, Wall Street, Hollywood, pro sports, and most of Big Tech. Ever wonder why US politicians retire with fabulous wealth?"

Adam said, "Sometimes it does seem like everyone is being paid off. But is that really possible?"

"No, not everyone. The vast majority are what Marx called useful idiots. Who knows why they do exactly what helps the

CPP and hurts the US?"

Dongfeng was not holding back. But Adam wanted to hear more and signaled the flight attendant to bring still another round.

Obviously feeling the booze, but still forming his words well, Dongfeng stiffened, sitting bolt upright, eyes gleaming. "The CPP knows no limits. Hell, the COVID-19 virus is a fucking bio weapon. Whether or not they released it deliberately, I don't know. If they did, that decision was made above my pay grade.

"Sure, it was messy, but it turned out very well for China. We lost far more people than reported, of course. But that's no problem. The impact on the rest of the world was much worse, so for the CPP it was a big win. For a hegemon, remember, people don't matter.

"In fact, in the CPP's eyes, their ability to handle loss of life with minimum blowback demonstrates the superiority of their system. They've got plenty of people and can definitely spare however many it takes. It's just a matter of controlling the news and minimizing the blowback. Contrast that with the US, where you guys tore into each other for not handling the crisis correctly."

As the hours passed and their level of inebriation rose, the revelations kept coming.

At one point, Adam asked, "Hey, for years there were rumors about something called project Shashoujian. What was that all about?"

"Shashoujian! Means assassin's mace. There's no delicate way to say it: China figured out how to rig US elections.

"Took years and years. And the eager help of a coterie of power-hungry American co-conspirators. But after an investment of over three billion US, we pulled it off. Faked millions of ballots and, shall we say, subverted Domain voting machines. It was one beautiful sucker-punch PSYOP.

"Course, you can't pull off something that big without word getting out. Claims and obvious evidence of election fraud make things a little tense. That's where information dominance—control over the media and Big Tech—comes in handy. You make it off-limits to even mention election fraud, and when it is mentioned you repeat over and over that there is zero evidence. Also, when there's any effort to prevent future election rigging, you call it voter suppression."

*   *   *

Dongfeng wasn't holding back. His years on the front lines of unrestricted warfare gave his words devastating clarity. The litany of malign, horrible deeds confirmed what Adam already suspected and left him boiling mad.

Under assault for decades, America had been brought to her knees, yet she was not fighting back, with half her citizens not even willing to acknowledge the onslaught.

What democratic country could survive such an insidious, ongoing, multi-pronged blitzkrieg that exploited its very openness and freedoms.

In a world of unrestricted warfare, was an open, free society even possible? Dammit, it had to be. There had to be a way for a free and open society to withstand such attacks.

CHAPTER 47
SAN FRANCISCO

Upon landing in San Francisco, Adam walked off the plane into the arms of Tripnee and his uncle Peace, their faces streaked with tears of joy and relief. Admiral Ty Jeppesen, BC Calhoun, Harry Bellacozy, Ike and two squads of armed Marines were also present, mainly to welcome Adam but also to receive Dongfeng.

Adam introduced the former Chinese spy, who stepped forward and bowed deferentially. Jeppesen, representing the feds, and BC, the Oakland police, welcomed him and explained that he would be in their custody.

As they made their way out of the airport, Jeppesen took Adam and BC aside. His voice was strained, full of urgency. "While you've been gone, Adam, things have been heating up all over. I'm throwing out normal procedure, and the five of us will debrief Dongfeng."

BC was even more direct. "China's unrestricted warfare has America on its knees. Has to be confronted. The sooner the better. It's a fucking crisis. Man, we gotta save America and steer China onto a better path."

A caravan of black government SUVs awaited them at the curb. Jeppesen, Dongfeng, BC and Adam piled into one in the middle, while the Marines climbed into similar no-doubt bulletproof vehicles leading the procession and bringing up the rear.

The caravan raced south down the San Francisco peninsula on Hwy 101 for twenty or so minutes, then, after ten minutes on surface streets, filed into the secure basement parking lot of what Jeppesen called a "secret safe house." The place, in fact, was no house, but a nondescript, sterile office building.

At the outset of his debriefing, Dongfeng promised to help them but insisted on full immunity in exchange for his cooperation.

BC exploded. "Absolutely no way! No immunity! We know you orchestrated Dave Dorman's murder—and maybe you pulled the trigger yourself! Dave was my friend! He's gotta—he's gonna—be avenged. Dongfeng, you gotta be held accountable."

Looking thoughtful and reluctant, admiral Jeppesen shook his head. "We're in a war, BC—an unrestricted war—going full bore. It's more important to learn everything we can and gain every possible advantage in this conflict, than to convict one man for his crimes." Turning to Dongfeng, he said, "So, yes, in exchange for your full, complete cooperation, we'll grant immunity."

Dongfeng poured forth a wealth of information, and the debriefing went on for some twenty hours, with occasional short breaks. There would be more debriefings later, but it was time for Bellacozy's team, after getting some rest, to incorporate what they'd learned into their strategy to save American democracy.

As the meeting was breaking up, BC said to Admiral Jeppesen, "You know, during the breaks I've been talking to Dongfeng. The guy was just doing what he'd been taught. What he thought was his patriotic duty. I can tell he feels bad about it. I've been a cop my whole life and I can tell when someone is lying. This guy feels remorse, real remorse. I was thinking he can stay with me on my boat until these briefings are done and we all figure out what to do. Very likely, he'll be a huge help to us dealing with the CPP going forward."

Jeppesen didn't like it. "No disrespect—but it's way too soon to trust this guy—a lifelong Chinese spy—with access to both you and the computer lab on your boat."

"My computers are all triple password-protected," BC said. "Totally locked down and secure. And what better way to keep a close eye on him and really figure the guy out?"

Jeppesen still didn't like it. "Too irregular."

But BC didn't let up. The six-foot-five-inch black cop kept pointing out advantages to letting Dongfeng come stay on his boat on the Oakland waterfront, concluding with, "The guy has given up his whole country and his entire former life. Instead of keeping him here in what amounts to a prison cell in this sterile building, wouldn't it make more sense for him to feel way more at home—and be way more inclined to help to us—if I invite him to hang out for a while on my Chinese junk, Big Zen. After all, where's he going to run to? Anywhere he goes, the Chinese find him, he's toast."

Finally, Jeppesen relented.

CHAPTER 48
THE PLAN

Time to refine *The Plan.* For the next several days, Adam, Tripnee, Jeppesen, BC, Ike, Qichang, Ling and Harry met in Harry's cyber war room with Prophecy's team of genius-level cyber ninjas and white-hat hackers.

Ike, who was not only Prophecy's head of cyber security but also one of its key thinkers and innovators, summarized the situation: "China's infamous Great Fire Wall is hands down the world's most sophisticated system for internet censorship and surveillance. It blocks foreign websites, excludes all but approved CPP party-line orthodoxy, and smothers thought."

Adam asked, "So how do we open up the flow of ideas and information?"

Tripnee added, "And do it under the radar, without them knowing?"

"Aye, there's the rub," Ike said. "With our root-level, back-door access to their BeiDou search-engine, we can disrupt the firewall. But the CPP would quickly fix any obvious breach."

Jeppesen, looking around approvingly at the Prophecy team, said, "This is where I have to hand it to you cyber ninjas. You've created a truly ingenious set of algorithms."

Adam's and Tripnee's eyes widened. "Yeah?" "Tell us."

Harry said with obvious pride, "For the vast majority of ordinary Chinese citizens, the new algorithms will provide complete, uncensored search results on the world-wide web.

While at the same time, everyone official or connected with the CPP will get only censored, party-line CPP approved results."

Tripnee asked, "Is that possible?"

Adam asked, "How are you going to do that?"

"We'll use their entire, 24/7, birth-to-grave, social credit surveillance system against them," Harry said. "The CPP, of course, uses it to coerce people into party-line conformity and groupthink.

"We'll turn it around and use it in reverse. The further a person is from CPP power and privilege, the more they will be rewarded with uncensored information.

"Conversely, the more powerful and connected to the CPP a person is, the more they'll receive only censored, party-approved search results. Brainwashing and propaganda prey on ignorance, and their effectiveness evaporates with awareness. Eventually, subtly and slowly, we'll also uncensor information going to CPP stalwarts. Overtime, we hope to open even their minds and reduce lockstep groupthink."

"That's just half *The Plan*," BC said. "The other half involves the CPP's damn near infinite BeiDou database of incriminating blackmail videos."

Adam nodded. "Such as an ex-president's wife ordering an assassination?"

"Absolutely. They've got devastating footage on pretty much everyone with power and influence—both inside and outside China."

Tripnee's mouth fell open. "Both inside and outside China?!"

"Yep. Everywhere. Especially China and America. Compromising videos that, if released, would guarantee public disgrace and jail time. It's almost as though, in order for people to advance, the CPP had to have dirt on them so they could be controlled."

The young black kid Vocab spoke up, "Rasheed and I are

editing this material to make 'white-mail' videos. Short exposé films, which, if put online, would go viral worldwide and destroy the person's reputation, career, entire life. The purpose is not to release them. Instead, it's to use them to persuade CPP honchos and complicit bought-and-paid-for US elites to mend their ways."

"Mend their ways?"

"How's that gonna work?"

"Well, for example," BC continued, "we'll use the BeiDou System to 'white-mail' them into stopping the full range of unrestricted warfare misdeeds. They'll have to stop all sales of meth and fentanyl; stop messing with US elections; stop bribing, blackmailing and covertly influencing US politicians, media, academia, Wall Street, Hollywood, and pro sports. They'll have to stop funding ACAB, FH and CRT; and stop cyber attacks, hacking, and data and IT theft."

Qichang, who had been playing a vital role in fine-tuning The Plan and writing the algorithm, jumped in. "They'll have to stop involuntary organ harvesting; stop persecuting Falun Gong, Uighurs and pro-democracy dissidents; stop arresting people for no reason; stop forced labor; and lift restrictions on artists like Wei Wei—who are working to inspire a new beginning in China."

Harry added, "The CPP will have to stop illicit technology acquisition; stop black ops guanxi—especially assassinations; stop arbitrary seizure of people's property; stop stealing billions and billions from the Chinese people; and stop censorship. Also, they'll have to repeal repressive laws like the ones squashing Hong Kong independence, and the law that inflicts prison time and even death for so-called spreading rumors. Over time, we hope to even get them to stop territorial expansion and intimidating neighbors."

Jeppesen said, "We'll use the worldwide BeiDou system to

force complicit US elites—and there are thousands—to stop taking bribes and orders from the CPP, and stop sending US jobs overseas. We'll make them: follow the constitution; run honest elections; protect the US electric grid; defend our borders; and maintain orderly immigration. Stop defunding the police. And stop using biased 'fact checkers' to censor the U.S. media."

BC added, "Also, a pet peeve of mine: We'll use the system to encourage civility, forgiveness and kindness. The message will be: Don't shout people down. Let them speak. Don't harass, stalk, cancel, beat, dox or threaten people."

Ike said, "It won't be easy. It's got to be done with great care. But the BeiDou system will tell us precisely who is responsible for what and who's doing what."

"Yes," Qichang said, "it will indeed take patient and thorough ongoing monitoring—and probably occasional quick cyber adjustments and algorithmic fixes. But the sheer quantity of black skeletons in these people's closets—hidden shameful things on video—makes pretty much all of the complicit players totally vulnerable to our pressure. A big part of our focus will be on preventing any of these people from taking countermeasures or pressuring one another not to comply with *The Plan*."

"What we're doing from one perspective, of course, is downright dastardly," Jeppesen said. "But this all-powerful BeiDou system is right now being used to do horrible, horrible, unspeakable things, and the only way to defeat it is to use it against itself."

"I love it," Tripnee said. "Simply exposing and destroying these people wouldn't really change anything, because they'd just be replaced by other corrupt characters. *The Plan* uses their own Beidou system to monitor them and make sure they really do mend their ways."

"Thank God," Adam said, "we're finally fighting back against a system determined to destroy us."

CHAPTER 49
THE PLANS OF MICE AND MEN

A few days later, late in the afternoon, the team feverishly labored away in the Prophecy cyber war room—putting finishing touches on *The Plan.*

All seemed good. Until, that is, Ike and Jeppesen burst into the big room and asked BC to step into Ike's private office. Half an hour later the three of them returned.

Jeppesen announced to the room, "An hour ago, Ike's people found a tiny ultra-ultra-high-frequency receiver-transmitter booster hidden in the wheel well of BC's Tesla Model 3. This device was relaying and boosting an audio signal and data stream emanating from a nano spyware transmitter inside a ball point pen planted on BC. There's only one likely source: Dongfeng."

A moment of stunned silence was followed by a collective gasp. Jeppesen continued, "Its super tiny, super sophisticated. My crew missed it."

"And my people almost missed it too," Ike said.

"But, thankfully," Jeppesen said, "Ike's cyber-security team did catch it."

Hearing this, something fell into place for Adam. "Very, very interesting," he said, nodding. "I've been thinking about Dongfeng's debriefing. When I analyze it carefully, he didn't reveal anything that we didn't already know or at least strongly suspect. Also, he omitted any useful details on black ops guanxi—such as assassinations as favors for U.S. elites."

Jeppesen asked, "On your flight together, could he have been only pretending? His whole defection an act to fool us?"

Adam shook his head. "It's hard to believe. He had me convinced. But the guy is a master spy—and dissembler."

BC looked thoughtful."Come to think of it, Dongfeng has been asking some rather suspicious questions. Like how and why we followed him around the Bay Area."

"The ball-point pen device and the micro booster pretty much prove it," Ike said. "We've got a fake turncoat working for the other side."

"This intel breach is serious," Jeppesen said. "We have to assume Dongfeng and his bosses know about The Plan."

"Which puts the whole thing—our entire plan to save the world—in jeopardy," Tripnee said. "It's fucking kaput."

* * *

Donfeng was staying below deck on BC's 65-foot Chinese junk Big Zen, which was back in its mooring in the Jack London Square Marina at the foot of Broadway in Oakland.

When Adam, Tripnee, BC, Jeppesen, Ike, and Harry Bellacozy all showed up fully armed in the evening twilight, Dongfeng had to know the jig was up. A search under the floorboards of his cabin revealed an ultra-miniature device receiving and recording audio and data streams from the ball-point-pen spy bug planted on BC.

Caught red handed, Dongfeng had the grace to come clean.

Adam asked, "Help me understand something. If you go back, Aiguo will kill you, and Xu will let him. Why waste your loyalty on such unworthy leaders?"

Dongfeng said, "If I return with vital information—the very

information they desperately need right now—I can negotiate my way back into Xu's good graces—and he'll protect me from Aiguo."

Tripnee said, "Good luck with that. You go back, you'd be toast."

Dongfeng first met her gaze, then calmly looked around at the rest of them, and said, "Even if my boss kills me, I'm still Chinese. You think my loyalty is only for my personal gain? I stand with my people. You have no idea what more than a century of humiliation at the hands of the West has done to my country—and to me."

Adam asked, "What about all the things you said on the plane? Did you mean any of it?"

"What I said was true, that is, true from a Western perspective," Dongfeng replied. "But from a Chinese perspective, not so much. Look at all China has done in the last forty years: We built forty thousand miles of high speed rail. We built the world's largest navy. We built airports everywhere. We built five hundred cities from the ground up. We built a 57 story building in nineteen days. We built a bridge in forty three hours. We did all this while saving up a four hundred billion dollar surplus. And most important of all, at the very same time, we lifted hundreds of millions of people out of poverty.

"To make omelets you've got to break eggs. We're on a roll, and we're doing great things. Meanwhile, you in the West attack each other, tear down your own history, and squabble over gender pronouns. We are serious and you are not.

"China was held down and humiliated for over a century by western barbarians. Now it's time for us to reclaim our rightful position of dominance. Our time has come.Yours has passed. We deserve to ascend to the top."

BC replied, "The CPP did all that by literally ripping off and undermining the West. Stealing our intellectual property, our technology, our methods. Constantly breaking agreements. Exploiting our trust and openness. That makes you greater, deserving to be dominant? I don't think so."

Jeppesen added, "Besides that, if for half a minute China stopped its relentless PSYOPs, turning Americans against one another, we could find common ground and unite—and we'd be indomitable."

Dongfeng sat with perfect posture, shoulders back, neck exposed. "There's some truth to that. But right there you see one of the advantages of our system. This is the real world. Chaos, discord, and internal struggle are ever present in your system—and a real vulnerability open to manipulation by your enemies. This is not so with China. We create and enforce harmony."

Adam said, "Phony, completely fake harmony. Where you cover up and deny the starvation of 40 million people. Where you cover up and deny the murder of 10,000 people on Tiananmen Square. Where people censor themselves, afraid to express their thoughts, afraid of their own shadow. Where they can be arrested for anything, can have their property taken away for no reason, can have loved ones dragged away at any time."

"I see your point. I do," Dongfeng said. "But sometimes harsh methods are the only way to maintain order among 1.4 billion people."

Harry said, "That right there has always been the CPP's bottom-line, default excuse for all its totalitarian brutality. But it just doesn't wash. India at 1.2 billion has nearly as many people and is a successful democracy. Taiwan combines the rich, true cultural traditions of China with democracy and is thriving. The naked fact is the CPP is a mafia-style gang ruthlessly doing whatever it takes to maintain power, quashing people, smashing liberty, crushing human rights. America just needs to awaken and unite—and the CPP will be in trouble."

Dongfeng smiled. "Dream on. You Americans always assume everything you do is altruistic, that you're always on the side of good. You're not.

"A heck of a lot of what the CPP does is actually modeled after the US. For example, our Belt and Road Initiative, a strategy you call debt trap diplomacy, is in fact directly modeled on American corporations' tactic of selling infrastructure projects to the third world—projects more expensive than they can ever pay for—that lock them into commitments that allow your corporations to exploit them indefinitely. We're just following your lead."

'Harry said, "Overall when you look at what America stands for in the world and what it has done, there is just no comparison. Look at the Korean war, for example. We sacrificed thousands of soldiers simply so that South Koreans could live free and thrive. One only has to compare South and North Korea to see the difference between what the United States and the CPP stand for."

"Is the CPP perfect?" Dongfeng asked. "No, of course not. And, of course, neither is America. Yes, I want China to evolve, to take its place in the family of nations, to be a leader among leaders. Above all, I want China to do what is truly best for the Chinese people—and not just for an elite bunch of gangsters. But fundamentally I simply cannot take the US side against China."

Dongfeng looked directly at Adam. "Besides, be honest, you're hacking the Chinese system. Whether you call it white mailing or blackmailing, aren't you just as bad as the CPP?

"I'm going back—come what may—to work on the inside to help China evolve. In China we have a problem that you don't. We have so many people with no history and no understanding of autonomy.

"Have you ever wondered why Chinese people seem to like to be told what to do?"

Dongfeng paused to look out a porthole at the pitch black night, then turned to survey his armed captors, studying each in turn. "I have a terrible fear. I'm afraid if the Chinese people themselves gained power, they would either be far more nationalistic and aggressive toward the West—or China would erupt in a civil war like no other, in which blood would flow like a river."

Ike said, "The idea that the Chinese people are not ready for democracy is absurd. Like Harry says, Taiwan is proof of that."

Adam said, "For the CPP to take credit for lifting hundreds of millions out of poverty is baloney. The credit goes to the Chinese people themselves. The CPP simply got out of the way enough for those people to lift themselves out of poverty." Adam paused to let his point sink in. "Recently the true, inescapable, totalitarian gangster nature of the CPP has been reasserting itself, and those gains are likely to be lost."

Dongfeng made a small movement with his foot and the junk's main salon plunged into total darkness.

Damn! In the blackout, no one dared shoot, lest they hit one of their own. Adam immediately lunged toward the companionway, figuring Dongfeng would try to escape by that route.

Sure enough! Someone was there. Adam grabbed and tackled them, bringing them down. But the guy was way too big. Phooey, it was BC.

BC yelled, "He's going for the forward hatch." Then BC headed that way, moving fast through the junk's pitch black interior.

Meanwhile, Adam darted up the companionway and ran toward the bow. He'd gotten only half way when he heard a quiet splash. Dammit. Dongfeng was even then swimming away, losing himself in the dark of night, in the black waters of the Bay. Adam checked all around the junk, but there was no sign of Gong Dongfeng.

Despite his anger and frustration, Adam was impressed. Dongfeng had sat the whole time with his foot inches from the junk's main electric power switch. He'd played them perfectly, engaging them with his veneer of reasonableness, baiting them with his party-line arguments. Playing for time, he'd patiently waited for the gloom of twilight to turn into pitch black night. Then, as soon as it was sufficiently dark, he'd made his move.

The team began searching the marina. Jeppesen alerted the FBI, and BC called in the Oakland Police Department. Emergency teams from both—including two Oakland Police patrol boats—searched the entire area, but there was no sign of the clever Chinese spy.

Half an hour after Dongfeng disappeared overboard, a black military-grade whisper-quiet helicopter lifted off from the top of a tall building two blocks from Big Zen. The background light of the city glinted off the chopper as it made a beeline for nearby Oakland airport.

Seeing this, BC alerted his OPD buddy to dispatch three Oakland squad cars with sirens screaming to intercept the helicopter when it landed. Simultaneously, Jeppesen sent the FBI to do the same. But before either team got to the airport, the chopper touched down and a guy matching Dongfeng's description ran from it to a Chinese diplomatic plane. The jet took off immediately, with a flight plan showing China as its destination.

Damn. It started to really sink in.

The Plan to exploit Harry Bellacozy's back door to China's BeiDou surveillance network was soon to be exposed—if it hadn't been already. The Plan was, in fact, already kaput. A feeling of loss, gloom and hopelessness spread through the group. Exhausted, feeling about as low as they'd ever felt, they shared hugs and tears.

What else was there for them to do but go to their homes, get what sleep they could, and hope that somehow, against all odds, the new day would provide some positive path forward?

Just as they were about to depart, Tripnee's phone gave off an usual ringtone. "Hmmm. My spy drones in Roe Rosen's Belvedere house are picking up key-player activity. I wonder—?"

BC perked up. "Patch it through and I'll put it up on the big screen."

CHAPTER 50
MEET YOUR MAKER

There, big as life on the huge screen in the main salon of Big Zen, were Gong Dongfeng and blonde, blue-eyed Roe Rosen.

"I'll be damned," Tripnee said. "The icy cool professional passed up his opportunity to get away, and instead listened to the insane promptings of his own human heart—"

On the screen, Rosen shouted, "You fucking asshole! None of this would've happened if you'd done what you said. Why in hell didn't you pay off the Oakland Police and nip any investigation in the bud? Why? Why?"

"Baby, I did pay them off. And we applied pressure. But there was a rogue cop who wouldn't—"

"You put me in danger! I'm so mad I could kill you! You promised to stop any investigation before it began! You let me—me— down! I've been wronged!"

Dongfeng gently pulled Rosen to him and took her in his arms. At first, she pounded his chest with her fists, but then, gradually, she hugged him back, finally bursting into tears.

Dongfeng asked, "What's this about you promising to be with Aiguo?"

"Oh, sweetie, I had to," Rosen said, pulling away from him. "Aiguo is here in the Bay Area with his giant praetorian guards. He was searching for you. He was determined to track you down and kill you.

"I told him that if he killed you I would never see him again. But if he'd let you live, I'd be his, his alone."

"No! No baby. No!" Dongfeng pleaded. "You just can't. No matter what happens to me, you just can't do this!"

"I had to. I have to. It's what the kid has always wanted. It's the only way to keep you alive."

"What happens to me doesn't matter. You just can't. Besides, I won't let the little hegemon kill me."

The pair embraced, then began kissing passionately. Before long they were tearing off each other's clothes. Soon they were naked on the bed, immersed, consumed, lost in wild sex, oblivious to the world.

At that moment, Aiguo walked into Roe Rosen's bedroom.

"Nooooo!" he screamed. "How could you? You promised!"

Jolted out of their euphoria, the naked pair rolled apart. Rosen, her large breasts swinging, advanced off the bed toward Aiguo. "Sweetie, it's not how it looks—"

"Not how it looks?!" Aiguo screamed, pulling out a pistol. "I see with my own eyes. I see you're a gweilo whore!"

Bang. Bang. Bang. Bang. The first bullet entered right between her eyes, the others through her beautiful chest.

Meanwhile, Donfeng, knowing where Rosen kept her handgun, reached into a bedside drawer and whipped out a Glock pistol.

There were no words. Both men, white with rage, each moving at his top speed, shot the other point blank. Simultaneously.

EPILOGUE

A month and a half after the triple murder in Roe Rosen's house, Harry Bellacozy's team gathered with various compatriots in Peace Weldon's creekside garden. Adam 's cantankerous ex-Zen monk uncle Peace was a friend and mentor to many of the people present, including Adam, BC, Tripnee, Ike, Vocab, Rasheed, Su Jingfoi and especially Harry, who found in Peace a best friend, wise counselor, and kindred-spirit bon vivant. Peace had closely followed the group 's recent doings, and was hosting the get together on his East Bay property in order to commemorate Dave Dorman—and also to celebrate some good news: After a month monitoring the CPP's all-intrusive BeiDou spy surveillance system, there was no sign Dongfeng had exposed *The Plan*. Therefore, with *The Plan* still under the radar, they were about to set it in motion!

Lounging and mingling among Peace's tulips, thyme, aloe and bougainvillea, and redwood, avocado, cherry, lemon and orange trees, was just about everyone who had been caught up in BC's, Adam's and Harry's recent adventures. The Chungs, including a laughing Bo and Mingshu, a beaming Jia, and a very relaxed Mei, were teaching BC, Ike, Rasheed, two cyber ninjas and several of BC's police buddies some Falun Gong exercises.

Chinese gunslinger Ling and ex-gang-hitman Vocab sat drinking and laughing, very much appreciating, it seemed, each other's rip-roaring inner cowboy. Chung Qichang pumped

Harry's pilot/bodyguards Ben and Jerry for the inside scoop on how best to get a pilot's license. Adam and Tripnee circulated, engaging in all manner of conversations, all the while making a point of frequently coming together to surreptitiously bump hips and poke each other in the ribs.

As the smooth California wine flowed and the guests grew ever more animated, Harry, Ike, BC and Jeppesen took turns manning the grill, competing to outdo one another in serving up out-off-this-world delicious BBQ.

At one point, the conversation turned to Gong Dongfeng.

"That guy," Tripnee said, "was a regular Chinese James Bond."

Jeppesen said, "Gotta respect—and keep an eye on—any organization that has people like that."

Adam agreed. "The way he played me. Fooled me by mirroring my own point of view. Shows a nimbleness of thought beyond most people. I doubt I could match it."

"You kidding?" Tripnee said. "Dongfeng was one cool, clever spy. But, Adam, your nimbleness makes him look like a block of concrete."

At another point, Dave Dorman's mother thanked Harry and Adam for paying off Dave's home, and for funding full college scholarships for Dave's daughters Debbie and Darla.

And at still another point, Jeppesen said to Adam, "I have to admit, thank God you ignored my order and did what it took to bring out Qichang. He's playing a crucial role in fine-tuning *The Plan.* What I'm trying to say is: your pigheaded daring paid off. We couldn't do it without Chung Qichang."

*　　*　　*

As was known to happen sometimes at Peace's gatherings, at a certain point in the ebb and swirl of laughter, eating, mingling, and drinking, some of the guests, including Harry, BC and others, started chanting, "Talk, Peace, talk."

Peace pretended to ignore this for a while, but then he stood, spread his arms wide, smiled broadly, and spoke.

"Hello and welcome. It feels so so good to be right here right now with each of you on this auspicious occasion. As you all know—and thanks to you—*The Plan* is ingenious and shows promise. A toast to *The Plan* and its success!"

All glasses rose, and a cheer filled the air.

"Even as we all hope for—and do everything possible to create—the desired outcome, we don't know how long or how well *The Plan* will be effective. We don't even know if it'll work at all.

"You're wondering why I'm pointing out *The Plan* might fail? You're probably thinking: Hey you old hippie, don't be a downer."

They all laughed. Someone joked, "True. True."

"I'm pointing this out because there's some really good news even bigger than *The Plan.* Sure, we all hope the plan succeeds. But *the plan* isn't our only path to a good outcome.

"Why?

"Because the real key to winning this battle is awareness. The CPP has been waging all out unrestricted war against America for forty years—and for forty years we've willfully, deliberately turned a blind eye."

"Hell," BC said, "most Americans didn't even know a war was going on."

"That's right, BC," Peace said. "But now we're waking up and taking notice, seeing it for what it is. Unrestricted war is a deliberate attempt to manipulate, coerce and destroy. The more people realize this, the less effective the whole strategy will be.

"The more Americans are aware, the more effective America

will be in fighting back, in taking counter measures. We must impose increasingly heavy costs on the CPP if they continue.

"Increased awareness is happening even now, as I share these thoughts with you." Peace paused to slowly scan his audience. Beaming, he seemed to make eye contact with everyone. Then he said, "Aware, we will hold our own. Aware, we will value and defend our democracy, our Constitution, our freedoms."

The crowd was abuzz, jazzed. Even the serious Jeppesen gushed, "Peace! You're right! With or without Harry's back door hack, with awareness we'll win!"

"Well said!" "Amen!" "Talk, Peace, talk."

When things quieted down, Peace added, "We must prevail not only for ourselves, but also for the world. Can you imagine a world ruled by the CPP? A world torn apart, decimated, utterly demoralized by the savagery of wide spread all out unrestricted warfare?"

"What will become of China? Of course, the dragon that needs slaying is the CPP, not the Chinese people!! The rise and fall of nations takes time, usually, many, many lifetimes. China is a tremendously great land and people, rich in history, culture, and profound spiritual traditions. Taiwan is proof that the Chinese people can embrace democracy as well as anyone else. Ultimately, only the Chinese people can determine their path."

Qichang leapt to his feet and shouted, "Another toast! Here's to the people of America and China! May we all be free and live in peace."

Glasses were lifted, most came down fully drained.

Then, little Jia piped up in her surprisingly strong voice, "Since the important thing is spreading awareness, we should get someone to write up everything that's happened as a novel."

Peace grinned. "I think I might know just the person to do that."

"Goody, goody, goody!" Jia bubbled, "I'll sell it door to door. I'll tell everyone I meet about it, until everyone in America is aware!"

*   *   *

Later, everyone watched a film about Dave Dorman put together by Vocab and Rasheed. A month before, the film had gone viral on the internet and had inspired the creation of a nonprofit foundation dedicated to helping the children of fallen police officers. Donations to the fund had already topped ninety million and continued to pour in.

Adam overheard Dave's mother talking to the two young film makers. "It's so, so lovely. You captured Dave perfectly—the tender, brave, caring hero that he was. Such a wonderful gift for his daughters. Your film will mean the world to them helping them remember their father as they grow older."

In front of the assembly, as a row of uniformed police officers saluted, BC got on a police radio and, honoring a long tradition, issued a Last Call, one call to Officer Dave Dorman, followed by silence.

There was not a dry eye in the garden.

This concludes this novel,
but the story continues…

AUTHOR'S NOTE TO READER

If you enjoyed this book, please post a review—and tell your friends. The more reviews, the more the Amazon algorithm helps spread the word. Thank you so much!! —Bill.

Reading List

To learn more about subjects touched on in this novel, the author recommends the following:

China's Vision of Victory, by Jonathan D. T. Ward, 2019

The China Threat: How the People's Republic Targets America, by Bill Gertz, 2000

Chinese Espionage: Operations and Tactics, by Nicholas Eftimiades, 2020

Critical Race Theory: What It Is and How To Fight It, by Christopher F. Rufo, Imprimis, 3/2021—Vol 50, #3

Deceiving the Sky: Inside Communist China's Drive for Global Supremacy, by Bill Gertz, 2019

The Deep Rig, by Patrick Byrne, 2021

The Dying Citizen: How Progressive Elites, Tribalism, and Globalism Are Destroying the Idea of America, by Victor Davis Hanson

Hegemon: China's Plan to Dominate Asia and the World, by Stephan W. Mosher, 2000

The Hundred-Year Marathon: China's Secret Strategy to Replace America as the Global Superpower, by Michael Pillsbury, 2015

Irresistible Revolution: Marxism's Goal of Conquest and the Unmaking of the American Military, by Matthew Lohmeier

Kafka in China: The People's Republic of Corruption, 2016, and *Kafka in China: An American Near Death in the People's Republic of Black Jails*, 2018, by Warren Henry Rothman

Made in China: A Prisoner, an SOS Letter, and the Hidden Cost of America's Cheap Goods, by Amelia Pang, 2021

Monsoon: The Indian Ocean and the Future of American Power, by Robert D. Kaplan, 2010

The New Art of War: China's Deep Strategy Inside the United States, by William J Holstein, 2019

Political Warfare: Strategies for Combating China's Plan to "Win Without Fighting," by Kerry K. Gershaneck, 2020

The Real War Against America, by Brett Kingston, 2005

Secret Empires, by Peter Schweizer, 2018

Stealth War: How China Took Over While America's Elite Slept, by Brigadier General Robert Spalding, 2019

Surviving Chinese Communist Detention, by Steven Schaerer, 2021

Unmasked: Inside Antifa's Radical Plan to Destroy Democracy, by Andy Ngo, 2021

Un-Restricted Warfare: Translated from the Original People's Liberation Army Documents, by Col. Qiao Lian and Col. Wang Xiangsui, originally published in 1999

War on Cops: How the New Attack on Law and Order Makes Everyone Less Safe, by Heather McDonald, 2016

Woke Inc: The Unholy Alliance of Big Government, Big Business, and Woke Dogma, by Vivek Ramaswamy. 2021

The World Turned Upside Down: America, China, and the Struggle for Global Leadership, by Clyde Prestowitz, 2021

Nonprofits Helping Families of Fallen Police Officers

Children of Fallen Police Officers Foundation:
'We Have Their Six'
www.policeofficersfoundation.org

Badge of Honor Memorial Foundation
www.bohmf.org

Law Enforcement Charitable Foundation, Inc.
www.lecf-inc.org

Concerns of Police Survivors
www.concernsofpolicesurvivors.org

WILLIAM MCGINNIS BIOGRAPHY

A California native, William McGinnis grew up in the San Francisco Bay Area. From his youth through college and graduate school and to this day, McGinnis seized—and seizes—every opportunity to sail, raft, canoe and hike the natural wonders of California and beyond.

At Richmond's Harry Ells High School, he presided over the school chess club, served on the senior board, competed in impromptu and extemporaneous tournament public speaking, and wrote poetic, satiric and philosophic tidbits.

Making lemonade out of lemons: When he graduated with a BA and an MA in English literature from San Francisco State University, Bill applied to every junior college west of the Mississippi only to discover that there were literally no teaching jobs to be found. This turned out to be one of the best things that's ever happened to him.

Instead of teaching, Bill wrote *Whitewater Rafting,* which was published in 1975 in hardcover and softcover by Quadrangle: The New York Times Book Company. The first thorough guide to the art of river rafting, *Whitewater Rafting* was considered the bible of the sport for decades and was reprinted many times.

Also in 1975, with two rafts and a $500 gift from his grandmother, McGinnis founded Whitewater Voyages, which pioneered guided rafting trips on a number of California rivers and grew to become California's largest river outfitter. For many, many years he and his guides took more people down more California rivers than any other rafting company.

In recognition of his many contributions to the sport of rafting, in 2000, Bill was named one of the "Top 100 Paddlers of the Century" by Paddler Magazine, the leading national paddle-sport publication.

McGinnis published the original *Guide's Guide* in 1981 and the greatly expanded *Guide's Guide Augmented* in 2006. To this day, this comprehensive work serves as a bible for professional river guides worldwide.

While he has a slew of first descents and pioneering raft runs in California and throughout the world to his credit, McGinnis says it is his influence on guiding that he is most proud of. The essence of good guiding, he says, is "…appreciating and nurturing people. Helping them move from fear to confidence to joy, from being a stranger in a group to bonding, from feeling cut-off from nature to feeling in love with and at one with this planet, and from being somewhat scattered inside and maybe self-critical to feeling more self-accepting, more whole, more energized, more alive."

It's been said that we gain experience—and eventually wisdom—by making mistakes. This certainly applies to Bill. At least the making mistakes part! One such near-death misadventure is described in his short but hair-raising ebook, *Disaster on the Clearwater: Rafting Beyond the Limits.*

More recently, McGinnis has been drawing on his life of adventure travel and love of writing to create taut, rip-roaring, upbeat thriller novels. *Whitewater: A Thriller* (the first Adam Weldon Thriller) draws on decades guiding and outfitting on

California's Kern River. *Gold Bay: An Adam Weldon Thriller* celebrates a lifetime sailing San Francisco Bay. *Cyclops Conspiracy: An Adam Weldon Thriller* retraces the author's itinerary sailing the Greek Islands. And *Slay the Dragon: An Adam Weldon Action-Adventure Mystery Suspense Thriller* reflects McGinnis' off-grid travels in and long fascination with China.

McGinnis' other works include, *Sailing the Greek Islands: Dancing with Cyclops, The Class V Briefing*, and numerous magazine articles.

McGinnis' passions, in addition to writing, rafting and sailing, include hiking, woodworking, staring into space, audiobooks and exploring new paths to adventure, friendship, and growth. He lives in the San Francisco Bay Area. His author website is www.WilliamMcGinnis.com.

BOOKS BY WILLIAM MCGINNIS

Note: Adam Weldon thrillers stand alone and the novels can be read in any order.

Whitewater Rafting

The Class V Briefing

The Guide's Guide Augmented: Reflections on Guiding Professional River Trips

Sailing the Greek islands: Dancing with Cyclops

Disaster on the Clearwater: Rafting Beyond the Limit

Whitewater: A Thriller (Adam Weldon Thriller #1)

Gold Bay: An Adam Weldon Thriller (#2)

Cyclops Conspiracy: An Adam Weldon Thriller (#3)

Slay the Dragon: An Adam Weldon Action-Adventure Mystery Suspense Thriller (#4)

Made in the USA
Middletown, DE
13 October 2021